☙ ❧ L A V A ☙ ❧

LAVA

By ARMINE VON TEMPSKI

"When life is ready to use you, you are drawn unto it ... you cannot hasten your tides, but when the waves begin breaking on the beach you cannot stop them."

This truth comes to the unusual heroine of this romance through an experience that tries her as fine metal is tried. Shouldered with responsibility for a Hawaiian ranch, she carries on through a terrific earthquake and volcanic eruption that threatens to wipe out the place and the people she loves. It is a very human story, moved by the great elementary forces of life — birth, passion, danger, love. Under the shadow of the volcano Hualalai a drama of hearts and souls takes place, accompanied by the terrible shudder of moving earth and the sullen glare of volcanic light, as ravines fill with molten fire and forests disappear like feathers in flame.

Never has Miss Von Tempski, lover and interpreter of Hawaii, given a more powerful and enchanting presentation of this place and people.

BOOKS BY ARMINE VON TEMPSKI

HULA · DUST · FIRE · LAVA
HAWAIIAN HARVEST
RIPE BREADFRUIT
BORN IN PARADISE
THUNDER IN HEAVEN
ALOHA

Juveniles

PAM'S PARADISE RANCH
JUDY OF THE ISLANDS
BRIGHT SPURS

*L*AVA
A Saga of Hawaii

By ARMINE VON TEMPSKI

OX BOW PRESS
Woodbridge, Connecticut

Copyright 1930, copyright renewed 1957

1991 reprint by
Ox Bow Press
P.O. Box 4045
Woodbridge, CT 06525

Paperback cover painting by Cecelia Rodriquez

Library of Congress Cataloging-in-Publication Data
Von Tempski, Armine, 1892–1943.
Lava : a saga of Hawaii / by Armine Von Tempski.
     p. cm.
ISBN 0–918024–88–9. — ISBN 0–918024–89–7 (pbk.)
  I. Title.
     PS3543.0647L38 1991
813'.52—dc20   91-27404
                                                              CIP

The paper used in this book meets the guidelines for permanence
and durability of the Committee on Production Guidelines for
Book Longevity of the Council on Library Resources.

Printed in the United States of America

TO

MY DAD AND "KA-KINA"
(L. A. THURSTON)

THE GODS OF
MY
CHILDHOOD

AND

TO

MONA KE-KAHA-KU-LANI HIND

WHO WAS THE INSPIRATION
FOR IT

LAVA

LAVA

CHAPTER I

Dirk Van Dyke closed the book he had been reading, a mild protest growing in his kind brown eyes. In some extraordinary way his surroundings persistently injected themselves into his consciousness.

The air was sweet with the fragrance of rotting guavas and smelt vaguely of drying coffee beans, sugar cane and, lingeringly, of fat cattle which had been driven past. He glimpsed, beneath the vermilion curve of a flame tree the long, molten slopes of Hawaii pouring with a sort of leisurely, magnificent abandon down to the sea, huge, serene, rimming the world with fierce blue. He stared thoughtfully at the spectacular coast line, then resumed reading.

His long, intelligent fingers held the beautifully tooled, worn, limp-leather volume affectionately and his eyes followed the lines with absorbed interest. Once or twice he glanced up as though the island had addressed him, politely attentive, but deliberately and entirely detached.

A step sounded and he turned his head.

An elderly man came down the veranda with heavy unsteadiness, touching the wall occasionally with an outstretched hand. Van watched compassionately. His ap-

LAVA

proach was somehow suggestive of a mammoth ship plowing into head seas that threatened to overwhelm it. As he drew nearer Van rose with quick courtesy.

"I thought I'd find you here, Van Dyke," the man said in a pleased voice.

Van started to guide him toward a chair, then restrained himself knowing that to be the greater kindness. The old man put out a groping, unsteady hand but there was no suggestion of weakness in the gesture, rather of great force chained by darkness. He touched a rocker, drew it forward and seated himself facing the sweep of the island.

Polished scarlet and green coffee plantations, rivers of clustering kukui trees showed delicately green against distant wastes of black lava that spilled through the land marring and emphasizing its beauty. Orange and amethyst air plants crowded against sturdy stone walls lining a road going away from the house. On a far-off rise a sugar mill shook the air with its muffled vibrations. Japanese, diminished by distance to the proportions of ants, toiled about cars loaded with ruddy stalked cane. Mango trees like huge volcanic bombs dotted hills and pastures, and beyond the green bulge of a ridge the long, sullen slope of Mauna Loa was finely etched against the sky.

After a brief silence, during which the blind man sat gripping the arms of his chair, he indicated with a sweep of his arm the slumbering mass of the island.

"I'll wager, Van Dyke, that in all your wanderings, for I gathered from your conversation at lunch that you're a great traveler, you've never seen anything finer than this."

LAVA

Some inflection in the man's voice made Van glance at him and he saw a terrible, restrained hunger in the rugged old face. Evidently blindness had descended upon this giant and Van experienced a tiny, inner pang.

"This is an overwhelming island, Mr. Lowell."

The blind man moved his head in assent.

"How long are you planning to stay, Van Dyke?"

"Possibly a week."

Lowell nodded in a pleased fashion. Van closed his book and slid it quietly into his pocket and they sat for a while in a warm, friendly silence.

Stretching his long figure contentedly in the wicker chair on the narrow sunny veranda, Van weighed his surroundings with well-bred, restrained interest as though he sought to get at the core of them in order better to appreciate and remember them when he was gone.

The locality seemed to be endowed with some extraordinary significance and, despite the drugged peace of the afternoon, he was dimly conscious of warring forces, struggling for supremacy, at work all about him. His gentle eyes considered the house thoughtfully; two-storied, white, with small deep windows shuttered in green, it somehow suggested a face with eyes closed lest it see something improper. Mad magenta bougainvilleas and orange huapala vines swathed the building as though they sought, resentfully, to strangle a structure so alien. Hibiscuses, with blossoms like storms of gaudy butterflies splashed their colors against the eaves. Snap-dragons, gardenias, begonias, Spanish daggers, yucca and jasmine, Chinese violets and golden sprawls of California poppies, Japanese musk and Bird of Paradise lilies grew above prim English daisies bordering the beds.

"Before I leave I'm going to list the flowers and shrubs in this garden," Van said. "They represent almost every country under the sun," and he studied the lawn, green, tree-shaded, jeweled with color, tilting toward the staggering blue of the sea which seemed to be waiting, with immense patience, for some event which was already on its way.

Lowell nodded and Van turned in order to face his companion.

"When I booked passage for the Orient I had no intention of stopping off in Hawaii, though islands enchant me."

The blind man made an assenting sound as though that went without saying.

"A week before I sailed, at a Club in Los Angeles, I ran into a man I hadn't seen for years. When he found out that I would be passing through the Islands he asked me, knowing that time is of absolutely no consequence to me, if I'd stop over a boat and try to look up a girl he'd known here, and apparently thinks the world of—Ku-lani Garland."

Lowell's heavy body jerked up.

"What was his name?"

"Allan White. I met him in China a few years ago when he was auditor of a chain of tea plantations. If I remember correctly he told me he'd worked in Kona about twenty years ago."

LAVA

"He was auditor here when Ku-lani was a kid."

"He said he'd seen her, about seven years ago, when she was at school in the East. He said she was the most unusual girl he'd ever known and he wanted me to find out, if possible, what had become of her."

"Ku-lani is—" Lowell paused, "magnificent. There's nobody, absolutely nobody like her."

"As you know, White gave me a letter of introduction to Mr. Garland but when I presented it this morning I never dreamed he'd insist upon my being his guest while I'm in Kona. It seems an imposition."

"Garland is practically a king here and is accustomed to having his own way and an unexpected guest is never an imposition in Hawaii. He owns almost all of North and South Kona. The Hawaiians call him," the blind man chuckled, "Ha-ole Hao."

"Which means?"

"Iron White Man."

Van sat silent thinking about his host, unknown to him until that morning, an immoderately tall man with carefully brushed hair which exactly matched his dry, gray skin. Van had felt, immediately, the impact of Garland's personality. His yellowish eyes, set queerly above prominent cheek bones emphasized the unusual width of his face and he had a slightly musty odor about him, as though he had been kept in the dark.

From conversations with Allan White he knew that Garland had been established in Kona about forty-five years and that he had had several sons and a daughter by a first wife. When he met the second Mrs. Garland, at lunch, he surmised that Garland had undoubtedly married her for lands which she probably possessed and, being as he was, he had seen to it that there was no second family.

Loki Garland had charmed Van. She was unaware of herself as a child and, despite her bulk, moved with the easy, sure grace of a cat. A voluminous black holoku had failed to conceal the noble curves of her body, sumptuous as the land. She had heavily lashed eyes, curiously young, a proud merry mouth and carried her head imperiously. In her manner she was typically Polynesian, dignified and friendly.

"I glad John ask you to stay with us." she had said, pressing his long, browned hands between hers, plump and dainty.

The sons, Luke, Benjamin and David, had materialized at lunch, the two elder ones colorless replicas of their father, the youngest a dark, vivid boy of nineteen. As yet he had not seen Ku-lani but from conversation during the meal he gathered that she managed some ranch in North Kona and was expected over during the course of the afternoon.

He wondered, almost indifferently, what qualities she possessed to make Allan White, a man well over fifty, retain interest in her destiny and make this quiet giant assert, so emphatically, that there was nobody like her.

"You know, Van Dyke," Lowell said as though in answer to his thought, "occasionally you run into a man or woman with, well, let us say an extra dimension."

"Yes."

LAVA

"Ku-lani is one of them. To outward appearances she was just an ordinary, lovable child whose most outstanding characteristics were an enormous affection for her fellow men and all living creatures and a passionate love of the land. She was educated by governesses until she was sixteen. Then her father sent her East to a finishing school, but she, finally," the old man laughed heartily, "finished them!"

Van waited.

"When she came back," Lowell paused and Van knew instinctively that he was deliberately omitting a chapter of her life, "she asked Garland if she might take over the management of Kilo-hana ranch, one of his many holdings. Garland was reluctant to let her for many reasons. Kilohana is isolated from the rest of the island by forests and lava flows and she had not been trained for such work. Finally, he agreed to allow her to try to run it for a year."

Lowell paused, his blind eyes fixed on the extravagant slope of the island.

"Unfortunately, Garland and his daughter are naturally rather antagonistic in temperament but she proved to his satisfaction that she was competent to run the place successfully. That was five years ago. Since then she has built up the herd to a peak unequaled by any other ranch on this island. All the stock on the place, Golden Guernseys, Herefords and Holsteins, are registered and even the sheep dogs she uses to round up the cattle are pedigreed. She has untiring energy, an immense pride in her work and a tremendous affection for everything pertaining to Kilo-hana.

LAVA

She has proved, convincingly, in my estimation that when you do your work, loving it, you fulfil earth's finest dream."

Van sat silent, feeling rebuked, perhaps because he had never worked. The riotous garden seemed to creep closer and the distant reaches of the island to stir slightly. He looked at the old man leaning upon the arms of his chair, his heavy figure sagged a little as though weary from wrestling with unending darkness but his fierce spirit burned on and by its very force lightened the eternal night enveloping him.

Van shifted his position a trifle, and waited.

"Ku-lani," Lowell resumed, "has pledged herself without knowing, I suspect, for she is young, to—life. She has no consciousness of herself as an individual and is magnificent in the singleness of her purpose. People criticize her, feel that she is wasting herself at Kilo-hana, but that is as one sees it. To me it seems that she squanders her force and youth to help life forward. She is selfless, and her affection, her feeling for Kilo-hana," he broke off, looking thoughtful, then continued, "is—extraordinary, but then it is an extraordinary place. Beautiful."

"Mr. Lowell," Van interrupted, "this whole island is, if such a thing is possible, *too* beautiful. I should think," he stared at the green fall of the island to the sea and felt or imagined he felt the soil throb, once, beneath him, "that it could easily enslave a man."

Lowell smiled. "It has—many."

"My father held that if a person wishes to pass through

LAVA

life with a minimum of suffering, he should never permit any person, cause or country to possess him."

"And?" Lowell inquired in a voice that was like a low rumble of distant thunder.

"It has been the principle upon which I've built my life."

Lowell started to speak, then a voice with a charming upward inflection called from inside the house:

"Kai-ko!"

"Loki wants me; you'll have to pardon me. We'll finish this some other time. I'm interested."

Van watched him make his slow way down the veranda and a hint of hurt showed in his eyes for a moment, then he relaxed and contemplated the blue afternoon with enormous contentment. Tawny sunlight prowled in fierce splendor across land and sea, piled clouds held mighty conferences above the horizon that towered, a menacing blue wall, up into the sky.

By a system of systematic wandering, by being an impermanent dweller in many lands and a permanent one in none he had succeeded in achieving a complete and satisfying sense of detachment. Deliberately, and in the full consciousness of what he was doing, he had elected to be a spectator of and not a participant in life but he gave to it the same polite attention he would have accorded actors in a play whose theme did not interest him particularly. He was invulnerable because elusive. But people who met him, even briefly, were attracted to him. He was invariably courteous, friendly despite his aloofness, cultured, and was the possessor of a delightful, ironical sense of humor about himself and life in general.

People liked to have him about. He had visited on African farms and Chinese tea plantations, on South American ranches and in Alaskan mining camps. He was a perfect guest, sufficient to himself when others were occupied but interested in everything going on about him. Over six feet tall, slim, and browned by many suns, somehow, he was, despite his length of limb, always graceful. His movements were deliberate as though he possessed all eternity to use for himself, but people instinctively divined that his leisurely manner was not laziness but rather an immense untroubled serenity, and it was obvious to even the most casual observer that he had never been, even remotely, touched by life.

His fine intelligent face seemed longer than it was because of a becoming baldness and when he smiled his skin seemed to glow faintly as though the inner man lighted with a sudden warm impulse of liking for his fellow men. People were reluctant to have him move on because he created an impression, or illusion, of being an interested visitor from some remote planet, only temporarily of the earth, therefore desirable.

A Hawaiian rode up, dismounted, tied his horse to the flame tree and crossing to the house seated himself on stone steps leading to Garland's office, half glimpsed through an open door and window that broke the warmth of the time-mellowed wall with a sort of chilly emptiness. The man drew out a pipe, short, dark, diminished with years, like himself, and contemplated the mouth piece, fashioned out of steer's horn, thoughtfully. In his eyes was a vaguely bewildered expression as though he had never been quite able to grasp the why of life and he sat as though all his days had been spent waiting to do Garland's bidding. Van experienced an instant of compassion, then a sense of satisfaction spread through him at the wisdom of his own untrammeled existence.

"Puhi!" Garland's voice called.

The Hawaiian rose, a trifle stiffly and crossed the veranda walking a little sidewise like a crab. He was brown, and cramped from years in the saddle.

"*Ae*, Ha-ole Hao."

Leveling rays of sunshine flooding the room, bare as a cell save for a polished *koa* desk and chairs set uncomfortably about, showed Garland's stiff figure bending over the paper-littered desk and in a corner, rocking placidly, Loki.

The Hawaiian crossed the threshold, hat in hand, and waited.

"When Luke and Ben come in send them to me," Garland ordered.

"*Ae*, Ha-ole Hao."

"Where's David?"

"He go mountain after lunch to bring down steers with the boys to ship to Honolulu Monday."

"I want to see him the minute he comes in."

"*Ae*, Ha-ole Hao."

"Tomorrow is Sunday. I want to give a *luau* for the

malihini who is staying here. Tell the boys to kill five hogs and a fat heifer."

"*Ae*, Ha-ole Hao."

Puhi started to replace his hat and the withered wreath dropped off the crown at Garland's feet. Puhi started slightly and his eyes went apprehensively and instinctively to Loki's.

"Bad luck, John, when a *lei* falls," the woman remarked, looking at her husband.

"I'm not a Hawaiian to be alarmed."

"I not scare, but I take notice," Loki said and Van smiled involuntarily.

Puhi picked up the wilted wreath, looking at it reproachfully and accusingly. He replaced it upon his hat and his eyes went, carefully and remindingly, to Loki's.

"You know, John," the woman said in a voice that, because of its seductive inflections, compelled Van to listen, "the Hawaiians not liking much because you build your new mill on that old *heiau* site. Before they Christian those places just like church to them. Good chance tomorrow to make just small sacrifice. You rich, never miss a few chicken and a pig. Bring good luck anyway."

"I'm not a Hawaiian—"

"Oh, I know, you are Ha-ole Hao," the woman conceded with a merry laugh, "strong as the iron for which you are named, but not good sense to make gods mad when just as easy to make them glad. Those little things you give just respect."

LAVA

Garland pushed back his chair and a secret smile devoured his wide gray mask of a face.

"Any more you like tell me, Ha-ole Hao?" Puhi asked.

"Not now."

The man went out as though relieved to escape from the chilly atmosphere of the room into the stupendous sunshine.

Loki rocked, looking thoughtfully at her husband.

"Much fun tomorrow, everyone getting ferns for the table and *maile* to make *leis*." She waited. "John."

"Yes?"

"You going to ask Napier to come?"

Garland's face closed.

"Better ask, he your own boy. Seven years, nearly eight, since he went to live on that poor ranch in Kau and three times that damn lava come down and spoil plenty land. When he marry las' year you never go over and now his wife going to have baby. No sense stay mad, only waste time."

"Napier defied me!"

Van felt a faint shock of astonishment realizing that Garland had another son who evidently no longer existed for his father. The fact was unpleasantly illuminative of an unsuspected side of his host's character.

"I know," Loki brushed it aside, "I hear what kind you two saying that time you fight in this office. You say, 'Napier, you're a bad son. I've given you every advantage that education and money can give but you are just like a Hawaiian. All you want to do is to sing and make love and wear *leis*.' Then Naps get sassy and talk back. 'What better things are there to do? If I'm a bad son you're a worse father for you are greedy and want to live my life as well as your own. I'm not a vegetable like Ben and Luke.' I picking flowers outside and have to laugh it sound so funny, then I shame to listen any more and go away."

"If Napier had been willing to be guided by me he'd be as well fixed as his brothers. I've made a success of my own life and it stands to reason that I can make successes of my sons."

Loki stared at her husband, then at the lawless land, drunk with its own beauty.

"John, you are just like your house, white and stiff. It always remind me of a dead *koa* tree in the green forest. Long time those old fellas stand up but after by and by the young trees get more strong and push them over. Luke and Ben do just like you say but they not much account, just cabbages; Napier and David and your girl Ku-lani—"

Garland tossed his wife a letter which she read painstakingly then looked up.

"Now, John," she protested, "why after you say Ku-lani can buy Kilo-hana do you change your mind? Why, she have it half buy right now."

"On giving the matter further thought I feel it will be wiser not to let her have it outright."

"Why, because you scared then she do just what she like?"

"Partly."

"You think she no do that now?" Loki asked with a

LAVA

magnificent peal of laughter. "Everyone in Kona little scare of you, John, except me, but I your wife. I know you marry me for my land but I not care. I proud to have swell white man for my husband. You smart but not with your children. Always you fighting with the best ones. Already you lose Naps and sure you lose David and Ku-lani if you not looking out. I bet she wild like hell about this," and Loki indicated the letter lying on her broad expanse of lap.

Garland's face tightened.

"Better you go little easy, John," Loki's amazing voice, holding all the warmth of the afternoon, went on. "Pity you trap Danvers Lowell into marrying with your niece Drina when he always love Ku-lani. If I Drina I shame to marry my own cousin's sweetheart but she so ugly I guess she scare maybe she never catch 'nother man. Danvers good boy and always I sorry for him marry to that stick. He just like Kai-ko. Pity Kai-ko get blind when he trying to help you with that rivet in your old mill. Before he busy man, now he just sit and wait."

Van stared at the mighty clouds holding secret consultations above the polished sea.

"That time when Kai-ko mortgage his land to you, when Ku-lani in America, you tell Danvers that Ku-lani going to marry with rich swell fella and if he take Drina you cancel Kai-ko's mortgage. Danvers sore because he believe that lie you been telling and he half crazy because his father get blind so he marry Drina to help the old man out. Then when Ku-lani hear about it she marry first fella who ask

LAVA

her to pay Danvers out. All your fault, John. Why you not let the kids alone?"

"I did not think Ku-lani and Danvers would make a good match."

"You think but you don't know! I feel sorry when Ku-lani come back all divorce and with a baby."

Van glanced up. So that was the chapter Kai-ko Lowell had left out. He smiled faintly. Sent to school to be finished and returning divorced and with a baby. Delicious!

"Dudie nice kid," Loki's voice went on, "but kid not enough when woman is young. Need a man too. That time she ask you to let her run Kilo-hana you think she no can but she make good money for you. Ku-lani swell girl but I very shame because before she begin to buy it, you only pay her one hundred dollars a month and she doing the work of three men. She keep the books, run the ranch, register the calves and boss the dairy. If Luke or Ben running Kilo-hana you pay them two or three times that much and throw a bookkeeper in, but because Ku-lani is a girl—"

"She did not have to work. I would have supported her."

"What she want to do hanging round here? Just sit? Better she work like she does."

A hard silence filled the room; then Loki rose and laid her plump, tapered hand on her husband's shoulder.

"John, you little mad because I telling you these things but inside you know I am right. You come to Kona, your kids all born here but because Hawaii not just like your old land you think it not very good; you scare that the kids going to turn out like it." She gazed out of the door, sharp-edged, shadowed with blue, at the lawless contours of the island. "John, you are strong but the land is stronger, no use to fight with it for your children. Ku-lani and Naps and David listen to the heart of this island beating, feel the lava running in its veins. By and by their kids be just like Hawaiians. Look at Kai-ko; he all white, his people missionary stock on both sides for three generations but he just like Hawaiian inside. If people live in America long time they get just like Americans, the same in Hawaii. You not liking much to admit it but inside you know I speak true."

Garland thrust his chair back.

"Ha-ole Hao."

He looked up and it was evident that he loved the title bestowed upon him by the Hawaiians.

"Yes?"

"Better you go little easy. Gods not like when men get too proud and hard. When that *lei* fall off Puhi's hat they warning you. You took Kona and Kona will take another of your kids as *mohai*, sacrifice in return, if you not careful. No use you try to get between them and the land. I not like that *lei* business much."

Garland smiled.

"Loki, you are a good wife and in many ways, despite your lack of education, a sound-thinking, intelligent woman, but that last speech proves you are all Hawaiian at heart."

"Maybe, but you wait and see. Sure some damn kind of thing going to happen."

She walked to the doorway, filling it, and Van marveled

LAVA

at the grace and beauty of mature Polynesians. With one hand she held a fold of her *holoku* against the splendid curves of her great breasts but the serene beauty of her face was marred by emotion.

Van looked at her compassionately. He had no consciousness of eavesdropping because he was in no wise concerned with the affairs of his fellow men, but when he saw someone involved in life he felt as though he had witnessed a deed of violence. It had been merest chance that he had met Allan White and come to Kona. The complications of the Garland family were not his affair, but this fine mountain of a woman was perturbed because she had permitted the thread of her life to become entangled with other people's. He moved uneasily and picking up his book began reading.

After a little he closed the worn volume with a frown. For the first time since he could remember he found himself unable to detach himself completely from his surroundings. Puhi returned and sat down on the steps staring at the austere house buried in its mad growth of orange and purple flowers. Luke and Benjamin rode in and Puhi went to take their tired horses. They barely acknowledged the old man's presence and Van watched them walking toward the office with great, leisurely strides. Men with large, flat, vacant faces, wooden, moving mechanically but apparently always conscious of themselves in a pleased way. They passed up the steps and through the cold doorway which was like a shark's mouth.

Hawaiians in checked *palakas*, lasso-soiled breeches, dusty

LAVA

leggings and flower-weighted hats rode past and vanished behind pink, flowering oleanders hiding the barns. The sun was falling rapidly down the last slope of the sky and the tremendous blue of the sea had dimmed to a smoky purple save where the fierce light struck it until it almost clanged like metal.

From within the office came voices. "The *makai* lands . . . seven tons of sugar to the acre . . . Coffee gone up six cents the hundred pounds . . . Shipping a hundred and fifty head Monday."

Van moved restlessly and opened his book. Sounds disturbed him, the busy scratching of a pen adding up profits, the echo of the sea against lava promontories, horses being ridden into dusty corrals, the hearty slap of men's hands on sweat-caked haunches as tired mounts were sent out to pasture. From behind the barns came the indignant outraged squealing of pigs being dragged to slaughter, voices, laughter and the throbbing of a guitar.

Van rose and walked away through the still aisles of the garden staring at the landscape that poured seaward and at the sea, which seemed to pour toward the land. Probably the illusion was created by the steep pitch of the country. He estimated that Garland's house must be somewhere in the neighborhood of fifteen hundred feet above sea level and it could not be more than a mile and a half to the shore.

Strolling across the lush grass he was amazed to feel the crunch of cinders beneath the sod. He passed under the vast, peaceful green umbrellas of monkey pods and through

LAVA

the pungent, purple shade of mangoes. To the south the long outlines of Mauna Loa showed and to the northeast Hualalai, its rimline broken by savage volcanic cones showing like purple boils against the sky.

Book in hand he stood noting stone walls undulating like slow gray serpents over the land and the arrested flight of forests seaward. The very contours of the district attested to a once-liquid condition. He felt vaguely uneasy and perturbed and walked quietly as though fearful of awakening malevolent forces silently at work about him.

A battered Packard of ancient make smoked up the strip of dusty road and came to a noisy halt in the quadrangle. A girl got out of it, spoke to the lusty Hawaiian at the wheel, then started toward the office. . . . Ku-lani, in all likelihood, coming to battle with her father.

Van realized, with relief, that her advent had shattered the eerie quality of the evening. He looked at her with interest. She was not pretty but had an odd, arresting face, guiltless of powder or rouge, and she walked as though bent upon reaching the heart of life. She gave an impression of vitality and strong, tired youth. Hatless, clad in dusty faded blue dungarees with a shirt open at the neck she was forceful without being in the least masculine. Her brown hair was parted simply to one side and knotted at the nape of her neck. With hasty, determined strides she went up the steps, paused for an instant to lay her hand on Puhi's shoulder, then vanished into the room that was like a shark's belly filled with swallowed Garlands.

The old Hawaiian's eyes followed her adoringly and a

LAVA

trifle apprehensively, then with a sigh he leaned back against the post. Watch-dog of Garland interests, Van suspected, on duty practically all day and night and in all likelihood sleeping anywhere but always at his post outside the office until the extinguished lights in the big house told him the man he served had retired.

Van saw Kai-ko come out and feel his way to his chair. Presently Loki joined him and her relaxing figure spread over the edges of the rocker like *poi* gathered into a monstrous calico bag. They seemed very merry in a quiet way.

He strolled to the bottom of the garden and stared at the twilight-dimmed acres Garland had stamped with his brand. Leaning his elbows on a gate that gave onto a guava grown pasture he looked at little paths which wound away on doubtful errands. Below, green avalanches of vegetation plunged, with a surprising send, to the sharply defined line of the coast. The slopes of the quiescent volcanoes had, all at once, grown gray and old, hinting at threatening, terrific, impossible upheavals and the straight, strong line of the horizon had mounted upward, invading the sky, thrusting it back.

He was conscious of the stillness of the island brooding under his feet and of a sacred quality charging the hushed evening. He straightened up and took his arms off the gate as though resisting the spell of his surroundings and turned and stared thoughtfully at the vine-smothered house.

A Hawaiian girl passed with noiseless bare feet down the veranda carrying a lighted lamp and the office door engulfed her. Rosy smoke spirals uncurled behind the roof-

LAVA

line of the barn just visible above the blossoming tops of the oleanders. The despairing screams of pigs being killed rent the dusk. Van took a deep, fortifying breath. He would go indoors, up to his room, escape from the peculiar atmosphere enveloping him.

As he crossed the quadrangle he heard raised voices and saw through the open door of the office huge shadows, cast by the lamp, confronting each other.

Ku-lani's voice reached him, outraged, indignant.

"Look! Look at *my* hands! Can either of you lay pipe lines, milk cows, mend tractors? I can run Kilo-hana better than the pair of you. I love it. I want it. It's my life! You are both jealous of me because I've had from life what you've never had—a little independence. You are a pair of mechanical toys. Father pulls the strings and you move but you can't even think for yourselves. Father, don't let Luke and Ben persuade you to—"

Van went hastily into the house and saw Loki and Kai-ko's shadowy, rocking shapes, heard Loki's voice of a sudden concerned.

"Kai-ko, I think better I go and help Ku-lani, she not got much chance against three fellas." Then the faint rustle of her dress as she rose, like dry grass stirred by wind.

He hurried up the narrow stair to the front bedroom and closed the door hastily with a gesture of shutting out the world. A tall white ghost he showed in the mirror, his face surprisingly brown above his white shirt and flannels. He laid his book on the dresser and walking to the great four-poster bed, seated himself upon it and began removing his shoes. From below came the continued rise and fall of voices. He stared at the window opening on the great charged darkness without, seeing in his mind again the shadow of Ku-lani's outstretched hands against the white office wall.

"Incredible, I am—indignant," he murmured to himself amazed that such a thing could be possible.

CHAPTER II

When Van was dressed he drew a chair up to the window and sat looking into the scented dark. He had a taste for solitude, outgrowth of a wandering, unattached existence made possible by the substantial inheritance left to him by his father.

He neither liked nor disliked his fellow men; rather he was interested or not interested in them, up to a certain point. His boyhood and young manhood had been spent mostly in a great dark old house in Amsterdam. He had never known his mother but he remembered his father's pale, distinguished face with a sort of regretful affection. Even as a child he had appreciated that his father was a weary, harried soul dissatisfied with the tawdry civilization of the age in which he had been unfortunate enough to be born and had withdrawn from it in body and spirit, a man who for some reason had a profound mistrust of life which he had succeeded in implanting in his son. The years of constant companionship with his father, lack of sufficient contact, until maturity, with others had left their impression upon Van, sensitive and sufficiently young to be seduced by the older man's teachings.

Since his father's death, some fifteen years previously, he had wandered, observing life and people in obscure corners of the world, friendly, courteous, but obviously belonging to himself. A man with sufficient leisure to be kind, by nature gentle, ready enough to help others out of difficulties if it were possible, but never permitting himself to become involved in them.

He had succeeded in passing through life unscathed, untouched but not uncompassionate, reflective but never cynical, an independent—observer.

He looked at his room with satisfaction; its restraint found an echo in him. The white plaster walls without pictures to mar them, the four-poster bed with its starched muslin canopy and the *koa* dresser with its low-turned lamp.

He experienced a moment of regret knowing that he must go down and feel the disturbed vibrations of others washing against him. He realized, almost with dismay, that the events of the afternoon had, in some extraordinary way, left a faint impression upon him. The hunger in Kai-ko's face to see again the barbarically beautiful district of Kona, and Ku-lani's cry to possess the acres upon which she was squandering her force and her youth. Why did people want things? Why want some certain thing more than another? He got to his feet and his long figure stiffened, then relaxed. If it were only possible to pass on to others less fortunate the wisdom bequeathed to him by his father!

Going down the stairs he walked slowly through the living room onto the dark veranda and came upon Kai-ko and Ku-lani seated upon the steps, talking earnestly. He would have retreated but at the sound of his footfall the blind man turned his head.

"That you, Van Dyke?"

"Yes."

"I wondered where you'd got to. Ku-lani, this is Van Dyke, a friend of Allan White's."

The girl said "Hello," as though her mind were occupied with other matters but she glanced up and Van saw she had been crying. She made no effort to conceal the fact and he felt dismayed and evidently showed it, for she said:

"Don't mind; you just happened to be unlucky enough to walk into a family row." And she smiled a trifle disdainfully.

"Sit down, Van," Kai-ko said. "I've just been telling Ku-lani that her father is a very wonderful man but—"

"But I won't be compelled!" Ku-lani interrupted in low, fierce tones and Van smiled and seated himself on the step beside her.

She put out her hand to him sideways as though subconsciously obeying the demands of courtesy and he took her fingers mechanically into his for an instant. Then she withdrew them and laced them tightly into their mates.

"Kai-ko, Father is drunk with authority; his position and power have been too much for him. They've gone to his head! As long as people live to suit him—"

She broke off and stared into the dark.

Van's eyes went, involuntarily, to her locked hands. He had seen their shadow on the wall and an immense compassion filled him. Rough, toil-worn, eloquent. She was still in her dusty dungarees and her hair needed brushing. She was not beautiful in the accepted sense of the word but there was that in her that conjured up visions of strong saplings bent by wind and green hilltops against a blue sky. She sat with her elbows on her knees, her vigorous, beautifully frank body thrusting forward as though trying to peer into the future, in all likelihood, heavy, dark as the night for her.

The light from the opened door cut resentfully into the still, perfumed garden but died when it met the solid massed mangoes standing like green and purple islands above the wild sprawl of lesser tropical growth. Van glanced down at his own hands, browned, fine-skinned, well cared for and his eyes grew thoughtful. Ku-lani seemed entirely engrossed with her thoughts, with what she was saying, unaware or uncaring of his presence. Then suddenly, she seemed to recollect herself. Her strong fingers closed on his wrist in a brief comradely pressure and she turned her face toward him for an instant.

"Forgive me; this is rude, unconventional, but if you'd lived as I do you'd realize that the forms of life don't really matter."

Van looked into her dark eyes, lighted with inner fire, and placed his hand over hers briefly. His touch was impersonal and very gentle, the same with which he would have attempted to console a child.

"I am sure," he said in his courteous way, "that you are entirely right. Would you prefer me to go?"

She shook her head, glanced at him and seemed to see him for the first time.

"I think, if I had time," she said disconcertingly, "that I'd like you, but I'm so busy at present fighting with my father and two elder brothers that I haven't room in my mind for anything else."

Van was mildly astonished, then smiled.

"I am sorry you are so occupied," he said with a hint of playfulness which seemed to be the very essence of him.

"Suppose, Sister-dear," Kai-ko suggested, laying a heavy, affectionate arm across her shoulder, "that you go and clean up a bit. It's about dinner time and your father will be down directly."

"Has David come back yet?" she asked with quick concern.

"I don't think so."

"He'll catch it when he does," Ku-lani said with a kind of indignant sympathy, getting to her feet. She passed through the lighted doorway and a sudden weariness weighted her erect body.

Kai-ko placed his elbows on his knees leaning his weight upon them and Van sat in sympathetic silence. He divined that there was an enormous sympathy between Kai-ko and Ku-lani, the sympathy of those who know the same things, who talk the same language and look at life through the same colored glasses. After a little he said, thoughtfully:

"There *is* something unusually fine about that girl."

Kai-ko inclined his head slightly, and Van saw his blind black eyes burning under their overhanging brows.

"You cannot hasten—tides," Kai-ko said in his deep, resonant voice, "but sometimes it's extremely difficult for a person to sit back and watch another getting experience, painfully. Ku-lani has always been a favorite of mine.

LAVA

It is the boundless in her that I love. I had hoped that she would marry my son Danvers but she is no less my daughter because she did not. I spend more than half my time with her at Kilo-hana. Tomorrow I'm going back with her."

Van stared thoughtfully at the lighted walk that divided the two halves of the garden.

"Kilo-hana is," Kai-ko paused as though searching for the right words, "a hang-over from an older, happier Hawaii. You should see it."

Van started to answer but steps sounded and he turned. Luke stood in the doorway.

"Supper, you two."

Van rose and waited for Kai-ko. He groped, found the pillar, got to his feet and brushing against Van took hold of his arm.

"Where is the sill?"

Van guided him across it and they entered the stiff uncomfortable drawing-room where the various pieces of furniture seemed to be watching one another suspiciously. Luke walked ahead, his long limbs moving jerkily and even the back of his head looked futile, vacant, intent upon nothing.

Garland glanced up as they entered. He stood with his hand grasping the back of his chair, casting a monstrous shadow on the wall. Loki was already seated at the opposite end of the table, a fresh wreath of flowers about her neck and a flower stuck into her high-piled, wavy hair. She put out a hand and touched Kai-ko affectionately on the arm.

LAVA

"Here," and she guided him toward the chair on her left. He found it and sat down.

"And you here," she signaled to the one on her right and Van went to it. Benjamin came in poking his head about like a turkey. He had a colorless face, flat as a pie and when his eyes met his brother's he grinned vapidly as though they shared an obscene secret.

"Where is Ku-lani?" Garland asked sharply as he seated himself. His sons followed suit. Van waited.

"Oh, she come in a minute," Loki said airily. "Sit down." She smiled up at Van, and he obeyed.

Beside him was a vacant chair, opposite another, David's probably. Garland began eating his soup furiously and Luke and Benjamin ate also.

Loki found Kai-ko's napkins and laid it across his knees.

"There your soup, old man." She steered his hand a little. "Look out, got alligator pear in it and I don't want it all splashed on my nice clean *holoku*," and she laughed and patted Kai-ko's unsteady, mottled hand.

Kai-ko smiled, found his spoon and was just raising it when Ku-lani entered. She paused for the ghost of a second in the doorway and Van glanced up. Her hair had been brushed and he suspected she had powdered her face, from its whiteness. Kai-ko turned as though to see her and as she crossed to the table Van rose. She pulled out the empty chair by Kai-ko and sat down, but her eyes met Van's for an instant, surprised, appreciative and friendly.

Luke and Benjamin glanced at her and something in

LAVA

their blank, expressionless faces called Van's attention to the fact that she had not changed her clothes. Above the rough blue calico shirt her face showed strained and tired. Her eyelids were still red and under the youthful curve of her cheek which was like a bird's folded wing, delicate and strong, he could see the determined set of her jaw. Her eyes swept her brothers' faces contemptuously, then went to her soup plate. She ate mechanically without tasting her food. Once, seeing the empty chair she frowned.

Garland addressed a few remarks to Van, wiped his mouth and laid his spoon down in his empty plate. He looked around impatiently and Loki called, "Helen" and a barefooted Hawaiian girl slid in noiselessly and removed the empty plate, replacing it with another.

Outside the dark night seemed to hold its breath waiting.

"What time tomorrow the *luau?*" Loki asked, looking down the length of the table at her husband entirely occupied with the business of eating.

"About two."

"You ever been to a *luau*, Van?" she asked.

"Never."

"Good fun. Tomorrow I make a *lei* for you my own self."

He smiled at her. She was delightful and the charm of her voice affected him subtly. Years of being married to Garland seemed not to have dimmed her enjoyment of life. She brushed aside the unpleasant as though it did not exist. Frankly, despite the charged atmosphere, she appreciated her food, making delighted asides to Kai-ko and Van alternately while the others ate on.

"You like that fine squid, Kai-ko? I send boy down to-day just to get for you. Now you try a little of this chicken stewed in coconut, Van. Sure you like. Ku-lani, this fine mutton you bring over from Kilo-hana today. I never taste any more good."

She lifted the wreath about her neck as though to give herself more air in order that she might utilize her capacity to the utmost.

"John, you getting on all right?"

A nod.

"Ben, why you no eating this fine mutton Ku-lani bring over?"

A mumbled reply of not liking mutton.

"Sha! What for you lie? Everytime you eating mutton. Just little mad with Ku-lani so you no eat and miss out. Silly!"

A footfall sounded on the veranda and Garland jerked up his head, his eyes fixed on the door.

"David?"

"David no come yet." Puhi's voice sounded apologetic. "I only come ask how many chickens you like the boys kill for tomorrow."

"Four dozen enough, John," Loki said. "Who you asking?"

"Danvers, Drina." Loki glanced at Ku-lani but she did not look up. "The Whites, Wallaces, Greenwells, Parises, Bryants, Anderson, and Louis Macfarlaine."

LAVA

"Pity you not bring Thelma and Dudie over, Ku-lani, but of course you not knowing that John feel like giving *luau* for this nice *haole*," and she smiled at Van as though he had conferred a favor upon them by being their guest.

Ku-lani lifted her head and her eyes went to her father's.

"You're staying," he announced.

"But I've work that I should attend to."

"It'll keep."

The girl's face closed.

"Just one day make no difference," Loki said mildly. "Always you working too hard. Good to rest little. Why you no send Pia over tomorrow to bring Dudie and Thelma? Good fun if they come. But that pretty long drive for Thelma, now, I guess. That Packard!" she laughed merrily, "I think better you buy new one, the poor old thing got seven year."

Ku-lani looked at Loki and smiled.

"Oh, I see, you—how you call it? Little strap?"

The girl nodded.

"Never mind, after you finish buying—" She stopped and for the first time her dark, long-lashed eyes held a hint of apprehension in their depths as they went, involuntarily, to her husband, but he did not appear to have heard her remark.

Puhi waited, his arms hanging unhappily and his eyes fixed upon the empty chair.

"You may go, Puhi," Garland said, seeming all at once

to recollect or realize the man's presence. The Hawaiian nodded and walking heavily across the veranda vanished into the black maw of the night.

All at once from behind the barns came a gust of joyous singing that as suddenly died away. Garland looked up, listened, then attacked his meat again. Ku-lani's eyes sought Loki's and she made as though to leave the table but Loki shook her head ever so little, watching Garland and his sons lest they see.

Van gave her a moment of sincere admiration. Despite her lack of education she possessed a quick tact and sure grasp of the moment. She probably accepted life with roars of delight or indignation but at times of stress could be still, deft.

The singing recommenced and Luke lifted his head and listened, Ku-lani watching him with resentful eyes. He saw it, gave a slow smile, wiped his mouth and glanced at his brother.

Van watched the faces about the table but his mind was intent upon the music which came now faint, now loud. He had heard more-or-less Hawaiian music but this seemed the very essence, the voice of the towering island, exultant, joyous, young, elemental.

Luke turned to his father.

"Listen to David singing."

"David! That's a Hawaiian," Garland said coldly; then an extraordinary expression went over his face making it more angular.

"Puhi!" he almost bellowed.

LAVA

The man came in hastily and stood as though he expected a blow.

"Tell David to stop that catawalling and go to my office and wait until I have finished dinner."

"*Ae*, Ha-ole Hao."

Ku-lani's brown eyes had turned black as they went to Luke and her face blanched and Van realized that it had not been powder but some terrific emotion that had drained the blood out of it leaving it the ghastly, clouded white of chalk.

The meal wore to its end.

Garland pushed his chair back and his shadow went upward like a python's uncoiling. His eyes met Van's and he seemed to recollect himself.

"You'll have to pardon me, Van Dyke. I have work that I must attend to. Make yourself at home."

"Thanks, I will, pray do not concern yourself about me."

He watched Garland go out, marveling that one person without actual violence could succeed in making so many others uneasy and unhappy. Loki leaned over and made an aside to Kai-ko in Hawaiian. Then she rose, sweeping her *holoku* about her.

"Ku-lani."

The girl appeared not to hear her.

"Ku-lani."

Van recognized the upward inflection in the woman's voice which had so charmed him that afternoon when she had called to Kai-ko from inside the house.

LAVA

The girl started and Van was amazed at the absolute blackness of her eyes. The pupils were so dilated that it seemed as though she were listening with them.

Ben and Luke rose and went out looking secret and pleased and Ku-lani followed their great slack backs with indignant eyes. Van realized that the antagonism of these two brothers for their sister was the natural jealousy of the weak for the strong and Ku-lani's was the contempt of the strong for the weak. Although born of the same father and mother they had no common meeting ground.

"Ku-lani," Loki said, laying her plump brown hand on the girl's rigid arm. "Now don't you be doing anykind foolish. Tonight I talk with John. You want Kilohana?"

The girl's ashen face twitched.

"I think I can fix up for you but you do like I say and help me. Go outside and talk to this nice *haole* for a little while."

Loki's eyes met Van's. "Too bad all this family stuff happening just when you come," her lips said, but her eyes, merry as a child's above their concern, had a swift message —"I know I can count upon you to help me."

"I shall be delighted to talk to Miss Garland if she wishes."

Ku-lani looked at him with tired indifference, then seeing the kindness in his eyes said:

"Let's go into the garden."

She bent and kissed Kai-ko and the old man squeezed her hand. She straightened up and walked onto the veranda.

Van followed, a tall dark figure in his evening clothes. When they reached the steps Ku-lani stopped.

"I have no cigarettes."

"Let me find you some."

"There are some packages in a brass box on the *koa* table in the drawing-room."

He found them and asked the girl called Helen for matches. When he got to the veranda Ku-lani had vanished. Looking down the walk he saw her riding boots but the rest of her was engulfed by darkness. Van joined her and she lighted a cigarette with slightly unsteady fingers. For a moment they waited and Van felt the presence of trees and heard the infinitesimal whispering and rustling of shrubs and flowers about them settling down to sleep.

Ku-lani thrust the package and matches into her breeches pocket and halted for a moment in thought. Then she turned.

"I'm going around to listen to what Father is saying to David. Come with me."

Van smiled at her frank, avowed announcement that she intended to eavesdrop. It was eloquent of her emancipation from all the shams and accepted forms of life, somehow characteristic. She was honest about and unashamed of what she intended to do. It was youth allied with youth against age and the despotism of age.

She pushed through the thicket of Japanese musk and he followed more carefully lest he injure the fragrant branches already heavy and brittle with dew. They reached the edge of the lighted quadrangle and Ku-lani put out her hand, halting him.

"If you'd rather be alone," he began, but she signaled him, impatiently, to be quiet. The light from an upper window outlined her profile, pale, intent, resolute. Raised voices came from the office. Her hand found his and gripped it and he looked down at it with a sort of amazement. Somehow it was even more moving than her face, tired, kind and—strong.

"Father's at it!" she whispered with fierce contempt.

She went a little forward in order that she might see. By the light spilling out of the open door and window Van saw Puhi sitting at his post, somewhat in shadow. He moved once, miserably, and his hunched shoulders looked vaguely unhappy. Through the door he saw David facing his father, and the knuckles of his hand, gripping the back of a chair, showed shiny in the hard white light of the room. Dark, moist hair went backward off his forehead like the waves of a sun-burnished, wind-furrowed sea.

"I tell you I'll have no more of it!" Garland said. "You're nothing but a God-damned Kanaka like your brother Napier!"

"Naps is worth ten of Luke and Ben."

"Don't drag your brothers into this. They have sufficient brains—"

David laughed a doubting laugh. "They know which side their bread is buttered!" But it was evident from the expression of his face that he, like everyone else, was somewhat in awe of his father.

LAVA

Ku-lani's fingers gripped Van's coat sleeve.

"I see no cause for laughter," Garland said, "and I'll have you understand that I absolutely forbid—"

David threw up his head.

"I won't stop going to Hi-ball's, Dad, and you can't make me. I'm young. I want some fun. I like old Hi-ball and his kids, they enjoy life! I'm sick of pussyfooting around this house!"

Van's eyes clouded. Again, youth pitted against the despotism of age. Youth, chained but belonging to itself. At bay, but giving battle.

Ku-lani swallowed and her eyes went up to Van's and he saw terror in their depths. A cowboy passed through the quadrangle on his way to the barns, bucket and knife in hand. The black silhouette of his figure passing hastily through the light looked furtive and sinister. He vanished through a gap in the hedge of oleanders and Ku-lani caught her breath sharply as Garland took a step toward his son.

The boy threw up his arm and stepped back.

"Don't hit me, Dad," he warned.

Van saw Puhi make a tortured movement, dragging himself deeper into shadow like a mortally wounded animal trying to escape from pain. Ku-lani's hand shook and her fingers dug into Van's arm.

"They mustn't—fight," she said in a smothered voice.

"I can't very well interfere," Van said regretfully.

The office door closed with a slam that shattered the stillness of the night. Van felt curiously upset.

LAVA

"Do you want me to go in?" he asked. "I—will."

She gave a violent, protesting shake of the head, then sat down upon the grass and began tearing it up in handfuls.

"Now David'll get what Naps did and he'll go—too!" she said. "I suppose I'll be the next. The three of us were born into this family by mistake."

She rubbed her hands over her face several times in a bewildered fashion.

Van listened; the night was impregnated with dynamite and dreadfully still.

"Miss Garland—"

"I'm not a miss. I've been married, divorced, and have a child nearly six years old."

Van experienced a faint shock of surprise, then recalled that he had heard it that afternoon but it had not registered for then she had been only a name. Now she sat on the grass before him and her very stillness was more moving than tears. She was too young to be so frozen.

"If you want me to—" he began but she made a fierce dissenting gesture.

"It would be no use." Her voice sounded weary and utterly forlorn.

He seated himself on the grass beside her and took her rough hand into his smooth ones with a close, kind clasp.

"Hold it tight," she commanded. "I'm crying—inside."

Van felt profoundly shocked. He had an unpleasant sensation as though he were watching something beautiful being destroyed.

"What do you wish me to do?" he asked. "Pray command me."

She glanced at him as though she had suddenly discovered that she was in the company of some being who had strayed to earth by mistake.

"I am sorrier than I can tell you that you are so upset," he said.

"That doesn't help. Poor Naps, poor David and I—I want Kilo-hana dreadfully! It's my—life!"

Van winced a trifle. He had heard her affirming that once already that afternoon. He looked at her pure profile. In her eyes was the magic of wide spaces. Then he realized with a slight start that she was still talking to him, or to herself, more probably, thinking aloud; but he got the last words.

"And now Father's in a fury and I probably—won't get it."

Her voice seemed to drop like a winged bird.

Van felt inadequate and groped about in his mind for words that might help to console her.

"My father," his voice sounded forced and unlike his own, "always held that the only possible way for a person to pass through life without too much suffering was never to allow a cause, person or place to ensnare him."

"I don't understand."

"He meant that the wise person looks at life as he would look at a play but takes no active part in it."

The girl looked at him incredulously, her tired face gray in the dim light.

LAVA

"But," she protested, "isn't that—slacking?"

Her eyes opened with enormous surprise as though she could not credit that anyone could be guilty of such a thing, much less this tall, kind man sitting at her side.

Van was moved by the sincere accent of her words, simple but utterly disturbing. He shifted his position slightly and a sort of terror filled him for a moment, then resentment. Not for her, for whom he had an immense compassion, but because her words implied that his armor against life was a futile, crazy thing unworthy of him. He thought of Kai-ko's words of that afternoon. "She squanders her youth and her force—to help life forward!"

He looked into the night and it grew more dark; then a sharp beam of light cut it and their hands tightened instinctively.

David lurched onto the veranda, his young face livid. He went unsteadily to the steps, put his hand against a pillar for an instant, then went into the quadrangle. Garland called after him and his voice sounded as hollow as that of a man speaking from a tomb.

The boy did not turn.

Ku-lani scrambled up and ran after him grasping his arm. He started to shake himself free, then realizing who it was, stopped and planted a hasty, boyish kiss on her cheek.

"David."

"I'm *pau!*" he cried violently. "Puhi, get my horse."

The man started to rise but Garland stared at him and he sank back into his place. Ku-lani shot an indignant look at her father and for an instant brother and sister conferred

LAVA

hastily together. Van heard Ku-lani whisper, "Kilo-hana." The boy shook his head and muttered, "Can't. You'll sure lose it then."

Ku-lani's hand fell from his arm. Garland called out to her sharply and she turned.

"What!"

"Go inside!"

"Ha-ole Hao!"

The words sounded sharp as two whip lashes on bare flesh. Van looked up startled. Loki was sweeping down the veranda like a battleship bearing upon an enemy squadron. Garland's face changed. Loki saw Ku-lani in the quadrangle and signaled to her with her head to go into the house. She obeyed mechanically. Loki went up to her husband, her large, mild face indignant.

"Ha-ole Hao, I like to talk to you."

He stepped back into the office but she put out her hand anticipating his intention of closing the door. Like a man she faced him.

Van rose and went indoors. In the hall he saw Ku-lani bending over a small marble-topped table scribbling frantically. Seeing him, she looked up and held out a sheet of paper.

"Will you take that to my brother—please."

As he took the note from her, her eyelids went down as though she were utterly spent and he noticed fine lines traced about her eyes and one by her mouth. They shocked him for he was certain that they had not been there an hour before. In the hard overhead hall light she looked done,

LAVA

all her strength seemed to have gone out of her, leaving only her exhausted, spoiled youth. Then the sudden upward flash of her opened eyes startled him.

"Don't think I'm dreadful."

"Dreadful, how could you be dreadful?" Van asked, looking puzzled.

"Because I'm—selfish, for the time being."

"Selfish, Ku-lani?" But he was not conscious of having used her name nor did she seem to notice it.

"I want Kilo-hana so much. If it is mine then David can come."

Van realized with a shock her passionate desire to actually possess what was her own already in her heart.

"You should have it," he asserted to his own astonishment. She regarded him intently with her dark eyes and said nothing; then she shuddered and the line beside her mouth deepened.

"I'll take this—"

Her eyes thanked him.

"I think you should go to bed," he said over his shoulder as he went out. She answered but he did not hear what she said for he was wondering if Loki would be successful.

When Van returned to his room he thought, "I must compose myself. Sleep." But it was not as easy as it should have been. He undressed deliberately, hanging his clothes in the old-fashioned wardrobe. He moved a small table to the side of his bed and put the lamp carefully upon it.

LAVA

The cool linen sheets were soothing to his skin which was, to his amazement, heated. Picking up his book he opened it at a familiar passage but fragments of the evening kept getting between the words his eyes dutifully followed. He saw again David's astonished face as he hastily saddled when the stranger he had met briefly at lunch pushed through the oleanders to give him a note. He had read it and his eyes filled. "Tell Ku-lani I understand—perfectly," he had said, reaching for the girth dangling on the other side of his horse's belly. Deftly, feverishly, he worked and behind him Van had seen men busy scraping dead pigs which looked horribly white and naked in the dim hot glare of lanterns. Buckets of water steamed slowly, knives gleamed and beyond loomed the huge, shadowy barn filled with saddles and slickers hanging like empty yellow ghosts. Dogs edged up to piles of highly colored entrails carefully piled on clean strips of white canvas, men kicked at them and they slunk away.

Van turned on his side, drawing up his long legs. Pressing the book open he shaded his eyes with his hand. From downstairs came the murmur of voices, indistinguishable but disturbing. The absolute stillness outside shouted at him. He got up and went to the window, a long white figure in his silk pyjamas. He stood very quietly as though giving the night his utmost attention. The delicate fragrance of blossoming *inia* trees came to him and the clean sweetness of wet banks of blossoming ginger. The utter and absolute blackness without was impregnated with flower scents, gardenias and bell lilies, jasmine and Japanese musk

LAVA

and the stronger, cleaner smell of trees growing lustily out of rich earth. He felt the immense diapason of the teeming tropical land and was conscious of the strong silent power of vegetable growth. From below came the whisper of the sea against lava promontories and the tiny, persistent sound of thousands of land shells singing in the forests. He thought, "I should leave. This island affects me strangely." Then he smiled. It was not to be thought that the work of a lifetime could be undone in a day or a week. He was invulnerable, thanks to his father's teaching.

He was filled with languor, wrapped in a sense of impending disaster, outgrowth of events transpiring about him. The evening had been disturbing even for an onlooker. He was safe from the onslaughts of life but the fundamental kindness of his nature winced from witnessing the distress of others, defenseless against it. His interest was stirred by fortunes hanging in the balance about him. He went to bed and composed himself for reading.

He heard the minute rustling of night insects at work in the vines swathing the house. The murmur of voices had ceased and he felt or imagined that he felt the island breathing in its sleep. Somewhere a boy was riding away and a girl, sitting perhaps wide-eyed staring at specters menacing her possession of acres she loved. He turned the light higher as though its minute circle could dispel the feeling created by the dark, of an enormous, menacing curtain hiding preparations of violence.

The familiar lines of the pocket-sized volume began

LAVA

exerting their old magic and peace flowed into his limbs relaxing them pleasantly. He closed the book, marking his place with a long forefinger, looked at the title with affection, re-opened it and pursued his reading. Then, all at once the island moved beneath him as though it stirred in its sleep. Strange, he thought, to feel the earth quicken beneath you, but not strange in an island so frankly volcanic.

He recalled his impressions of the previous morning when he had leaned upon the rail of the little Inter-island steamer which had brought him to Kona. For a while it seemed to stalk the receding slopes of the island unsuccessfully. As it followed the curves of the coastline he had watched the three great mountains, Mauna Kea, Mauna Loa and Hualalai dodging and vanishing behind one another like Titans at play. As the ship drew nearer he had experienced a curious sensation; it seemed as though the island expanded as he watched it like a beast filling itself with a great breadth.

The instant he put foot on the soil he appreciated that it possessed a quality unlike that of any other land he had ever visited, or even of its sister islands.

He had seen in the growing light long flows of lava that had once poured relentlessly over the land, wiping out forests and pastures until they had won the huge blue jewel of the sea.

His eyelids grew heavy and he reached his hand out to extinguish the light. Again the earth stirred and was still. Van wondered sleepily if he were going to be fortunate enough to witness an eruption, then drawing a deep breath slid into oblivion.

He was awakened by the sharp rattling of doors and windows as though something were impatient to enter the house. He lighted the lamp and watched a small bouquet of flowers quivering on the dresser. He waited for the house to stop shaking, then as it did not, he put his legs over the side of the bed. The earth stilled, then jerked sharply in the direction of the sea. He heard voices below and from the men's quarters came a long cry, *"Oni-Oni!"* The word coming out of the dark in a strange language had a peculiar effect upon him. He picked up his wrapper, blew out the light, walked to the door and opened it.

Below someone had just finished lighting a lamp.

He saw Garland emerging from his room. Somehow in a bathrobe he looked horribly immoral. His gray hair was rumpled and his face indignant. His skin appeared to be stretched more tightly than ever over his prominent cheek bones. Luke and Ben stood blinking like owls and grinning nervously. Kai-ko emerged like a huge untidy old bear securing his pyjama pants hastily. Loki, coming down the hall carrying a lamp, let out a peal of laughter.

"Kai-ko! Sure sometime you get catch. Just all same Chinaman never sleeping in pants. Shame! You *kolohi* old man!"

She set the lamp on the marble-topped table and stood guarding it with her hand. Van put on his bathrobe and descended the stairs slowly. She looked up and began shaking with laughter.

LAVA

"Fine sight I look in my *mu-mu*," and she indicated the voluminous garment covering but not concealing her ample form. "I fat—like a sow!" and she shrieked with mirth.

Van smiled with his eyes and Loki picked up the lamp.

"Well, what we do—sit up or go back to bed?" she demanded of her husband.

The house swayed outward again in the direction of the sea, then came back sharply. The motion was peculiar and over almost instantly. Kai-ko thrust his hand through his sparse gray hair.

"I think I'll sit on the veranda for a bit. What time is it?"

Van glanced at the grandfather clock.

"Just one."

The old man looked around as though he hoped that Van would accompany him, and always ready to oblige he said:

"I think I'll join you, Kai-ko."

Kai-ko nodded in a pleased fashion and Van was aware of his liking and felt honored. Luke and Ben moved vaguely, tightening their bathrobes.

Garland asked:

"Where's Ku-lani?"

"No use waking her up, she sleeping I guess. Poor Ku-lani."

Loki lighted Kai-ko and Van through the living room.

"I leave here," she said, setting the lamp on the floor. "If shake again, Van, grab quick."

He nodded and guided Kai-ko to his rocker. For a while

they sat in silence and the dark night was filled with the vast, regular breathing of the sea. From the men's quarters came voices and lights showed between the sturdy treetrunks.

"Have you ever seen a volcano in eruption?" Kai-ko asked.

"Never."

"It's the most awe-inspiring and magnificent sight on earth. There is a terrible beauty to flowing lava. I saw Mauna Loa erupt first in 1868, when I was nine years old and it had been in eruption previously in '52, '55 and '59 but I was too young to remember it. Since then it has gone off in '72, '73, '76, '77, '81, '96, 1903, 1907 and several times in the last ten years; the most spectacular flows being in 1919 and 1926 but—I did not see them."

"Quite a record," Van laughed. "It would be rather wonderful luck if it went off during the week I expected to be here."

"Must you go in a week?" Kai-ko's voice sounded regretful.

"My passage to the Orient is engaged."

They talked for a while and Van thought of the forested, lava-blighted slopes hidden from sight by the dark. One by one the lights in the men's houses were extinguished and the night seemed to fold its wings more closely about the island. Conversation grew fitful and Van saw his companion was dozing. He noted the bare feet protruding from the end of Kai-ko's pyjamas; they were as perfect as those of a child, the feet of one who has gone barefoot more than half his life. He studied the old man. Despite the Ayran quality of his skin he was Hawaiian in appearance and manner. He had the generous magnificence, the leisurely dignity, the directness and simplicity which characterizes Polynesians.

His heavy head was sunk a little forward and the light tinged his gray mustache with yellow. His white cotton pyjamas outlined his figure which sagged a little even when he stood, but it was still charged with vitality and majestic as the hidden island. Van thought of Loki's words of that afternoon, realizing their truth. "Look at Kai-ko, he all white, his people missionary stock on both side for three generations but Kai-ko just like Hawaiian." It was inevitable that an environment so vital should affect those whose lives were lived under its influence. He stared at the garden and listened to Kai-ko's breathing, the faint, audible breathing of the aged. The night was without wind but an occasional vagrant air rustled the foliage below the veranda railing and hurried on, touched the guavas and coffee beyond the stone wall and died.

"Kai-ko, I'm afraid you'll get cold."

Kai-ko nodded, got to his feet and Van picked up the light. The old man's hand closed on his arm and Van led him, carefully, to his room, blew out the lamp and went upstairs to bed.

From below came voices, Loki's and Garland's. Evidently they had not gone to bed but were sitting on the veranda directly below.

"Now, John,"—Loki's voice sounded conciliatory—"it

LAVA

no use you getting mad. I tell you this afternoon some damn kind of thing going to happen but you no believe and no listen to me. You smart but you no got good sense! Now you been lose two boys. Luke and Ben look you with open mouth like you were God and it make you feel good. David and Naps not like that so you always licking them when they kids and fight with them when they grow up. After by and by, sure, you feel sorry and shame. If you just losing one boy people think, well, that kid no good; when you lose two they begin thinking more. Now if you damn fool with Ku-lani and she go too then everybody be talking like this, 'What the Hell the matter with that Ha-ole Hao? All his kids leave him.'"

Van smiled. Loki was the possessor of an enormous sagacity only possible in a primitive woman fighting, not for her own young in this case, but for members of the younger generation who, her instinct told her, were the most worthy and fitted to carry on the race. The instinct prompting her was as old as the beginning of time. She was remarkable in that she was unafraid of Garland; perhaps the enormous serenity wrapping her soul was impervious to outside disturbances.

"I little angry with you tonight, John, for I not liking my fine Ha-ole Hao to be stupid. No need getting mad because David go to Hi-ball's. He jolly old man. I like very much and his kids good kids. Just lively. You no born in Kona and you not able to understand—"

"I would like to destroy it, to see it destroyed, for it has destroyed two of my sons!"

LAVA

"Hush, John, don't speak so loud. Gods are walking tonight. Listen to them rustling the coffee and to the whisper of their feet on the sea."

Van's skin roughened slightly. He had encountered all sorts of strange experiences in odd corners of the earth, run into adventures, seen life in all its aspects, splendid and sordid, tragic and ludicrous, but somehow this drama was unlike any other he had ever witnessed, for it was one in which an island seemed to participate.

He heard the violent scrape of a chair being pushed back, footsteps pacing up and down and a rocker going serenely back and forth.

After a while:

"Well, John, what you decide?"

"By God, if I let her have it she need never expect to come to me for help if she cannot make it go!"

"She never come—don't trouble."

The pacing recommenced and the rocking. A quiver passed through the island.

"I'll tell her tomorrow."

"My good Ha-ole Hao. And now don't you be letting Luke and Ben—"

"My decisions, once they are made, are never influenced by anyone!"

"That right. You Ha-ole Hao, just like iron. And now I think better we go to bed. Tomorrow must feel fine for the *luau* you giving that nice friend of Allan's. I like very much."

Van smiled in the dark.

CHAPTER III

When he woke dawn was stirring the tree tops. He was, as a rule, a leisurely riser but some tingling quality of the morning, not of the atmosphere, stirred him. He got up and went to the window. Above the green domes of monkey pods he saw the blue wall of the sea swimming up to meet the paler blue of the sky. To the right, through a gap in the massed mangoes, was the summit of Hualalai, violently colored, scarred by fire, the cones showing like unsightly eruptions on the mountain's rough hide.

He dressed and went quietly downstairs. The house was in absolute silence. He glanced at the tall clock, and saw it was just half past six. Being Sunday, everyone doubtless slept late. The house looked conscious of itself in a virtuous way and he walked quickly through it into the gay, reckless garden. He halted for a moment looking about him and inhaled the exaggerated smells of early morning. Behind the barns he heard the stir of life but he wanted to be alone in the freshness of the new day.

The road curved enticingly. Rounding a turn the whole southern sweep of Hawaii showed and in the first clear sunlight the island looked naked with the newness of its recent birth. A line of donkeys passed soberly following a man riding a dilapidated gray mare. Below a vivid pasture the lavender haze of blossoming *inia* trees stood against the blue

LAVA

haze of the sea. The day seemed breathless, aghast at its own beauty, and a waiting stillness, akin to the hush of the first morning of creation, lay on land and sea.

Van pulled his hat over his eyes as though he faced a blinding light. He was subtly aware of the pulse of the sea and the throb of the soil underfoot. He passed a long-legged Hawaiian house. Underneath it pale-eyed, apologetic-looking dogs lay, and meditative fowls picked listlessly at flower beds. A dejected-looking peacock with a plucked neck sat on the stone wall surrounding the garden and he remembered that he had been told that island people coveted its feathers to wear on their hats. The bird seemed aggrieved and conscious of its withered, prune-colored neck. "Never mind, old fellow," Van thought with a smile, "I have a bald head."

A spear of sunlight touched the noble curve of a ruddy gourd hanging against the wall of the house and behind it a lone coconut tree stood sentinel over seas of guava. The growing warmth of the morning drew up smells: damp earth, young forests, tasseled cane, coffee that seemed to blossom and berry at once and the fragrance of fat stock hidden by the luxuriant growth of the land.

He seated himself on a rock and watched the speck of a canoe making its leisurely way around a black lava promontory that jutted beyond a jade green torrent of *kukuis*.

Van looked thoughtfully about him; in Kona shadows, clouds, contours conspired against one.

He glanced at his watch. Seven-thirty; he must go back, breakfast would probably be at eight. As he approached the house where he had seen the peacock, Ku-lani came out of the door followed by the huge Hawaiian he had seen at the wheel of her Packard the previous afternoon. There was passionate determination in the girl's face and the man looked concerned.

Seeing Van, Ku-lani smiled.

"Take the car, Pia, and go over and come back this afternoon for me."

The man nodded, lifted his hat and strode down the road. Ku-lani waited and Van lengthened his stride and caught up with her.

"I hope you had a good sleep; you looked dreadfully tired last night."

"I was, and I slept like a log. Pia said there were a few small earthquakes but I didn't feel them."

"We were all up for a while."

The girl nodded. Her freshly brushed hair had a glint of copper in it but the skin of her face was clouded and chalky. Reaching into her trouser pocket she brought out a smashed package of cigarettes, stopped, lighted one and went on.

"I sent Pia back to Kilo-hana." She spoke the word without a quiver but he knew she was deeply affected. "There is work that must be done and I wanted him to find out if my little Dudie and Thelma—"

"Who is Thelma?" Van asked gently.

"A girl who lives with me—now. We went away to school together." Something in Ku-lani's voice made Van glance at her. It was unemotional but remembering and he

LAVA

recalled that it was while Ku-lani was at school that Kaiko's son Danvers had been coerced into marrying the ugly cousin. Perhaps the girl Thelma had been unfortunate also in some way, thereby forging a bond. He wondered in an uncurious way what manner of man Danvers might be. Ku-lani was worthy of someone very fine.

"How long are you going to be here?" Ku-lani asked as they turned in at the gate.

"About a week. The real reason I'm in Kona is because a friend of yours asked me to look you up and let him know how you are getting on."

Ku-lani glanced up at him.

"Who?"

"Allan White."

She smiled. "He was very kind to me when I was a kid and when I was at school he came a couple of times to see me. And he was a dear to me—" she paused, "just before I came home. I promised to write once in a while and let him know how I was getting on but I never have time. When, if you write to him give him my love and tell him I'm making out all right."

Then a thought seemed to occur to her.

"Why don't you—would you like to come over to Kilohana for a night?"

"I should like to immensely."

"I'll send Pia for you."

"Please don't bother, I can get a car."

She did not appear to hear him. They crossed the quadrangle. Behind the barn men were digging holes in the ground and making fires under piles of porous black rocks. Half a dozen riders were departing with bags slung from their pommels. Ku-lani called out in Hawaiian and they made some laughing sally in reply.

The battered Packard had gone.

Breakfast over, Van took his book and found a shady strip of lawn. Stretching himself out on the warm grass he alternately read and watched the house. People came and went, horsemen rode out and returned, automobiles drove up, men went into Garland's office and came out again.

Loki came down the steps and walked among her flowers selecting them carefully and dropping them into a basket slung on her arm. When it was filled she went to a young banana tree with huge leaves that looked like green bronze with sunlight filtering through their juicy, transparent cells. She plucked at the moist bark with strong brown fingers and tore a long strip away. She repeated the process two or three times, then apparently was satisfied and laid a long gauzy strip like transparent ribbon over her plump arm. Spying Van on the lawn she signaled to him.

"Come! I make your *lei*."

He got to his feet and joined her.

"You look fine with a hat on." She weighed him critically and Van laughed and they were friends.

"How many year you got?"

"Thirty-six."

"Me—fifty!" and her massive body shook and she looked at him mischievously from beneath her upcurling lashes.

LAVA

She seated herself upon the steps placing the basket conveniently close and Van sat down on the step below her, in the sunlight, and watched her deft, tapered fingers busily at work.

"You know, Van," she said with child-like frankness, "before I marry with John I not much account. My father fine old man but in my day girls not go to school much. I no want to learn English, 'rithmetic, all that bunk. I just like to fool round, dance, swim, sing, eat a big feast. And I fine hula-dancer that time." She rolled her expressive eyes. "One time John see me at a *luau* and ask who I was and one fella tell to him, 'That old Ka-aina's girl.' That just little time after John's first wife die and he beginning to look around."

Van smiled involuntarily.

"My father own plenty land that time and I the only child so I guess old John get thinking, 'Never mind if she only native girl when the old man die she have plenty land,' so he ask Papa if he can marry with me. Papa glad for his girl to have swell white husband and I glad too. After we get marry all change, no more hula-dancing and playing around but I always have fun anyway. Ha-ole Hao good man but little hard with the kids. That his nature so no can help. But funny how some peoples never understanding about things. Man's kids not really his kids; they belonging to life. Always John worrying because Naps and David and Ku-lani not just like him, but that silly. Right for parents to give kids their love but not right when they always wanting to give them their thoughts. Those kids got right to their own thoughts. Today belong to us, sure, but tomorrow belonging to the kids and no sense making nuisance about something that we never going to reach, that their job. Sure they going to make some mistakes but better let alone because when they make mistakes they learn and remember when they learning themselves." She stared at the day, splendid with sunshine, then looked back at Van. "Now I wonder why I talking all this kind of stuff?" She smiled enchantingly. Her fine intelligent, lighted eyes were, momentarily, misted. Then she gestured, brushing seriousness aside, and continued deftly binding and weaving flowers to the strip of banana bark which lay like a glossy strip of silk across her ample knees. Van marveled at the wisdom of this uneducated woman.

"Sometimes," she smiled like a mischievous child, "when John going to the states we have little *luau*, just the kids and me and," she rolled her eyes, "and the cowboys. Good fun. Luke and Ben never join in with us but David and Naps and Ku-lani and me raise little Hell. But Luke and Ben never say nothing because"—she looked roguish—"they not so good!" and she elevated her eyebrows. "When Ha-ole Hao gone las' spring to California I send boy over to fetch Naps and his wife, and Ku-lani and Dudie and Thelma come from Kilo-hana and we drink little *Okolehao*, cook pig, dance, sing. Inside I just pure native girl, like to have a good time and make a big noise." She shook with immoderate laughter. "I dance hula to make everyone laugh. Too fat now, just wriggle around and make foolish—"

LAVA

"Loki," Van said, "I'm sure you would be delightful under any circumstances."

She beamed. "You nice. Pity you so bald." There was real regret in her voice.

Van smiled.

"There, that finish," she said, touching the wreath. "Give me your hat."

He handed it to her and she placed the garland upon it.

"Thank you, Loki."

Van accepted it, his hat which had been made by a Parisian hatter, and he turned it around thinking that the designer would experience considerable astonishment were he to stroll into the exclusive little shop with the head gear that the good man had fashioned expressly for him, so decorated.

Men crossed the lawn carrying bags sprouting ferns; others laid down tarpaulins and began covering them with the pungent plunder of moist forest glades. Ku-lani joined them and it was evident that her father's workers adored her. He heard rounds of laughter and wondered if Garland had made known to her his decision of the night before. But when she joined them he knew that he had not. Her lips were dry and the color of paper.

Van felt indignant at the unnecessary cruelty of prolonging her suspense. She sat down beside him as though she had known him a long time.

Loki glanced sharply at her.

"Ku-lani."

The girl looked around.

"Ha-ole Hao no been talk to you yet?"

LAVA

She shook her head and stared with hard eyes at a crack in the concrete.

"Ku-lani."

"Yes?"

"I tell you something."

The girl jerked up and in her eyes were the violent and somber hues of a tropical sunset.

"Last night I talk to Ha-ole Hao and he say he decide after all to let you finish buying Kilo-hana but no let on I tell you."

The smoldering fires in Ku-lani's dark, dilated pupils were extinguished. She pressed her dry lips together and swallowed and her work-ravaged hand gripped Van's arm painfully. He knew he had nothing whatsoever to do with her emotion; he merely happened to be the nearest human being in reach. But her emotion affected him and he wondered, with vague dismay, what it would be like to feel so dreadfully, so keenly.

He glanced at Loki, who was slowly wiping her eyes on a fold of her voluminous dress.

"Silly! I cry because I happy for you," she apologized.

"Loki," Ku-lani said, putting her hand back until it rested on the woman's knee, "I feel closer to you than I ever have to anyone in my life. You are like Kona, rich, warm, living."

She looked at the woman with immense affection and Van realized that these two, so utterly unlike, were fundamentally one metal, in that they were both acquainted with life's terrific realities.

LAVA

Loki made no reply but her hand went to the girl's head and caressed it, then she rose and walked slowly toward Garland's office.

They sat for a while in the sun without speaking and Van stared at the green fall of the island, at the teeming sea and steaming forests eternally brewing their magic. Ku-lani lighted a cigarette. When she was finished she tossed the butt away and it smoked hurriedly on the walk. A long shudder passed through the island but the girl did not appear to notice it nor did the expression of her face alter. From the workers on the lawn came the cry:

"*Oni-Oni! Oni-Oni!*"

Ku-lani seemed to come back from a great distance.

"I feel—undone. You brace for rotten things but happiness takes you off your guard. Have you ever loved anything fearfully?"

Van shook his head.

"Then you can't possibly understand what I'm feeling now." She looked at him thoughtfully. "You give me a peculiar feeling of being—well, a sort of ghost, of not being in life—really."

"I've made it my business to keep out of it."

"But you can't!"

"Can't what?"

"Keep out of life, because everyone's in it. *Part of it.*"

"My father held, as I told you last night, that every individual is entitled to absolute intellectual, moral and physical liberty."

"Only to a certain extent. Life to me," Ku-lani said,

"is like a snowball, a whole composed of atoms welded solidly together. If the particles didn't melt together the ball would fall apart."

"That's an interesting thought but it seems to me that people in general allow life to be thrust upon them; they permit themselves to become involved."

Ku-lani's hand went out protestingly.

"You can't become involved in a thing you are already in, for, as I said to you a moment ago, everyone is in life whether or not he wishes to be or realizes that he is."

Her words affected Van profoundly for they attacked the careful structure of his life which had been a masterpiece of aloofness. He had been lounging against the steps but he sat up and laid his crossed arms upon his knees. Ku-lani leaned down and flicked a piece of grass off her boot.

"Your words are disturbing, Miss Garland."

"Ku-lani."

"Ku-lani." He glanced at her—the absolute naturalness of that girl!

She weighed him curiously.

"I didn't mean them to be. The fact that I stated I can illustrate very simply." She found a cigarette but did not light it. "When I came back from school divorced and with a baby I felt lost, discarded. Things had happened too quickly to me, before I was ready for them, but I knew it was mostly my own fault so couldn't say anything. I was in a daze, sitting on the bank of a river which hurried by me eager to reach the sea. I was conscious in a dim way of life, work, going on about me, going forward and I

LAVA

was just—excess baggage. I finally asked Father to let me try to run Kilo-hana. I have always loved lonely places, and finally, through Loki's persuasions he agreed to let me have a shot at it. The work is hard," she smiled at her hands, "but after being at Kilo-hana a while I got something of the rhythm of life as a whole."

Van watched her absorbed face.

"I am in charge of two hundred and fifty thousand acres and five thousand head of cattle. They are dependent upon me for care and I upon them for a living. Men and women work for me. I need them to help me with the work and they need the work I give them to make a living." She took a deep breath. "It goes back and forth like waves going into each other. Kilo-hana isn't just a *place* to me. It was the key given to me to unlock the door of life, it was the door through which I went into life. Therefore it's sacred."

Her eyes, which had been fixed upon the sea, came around to his, fine, intelligent, lighted with dark fires and her candid gaze was infinitely upsetting.

"Perhaps because of my father's influence," Van said after a silence, "life has always seemed a clumsy comedy to me. You make me wonder."

His thoughtful brown eyes were concerned and his face serious. "You see in my case it's a bit different. I must defend my convictions in order to strengthen them with myself. I am dependent on no one and upon no locality for a living."

Ku-lani weighed his words. Then she looked up.

"But, Van, *that's only a part of it*—"

"Ku-lani, Father wants you," Luke said from the doorway.

The girl's thoughtful mood dropped from her and her eyes filled with distant defiance. She rose and entered the house without a word.

Van fixed his eyes upon the dizzying wall of blue sea. Then he got to his feet and strolled off in the direction of the barns. He did not want to reflect upon Kulani's words, he would rather have his mind taken off them.

He went through the gap in the oleanders and came upon groups of men sitting on over-turned buckets and boxes, gossiping. They smiled but did not try to include him in their talk. He felt their friendly, impersonal liking but worlds yawned between him and these simple brown folk. He saw mounds of freshly piled earth and surmised that they were the underground ovens in which pigs and chickens, breadfruit and sweet potatoes were being slowly steamed for the feast. There was a feeling of Sunday in the air. All the men had on fresh shirts and wreaths on their hats. A group of work horses with saddle-marked backs stood under a mango tree with lowered heads conferring softly together. Dogs stretched out in the sun.

He glanced at his watch. It was almost noon and people would begin arriving presently. Better clean up. He retraced his steps and was about to enter the house when he saw Ku-lani coming out of the office. Her face was white, with a peculiar expression upon it. Van stopped.

LAVA

"Ku-lani!"

"I've got it!" she said, "but Father always upsets me. We think in different directions." Then she pulled a folded sheet of paper out of her back breeches pocket. "There's my deed to it," she smiled. "Witnessed by Luke and Ben." She grinned boyishly and thrust the paper back into her pocket. "But I shall never feel quite safe until the last payment is made. Rotten thing to say, but it's true."

A warm glow rose into her face making it beautiful for an instant.

"I haven't realized, fully, yet that Kilo-hana is mine. Oh, Van, it's so beautiful. Wait till you see it!"

He smiled.

"Why are you smiling?"

"Because, Ku-lani, you enchant me. You are unlike anyone I've ever met."

"That's so true it isn't funny. Many people feel that way about me. Wait, you'll see at the *luau*." She flashed a radiant smile at him and ran down the steps across the quadrangle in the direction of the barns and Van knew that she was going to share her joy with the cowboys. It gave him a curious feeling. "It goes back and forth," she had said, "like waves going into each other." Joy, sorrow, courage, cowardice . . . the waves of life.

He went up to his room.

When he had changed into fresh flannels he drew the chair up to the vine-framed window. Over the green tree tops he saw the triumphant blue of the sea and directly

LAVA

below, beyond a green stretch of lawn, a group of young bananas moving their large glossy leaves lazily in the sun. He thought about Ku-lani. To the average onlooker, it must seem an utter waste for a girl of her education, intelligence and advantages to be running a ranch; it was not to be expected that, as a whole, they could understand the quality of her affection for acres which had helped her to find herself. Her words, "Kilo-hana isn't just a *place* to me, it was the key given to me to unlock the door of life, it was the door through which I passed into life—therefore sacred," passed through his mind, profoundly moving him.

About one the first automobile arrived. Loki in a freshly starched *holoku* with a wreath of crimson roses about her neck swept out with glad cries.

"Danvers! How's my boy?" she embraced a tall dark young man with affection. Van observed him interestedly. He had the strong figure of a horseman and his father's dark eyes.

"Drina, I glad you two can come."

Van smiled at the subtlety of the second greeting. Drina was slight, spectacled, and had a mincing walk. Her fair, oily hair was elaborately puffed over the ears and her dried-up-looking body was covered with a stiffly starched waist and skirt.

Van wondered, looking down from his window, how any man, even to help his father, could have taken such a pathetic apology for a woman when he might have had Ku-lani. Then his eyes grew serious; the young are in-

LAVA

fluenced, swayed by pressure, by emotion, by unforeseen circumstances or events.

They went talking into the house and he heard Kai-ko greeting his son. Other cars arrived. Loki called up to him and he went down. He found himself watching men and women crossing and recrossing the lawn carrying platters and bowls, darting here and there. Men in flaring leggings and flower-crowned hats, women in *holokus* with wreaths about their necks or upon their hair. Beyond the green swell of the island the satin smooth sea with the vermilion top of the flame tree against it.

Luke and Benjamin moved among the guests, immaculate, conscious of themselves in a pleased way like cats when they are being noticed. Young girls gazed at them with awed eyes, matrons made much of them, older, less fortunately fixed men deferred to them. Kai-ko sat in his rocker talking to a blue-eyed man with iron gray hair.

"Who is that rather distinguished-looking man, Loki?" Van asked as she passed.

"That one talking to Kai-ko?"

He nodded.

"That Louis Macfarlaine. He run the big coffee mill for John. He good fella. Having nice time, Van?"

"Yes, Loki," and Van realized with surprise how easily in Kona, forms, shams seemed to slide away. Overnight, in thoughts, conversation, it had come to first names. Naturally.

"That nice." Loki's hand fell on his arm and she went leaving him warmed.

LAVA

Garland appeared and there was a faint stir as when royalty enters a room.

Van watched groups collecting on the lawn. Ku-lani stood talking to a knot of men and women, her hand on Puhi's shoulder. The old fellow seemed invested with joy and importance. Some subtle extraordinary change had taken place in the girl. She looked lighted from within, and even her shirt seemed a brighter blue. Her hair was brushed and shining and a wreath of flowers lay about her neck, making her face younger and softer.

He went down the steps and when she saw him crossing the lawn signaled to him gaily. Women were tossing hibiscus flowers on the green ferns, wooden bowls shone, glasses winked in the sun. He appreciated that Ku-lani was one of these people; they felt no constraint in her presence. She introduced him and the Hawaiians seemed to become aware of him as a personality and were shyly friendly.

The day widened out.

"Well, are they desolated because I haven't put in an appearance?" Ku-lani asked mischievously, then went on, "Oh, they like me well enough but never feel quite at ease when I'm around because we talk different languages." She shifted the flowers about her neck and looked down. "I wish I had a clean shirt but I won't borrow from Luke or Ben."

"Help yourself to one of mine," Van said. "They are in the dresser, or would you prefer me to get one out for you?"

He felt amazed at the impulse that prompted him to

LAVA

offer his own wearing apparel to a person he had not known twenty-four hours but she did not seem surprised.

"Could I? Thanks. Perhaps you'd better find it for me."

They went into the house by a side door, and a moment later he brought her the shirt.

"Wait for me while I change, I'll just be a minute."

He half sat on the railing and heard her moving about in the room. She came out presently.

"I'm glad you brought me a blue one. White would have made my breeches look even dirtier. I had no intention of staying overnight when I came."

They descended the stair together and Van was conscious of a new sensation, the most real of his detached existence, of sincere liking and admiration for Ku-lani and the distinct pleasure her presence afforded him. He had been interested in many people temporarily, liked many after a fashion, but he knew that he would think about Ku-lani often when he was gone and wonder how things were going with her, even as Allan White had done.

When they got out everyone was assembled on the lawn. Ku-lani talked and shook hands, kissed a man with a delightfully humorous face whom she called "Uncle Bob."

"Now you're going to sit by me, Ku-lani," he insisted, "or my whole afternoon will be spoiled."

She grinned and groped for cigarettes.

The man considered her. "You look radiant today," he announced.

She whispered into his ear.

"You don't say so," he cried with delight. "Well, I shall have to give you another kiss for good luck."

Danvers came up with Drina walking possessively beside him. Van smiled, he could not imagine Ku-lani being guilty of such a stupidity as trying to hold a man. She was too well versed in life, too proud. Ku-lani greeted Danvers without emotion as she would have greeted another man, made some impudent aside to him, shook hands with Drina and strolled away.

Loki called out. "Eat! Eat! The pig getting cold. Van," she signaled to him. Kai-ko was already seated on the grass at her left. In her white dress with the green lawn behind her she was as delightful as the abundant island.

"Eat! Eat!" she insisted and the guests seated themselves. She bent toward Van. "This not real *luau*," she said in confidential lowered tones and Van marveled that her voice retained its charm even in whispering. "Everyone little scare of Ha-ole Hao so not can have a very good time, but the food good. Try that," she pointed at some seaweed. "Your *poi* all right, old man? Here your *opihis*," and she moved a dish of shell fish nearer to him.

Van looked at the spreading trees leaning indolently over the garden, at the highly colored shrubs crowding at the house, at the vivid stretches of lawn, at a bit of Hualalai raw and red against the fragile blue of the afternoon sky. Men in flannels, women in brightly colored dresses, sitting on the grass, eating. Green tables of fern splashed with orange and pink hibiscus which looked like gorgeous butterflies resting between the dishes. Exotic, unreal, unlike anything he had ever encountered in his wanderings.

The ghost of a shudder passed through the earth and he glanced up to see if he had imagined it. Everyone was occupied with food and conversation. Probably these people were accustomed. . . . Then the ground jerked upward viciously and suddenly. Everyone froze as animals freeze when they feel the bead of a rifle leveled on them. Hands were arrested in mid-air, eyes widened.

"Well," Loki said when the ground quieted, "I guess old Pele going to get busy," and she gazed at the long, blue dome of Mauna Loa stretched against the sky to the south.

"Pele?" Van inquired.

"That the Hawaiian goddess of volcanoes. She a *kolohi* old girl, sometimes. Like to kick up big fuss and splash lava over everything."

Kai-ko raised his blind eyes.

"If you're wise, Van, you'll come to Kilo-hana with Ku-lani and me tonight; then you can come back to this side in case of an eruption. You can't see any of the mountains from the house at Kilo-hana as its under a hill."

"I think that good idea, Van. You go with Kai-ko tonight, no sense miss anykind long as you here. Kilo-hana fine place, sure must see, but Ku-lani understand if you hurry back if Mauna Loa blow up. Maybe nothing happen for a while."

Van looked down the table; the girl was laughing with the man she called "Uncle Bob" but feeling Van's glance she turned.

LAVA

"I heard, and it's the best arrangement as it'll save Pia making an extra trip."

A curious thrill pierced Van's body. The very name Kilo-hana was musical and beckoning.

All at once the island began struggling violently under them; glasses were tipped over, trees and shrubs quivered, guests scrambled to their feet looking wildly about them. From a table lower on the lawn where Garland's workers feasted came the cry, *"Oni-Oni!"* but there was a note of fear in it this time instead of excitement.

Kai-ko braced himself with propped arms; Ku-lani stopped eating but did not get up. Loki's hand went to Van's arm but she made no effort to rise. Garland scrambled up looking outraged. Loki's eyes were fixed upon her husband's parchment-like face with a curious baffling expression. The ground continued to wrench and jerk and Van noted that the Hawaiians were regarding Garland accusingly as though it were entirely his fault that the earthquakes continued coming. The deep-cut corners of Loki's lips tightened with a hint of contempt as she continued to stare, remindingly, at her husband.

The ground came to a shuddering stop but the feast was broken up. Ku-lani came to Van.

"As soon as Pia comes we'll go. You'd better pack what you need. I don't imagine they've got this bad at Kilohana as it's on the slope of Hualalai and it hasn't been active since 1801. Here we are on a slope of Mauna Loa, but Thelma isn't well and she and Dudie are the only white people in the district and she may be nervous."

LAVA

Kai-ko put out his hand.

"Help me to pack, Sister-dear," and they went off together, comrades of two decades despite the difference in their years.

Garland came over.

"Loki tells me, Van Dyke, that you're going to Kilohana with Kai-ko for a couple of days. Don't feel you have to unless you like. Ku-lani—"

"Unless you have other plans I should like to go immensely," Van interrupted.

"I happen to be particularly busy and will be until the middle of next week."

"I appreciate that. It was good of you to ask me to be your guest and the less you concern yourself about me the more I shall enjoy myself."

"I felt that when I invited you," Garland said with a chilly smile.

"Then suppose I go and later in the week when you have more leisure you can let me know and I'll come back."

"That's a wise arrangement. When I am ready to show you around a bit I'll telephone and send the car over."

"Thanks."

Luke strolled up smiling inanely.

"Ku-lani tells me you're going to Kilo-hana."

"Yes."

"You may find things a bit—" he broke off and laughed, but his tone implied anything.

"I haven't been over there, to be frank," Garland said, "since Ku-lani took over the management of the place.

LAVA

She's done very well, however," there was a reluctant pride in his voice, "but either Luke or Ben go twice a year."

Van saw Ku-lani waiting in the doorway, a peculiar Mona Lisa smile curving her lips. Luke looked foolishly pleased and important and Van thought how it must irk her to have this half-stuffed effigy who passed for a man sent to check up on the running of the ranch which she loved. Her words he had overheard when he was entering the house echoed in his ears. "Can either of you lay pipe lines, milk cows, mend tractors!"

He glanced at Luke's unlined face and at his soft, carefully manicured hands.

"Well!" Ku-lani asked when he joined her.

"It seems to me," Van said, "that the male members of your family don't half appreciate—"

"Me, or the work I'm doing?" she asked smiling.

"Well—both."

"It doesn't matter. Life, work goes on with or without appreciation, and I, of necessity, with it."

"You interest me immensely, Ku-lani, and I'm glad I'm going to have an opportunity to know you better."

"I'll call you when Pia comes," she said as he went up to pack.

When he came down the last guests had dispersed. Loki, her duties over, sat rocking and fanning herself on the veranda with Kai-ko. When Van appeared she beckoned to him and finished what she had been saying, making him feel included in the conversation.

"I just telling Kai-ko that Ha-ole Hao, *paa-ki-ki*, stub-

LAVA

born. I tell to him yesterday when we talk in the office, better make small sacrifice but he no listen. I think my own self gods little angry because he building his mill on that old *heiau* site and the Hawaiians all talking today that these *oni-onis* last night and today—"

The island started beneath them.

"There another!" Loki said, opening her eyes. "I tell you Pele waking up and the old mountain going to get busy again."

Ku-lani appeared in the doorway.

"Pia's here," she announced.

Van and Kai-ko rose.

CHAPTER IV

The drive to Kilo-hana was accomplished mostly in silence and darkness. A prodigal sunset burned out hurriedly into an ashen twilight. The sea was the dead white of a bone and the long, liquid slopes of the island were leaden against it. Above the ghostly horizon, unbelievably withdrawn, contorted cloud masses heaped threateningly. Ku-lani drove until the macadam ended, then Pia took the wheel. Van watched the man's heavy shoulders silhouetted against the dashlight. Occasionally he and Ku-lani conferred in lowered voices. Pia drove with furious abandon, tires crunched the volcanic cinders of the roadbed viciously at each turn, headlights flashed on ragged forests growing out of black wastes of lava and the dark mass of Hualalai lowered above, the sinister quality of its outline exaggerated by the sickly light of a wan baby moon.

Once Van heard a cow calling to its mates and the sound emphasized the utter isolation of the country through which they were tearing.

After hours of driving they came to a gate and before the car stopped Ku-lani was out and had opened it. Van saw they were heading up the mountain. The engine roared up the long incline and the powerful lights snatched and flung away glimpses of crumbling lava covered with straggling *ohia* trees and scanty vegetation. An immense uneasy presence seemed to crouch in the black heart of the night. Presently Van saw the loom of a great wooded hill with lights winking at its foot. The car tore on as though assaulting the stronghold of gods, through a gate that opened onto a sudden surprising green meadow. Grazing horses and cattle raised startled heads as the car smoked up the dim white ribbon of road which followed the lower contours of the hill in a series of sharp turns. Pepper trees drooped gracefully into the dark, stone walls rushed up and vanished, then with a lunge the car jerked up a rise into a shadowy garden.

Van had a hasty impression of a huge lighted house banked with flowers and spilling light from every window. The engine came to a panting halt under some orange trees and Van jumped out and opened the door for Ku-lani. She got out, thanked him with a nod and leaned into the car talking to Pia. Servants came hurrying out, a little golden-haired girl went into Ku-lani's arms with a squeal of delight. Van was mildly surprised. Somehow he had not visualized Ku-lani in the rôle of a mother. She picked the child up, squeezed her and set her astride of her hip and went on with her talking. He glanced at her, serious, intent, and had an odd, vivid impression that she had completely detached herself from the world that existed outside of Kilo-hana. She was no longer an individual but an atom of a vast shadowy something that the dark jealously hid, but the presence of which he felt dominating the night. Dogs swarmed about Ku-lani's boots, wagging their tails, dogs with alert intelligent little faces and sharp pointed ears.

When she finished instructing her man she jerked the child higher, bent for a moment to caress the dogs, then taking Kai-ko by the arm started for the house. The old man's figure seemed invested with vigor and he turned his head this way and that as though looking at familiar, loved objects.

"Thelma!" he called.

A girl emerged from the shadows in a swift rush. She kissed Ku-lani and Kai-ko and looked at Van. Her fragility was shocking, her great dark eyes burned with a feverish luster and black curling hair framed a small face, absolutely white save for two burning spots of color low in the cheeks. There was a wistful wildness about her like bamboos shaken by wind. Then Van saw, with an inner start, that she was to be a mother.

Ku-lani introduced her and she directed a long, hostile stare at him, then thrust her arm through Kai-ko's, pressing it affectionately to her thin side. The house seemed to open welcoming arms as they passed under the eaves onto a small veranda littered with riding boots and level with the ground. It gave onto a lofty room. A fire burned brightly and an alabaster indirect light spilled a warm radiance on heavy carved teakwood furniture and a table set for five.

"Take Kai-ko to his room, Thelma," Ku-lani directed. "This way, Van."

He followed her through the vast room sweet with flowers and opening onto a long glassed-in veranda running the

LAVA

front length of the house. The fitful firelight was softly reflected in a grand piano and beyond were bookcases, screens, couches and objects of art.

Ku-lani flung open a door leading into a bedroom that showed beyond a white glimpse of bath.

"As soon as you're washed up we'll eat. It's after eight and I hate to keep the servants too late as we are all up before daylight."

A shy Hawaiian boy came in by a back entrance, set Van's suitcase on the floor and vanished like a spirit into the great darkness lurking without. Van slipped into a fresh coat and went out. The living room was empty and walking to the fire he recognized the smell of burning sandalwood. Its incense-like fragrance invested the room with an almost sacred quality. It was a kindly room full of warm lights and wide pleasing shadows, a hospitable room guarding the memories of other years. Huge Chinese vases stood in dim corners, costly rugs lay on the floor, intimate trifles of ivory and porcelain stood on slender-legged tables and glassed-in cabinets were filled with rare china.

He appreciated the immense affection Ku-lani must have for this spot isolated from the rest of the island by forests and flows. Magnificent two-handed hospitality breathed from the dark paneled walls in utter opposition to the meager and careful atmosphere of Garland's home.

Kai-ko came out of a door and made his way to the fire. Spreading his great hands to the blaze he let out a sigh of content.

"Great place, Kilo-hana, nothing quite like it left in the

Islands. I'm delighted you had this opportunity to see it."

"There is an almost feudal magnificence here."

"And those cod-fish Ben and Luke did their best to try to keep John from letting Ku-lani finish buying it. Why, it's her life. I believe she honestly has a real affection for every rock on the place and the people here who work for her worship her as they used to worship their chiefs, only she's a darn sight kinder to them than those high-stomached old devils ever were."

"I don't doubt it."

Ku-lani appeared with Dudie and Thelma and again Van was aware of the latter's antagonism. There was suspicion and resentment in her too brilliant eyes. Ku-lani had tied a bright silk handkerchief about her throat but still wore his shirt. She was radiant, glowing. Taking her place at the head of the table she called out and two Japanese women appeared, one like a gentle scurrying mouse and the other a portly wag with a large face, flat as a rag doll's. She swung Dudie into her chair, made a pass at Kai-ko's back and waddled away.

Ku-lani called out after her, "Otero!" and the woman stuck her face through the pantry door, grimaced, but her eyes were worshiping.

"What kind you like, Sweetheart?"

"Soup!" Ku-lani said, laughing.

From the kitchen came shrieks of merriment and the sound of a man's heavy footsteps dragging in. Then the night seemed to pause and Ku-lani's face grew thoughtful.

"You know, it's odd," she said, "but Thelma and the

LAVA

servants say they've had a dozen hard shakes here today, more than we had in Kona."

"That's extraordinary." Kai-ko jerked up. "You know, Van, this island is composed of four, some claim five, distinct volcanic mountain masses. Roughly Hawaii is shaped like a turtle, to the north is the head, formed by the Kohala mountains, old in formation but distinctly volcanic. To the south is Mauna Kea, extinct since time immemorial, south of that is Mauna Loa, the largest and one might say the most destructive mountain mass in the world, for it has, actually, covered and recovered hundreds of thousands of acres with lava. On its flank is Kilauea and to the northwest is Hualalai on whose slopes we are now. It has not been active since 1801." He paused. "It would be rather extraordinary—"

Thelma spoke for the first time.

"Don't say that, Kai-ko!"

Her face looked small, frightened but stubborn, as though by the very force of her will she could prevent a mountain from erupting. Kai-ko smiled and Ku-lani laughed aloud.

"Don't laugh," Thelma said. "It sounds as though you were challenging—gods! Mauna Loa can't do much damage because it's all done but if Haulalai erupted it would destroy—" She stopped as though she could not go on with her thought.

Kai-ko wiped his mustaches with a magnificent flourish.

"Mauna Loa has been the vent for over a century so I don't think you need worry your pretty head about it, my dear."

LAVA

"But I feel—uneasy," Thelma said.

"You needn't be scared, Thelma," Dudie broke in, "Mother wouldn't allow lava to come through Kilo-hana."

Van smiled and Ku-lani looked amused but her eyes rested affectionately on her child. Van studied the pair. Dudie had her mother's fine intelligent eyes but hers were blue and heavily fringed with golden lashes and he wondered, for the first time, what sort of a man her father had been.

The women came in and began moving the soup plates.

"Sizu—" Ku-lani began.

The house shook viciously and Van had an unpleasant impression of imprisoned forces thrusting against the crust of the earth.

Otero cried out, "Hi-Ya!" and set the tray she was carrying unceremoniously upon the table and her eyes went involuntarily to the door. Thelma started to her feet, caught her breath, and commenced coughing.

"Sit down, Thelma," Ku-lani said. "There's nothing to be scared of; it'll be over in a moment."

From the kitchen came the rattling of pans and the sound of chairs being pushed back hastily, raised voices, exclamations.

"Well, it seems as though you were in for a little excitement," Ku-lani said when the earth ceased trembling. "Hurry up Otero and Sizu—serve dinner. We may have more and harder shakes and I'm hungry."

Van glanced at her. Her face had an absorbed expression and he had an impression that she was withdrawn from them for an instant. He knew by her face that she was not frightened but she was thoughtful. There was an almost secret quality about her; it was impossible to guess at the thoughts behind her steady brown eyes. When the meal was over she rose.

"Make yourselves at home. I have to see the boys about the work tomorrow. Otero, put Dudie to bed."

She vanished through the pantry door followed by Thelma. Kai-ko settled himself in a deep leather chair hollowed from long holding of his ponderous body. He relaxed, looking about the room, inhaling its fragrance.

"If I could have all the other ranches in Hawaii or Kilohana I'd choose it," he said. "There's an atmosphere—"

He paused.

"I felt it the minute we turned in at the gate," Van said.

"The longer you stay here the more strongly you'll feel it. I used to know the old fellow who had it before John bought it. We were great friends and I spent half of my boyhood here with him. He was a magnificent old chap but like many of those magnificent old chaps he wasted his substance in riotous living. Ku-lani has done splendid work here. Wait until you see her stock tomorrow. While there isn't a fortune in Kilo-hana there's fat living. All this," he waved at the furnishings, "Ku-lani bought piece by piece out of her salary. That ceased when she began buying in, but, Lord Harry, they live off the land. The whole place teems with game. A man goes out twice a week with pack mules and brings them back laden with sheep, hogs and turkeys. All the workers are fed from the house except about a dozen who have homesteads about four miles away on an old mud flow."

A sharp wrench jerked the floor up under them and Van leaped to save a vase from falling.

"I wonder if it wouldn't be just as wise," Van said, "to put some of this bric-a-brac on the lounge."

"Ku-lani will be along presently," Kai-ko said. "My father was a missionary in Kau," he continued, "and he told me that during the years between '52 and '68 people living in the district used to put a spot of glue under small breakable objects in order that they would not be shaken down and broken."

"Incredible," Van murmured.

Kai-ko hitched his chair nearer the fire and Van stretched his long legs to the pleasant blaze. A feeling of absolute contentment stole through him.

The silence was so intense he fancied that he could hear the grass growing. Once a wild peacock shrieked from the hill and a dog gave an answering bark. He was intensely conscious of the uninhabited spaces about, shutting out the world and of some current passing through the night, but the room was filled with color, warmth and fragrance. Peace brooded in it. Once the island started sharply at some deep-seated pang, then relaxed against ocean bottom once more.

Ku-lani came in about ten and Van drew up a chair for her. She relaxed affectionately against the upholstery and stared into the fire which had died to a glowing heap of coals. Her face, imperfectly lighted, was grave and thoughtful, and her brown hair, parted and drawn back simply, looked like dark wings framing her face. He noticed, for the first time, her well-balanced forehead.

"You know," she said, "I'm going to have to squeeze a bit for a while to meet all my payments. I won't get behind!" Then she smiled brilliantly.

Kai-ko turned his head.

"Don't kill yourself, Sister-dear."

"The bit of me that may, that must be killed, will be the price of my freedom and—possession," she replied, looking about the room, her eyes filled with affection. A shudder ran through the earth and Kai-ko heaved around in his chair.

"Sister-dear, shouldn't you put some of your pretties on the couch, they may get broken."

Years seemed to have slid from him, he looked younger, vigorous, interested in life.

"Perhaps it would be as well; it'll be ages before I can afford to get more. Van, will you—"

The house lurched heavily like a ship struck by a great sea, pictures flapped noisily against the walls, flower vases pitched over, a small Winged Victory crashed to the floor. Van leaped to save a mirror and Ku-lani caught a teakwood mother-of-pearl inlaid screen from going over.

"Help me to lay this down, Van," Ku-lani called, "it's heavy."

"I wish I could do something, Sister-dear," Kai-ko said, gripping the arms of his chair while his head strained forward as his ears registered the untoward noises all about him.

Van helped Ku-lani place the screen on the floor.

"Thanks." Her eyes met his, dilated but unafraid. "Now I must go, Thelma will be scared."

The ground came to a quivering stop but little shudders continued to run through it like breezes ruffling the smooth surface of a lake. Ku-lani vanished through the door that led onto the veranda and Van heard her calling out in Hawaiian. Kai-ko sat tense and still.

All at once the room filled with people, men in their undershirts and hastily donned breeches, women with their hair down. Thelma fled in like an uneasy ghost securing her green wrapper. Her face was bloodless and Van noted, mechanically, the jerking of the silk fabric over the region of her heart. She ran to Kai-ko and seated herself upon his knee and he put his heavy arm kindly about her. Van switched off a tall lamp and removing the taffeta shade placed it carefully on a chair. Ku-lani came in with Dudie.

"There's Pia!" the child cried with delight.

The man smiled. "No scare, Dudie?"

"Of what?" she asked scornfully as her mother might have done.

"Of the *oni-onis*."

She shook her head and bounced into a chair.

Hawaiian cowboys and the two Japanese women began hastily collecting valuables. It was evident enough to Van that these people had no feeling of working for Ku-lani;

LAVA

they worked with her. They had an intense personal pride and concern lest her possessions be injured. Otero with much horseplay mounted chairs and took paintings from the wall; Sizu scurried about collecting bric-a-brac. Men clumsily and carefully removed china from cabinets and placed it on the floor. Pia vanished into one of the bedrooms and returned with armfuls of blankets and sheets which he dispensed among the various workers and they hurriedly wrapped them about breakable objects. Ku-lani moved about them assisting this one and that, joking them when they eyed the open door as though they expected something to come through it.

The telephone began ringing shrilly, impatiently. Ku-lani went out on the veranda and answered it and Van heard her talking.

"You bet we are! We've had a dozen since dinner. Only three? That's funny."

Kai-ko sat tense and still, frowning.

"You know, Van," he said, "this looks—*ugly*."

Van nodded, and a curious sensation passed through him, not fear. He listened to Ku-lani's clear, steady voice.

"Mostly little ones, but within the last hour two pretty stiff ones. I guess we are in for a lively night. Yes, I'll ring you up in the morning, Loki. I hear another coming—"

The house tilted sharply and Van watched with amazement furniture sliding across the room. The piano hit the lower wall with a hollow thud. Thelma started, caught back a scream and leaped to her feet. The workers fled

LAVA

across the long room toward the door. Van snatched up Dudie and thrust Kai-ko's chair aside as the furniture started back toward them. Ku-lani rushed through the men and women pouring out of the door. The house leveled but savage angry shudders continued to run through the earth. She placed a shaking hand on Van's shoulder and for the first time he was aware of the heart in his side, it gave three slow beats then died into its old inertia.

Ku-lani's eyes went up to his with a sort of fierce gratitude.

"You're not afraid?"

"I'm—amazed, I cannot believe my eyes."

"Well, I guess we better get out; if this darn furniture is going to fox-trot all over the place, someone will get hurt."

She took Kai-ko's arm and steadied him across the room and Van followed carrying Dudie. She clutched his neck but did not utter a sound.

They reached the garden. Dogs whimpered and men and women stared at the house, shaking continuously. All at once it had become utterly foreign, appalling. Thelma breathed painfully and Ku-lani laid a consoling hand upon her.

"It'll be over in a minute," she said, but the island kept straining beneath them.

Kai-ko said, "Sister—"

"I'm here. There, I think the damn thing is over. Gosh it was a long one. Pia—"

"*Ae.*"

"Take some of the boys and get blankets and cots out of the office. I guess we'd better sleep outside tonight."

"More better put beds under the bamboo," Otero said, "Japan style when *oni-onis* come, go quick under bamboo. Roots too thick, s'pose ground open no can go through."

"Jolly thought," Ku-lani laughed. "Nuhi, Joe, Shiba, Bill, go and help Pia."

They went without demur, some toward the office and others into the main house which looked, all at once, abandoned. Through the lighted windows furniture showed all askew. Van had a curious stifled feeling. The quality of the night had subtly altered; it seemed stilled and filled with grim ferocity. By the dim light of stars he made out the huge dark mass of the island girdled by the pale silver of the sea.

"It's lucky the house is electrically lighted," he said. "Lamps would have gone over. How is it that you have electricity here?"

"One of Father's economies—lamps," Ku-lani said in scornful tones. "I installed a dynamo as soon as I came over."

Pia and his fellows appeared carrying cots and blankets.

"Better all man sleep here, tonight," Otero said. "If I stop near you, Sweetheart, I no scare."

Ku-lani laughed.

When they finally retired Van lay sleepless. About him people stirred in their cots, exchanging comments when the ground jerked beneath them. Dogs edged closer. Kai-ko sat for a while in his cot facing the sweep of the island, then he lay down with a sigh heaping his blankets about his massive shoulders. Once the island contracted sharply and Ku-lani called out:

"Kondo."

The Japanese cook sat up.

"I think better put water—"

"Already I fix, before I come out I put water inside stove and on top of living-room fire."

Van lay still in his cot thinking. The loyalty of these people to Ku-lani and to Ku-lani's interests was eloquent of her equal devotion to theirs. He stared at the solemn tree tops massed darkly against the stars. Behind and overhead bamboos creaked softly and from somewhere below came the thin, sweet whinny of a mare. He was aware of silent forces at work about him, strange waves passing through the limitless night. He watched the constellations making their slow splendid arcs across the heavens and heard the distant muted stir of the sea. Finally he slept.

Dawn broke in the east, pale and exhausted and Ku-lani sat up and pulled on a sweater.

"Pia!" she called.

The man woke instantly.

"We must hurry with the milking. Nuhi and Joe saddle the horses. We've got to take steers to Ki-holo today, the boat is due tomorrow and it's my shipment."

The cook went off in the direction of the kitchen and all at once everybody was up except Thelma, who slept exhaustedly. Kai-ko bundled off and Ku-lani came over and laid her hand on Van's shoulder.

"I'm awake," he said, sitting up.

"What do you want to do, Van, go back or stay here?"

"If it's the same to you, I'd like to stay."

"Fine, I'll feel better today while I'm gone if I know you are here."

"I'm afraid I'm of no particular use."

"Well," she smiled, "I will feel better all the same. Thelma—"

"I'm afraid she doesn't like me," Van said.

"It's not you; it's people in general. They condemn—without understanding—circumstances. She was to be married but her poor boy got killed roping a wild bull."

The man looked at her. "Ku-lani, I don't know whether you are only a child or whether you represent something old as time."

She did not seem to hear him, her eyes were fixed on the hill behind him.

"I do believe the damn thing is cracked," she said, frowning.

He turned. The huge mass of earth, fluted like a sponge cake and densely wooded, showed a red jagged rent at the top of one of the ridges.

"It's been pretty dry lately and the earth is all loose. With a big jerk that ridge might come down," Ku-lani observed without visible emotion. "I've got to get my shipment of cattle together for tomorrow and can't stay around here waiting for something which, probably, won't happen." Her face hardened and Van appreciated that no earthquake or legion of earthquakes could halt the mighty mechanism

LAVA

of the work she directed. "If things get too lively I'll send you home tomorrow or the day after, with Pia. The day after would be better as I need him tomorrow for shipping."

"I'm in no hurry to return," he said.

She smiled as though she were pleased.

"When you have your bath it will be just as well to leave your door open."

He nodded and watched her walk away toward the tanks and barns, then rose and went into the house.

When he was bathed and dressed he went toward the kitchen. Through an open window he saw Kai-ko seated at table with a steaming bowl of coffee before him. Van halted for a moment in the garden. Land smells, tree smells, earth smells and the great clean smell of the sea assailed him. The lawn was gilded with sunlight, pheasants crowded from the hill, turkeys gobbled, cows lowed for their calves and from behind the barns and tanks and sheds came shouted orders.

The cook came out and rang a bell and the two Japanese women and the slight Hawaiian boy who had carried in Van's suitcase the night before appeared carrying steaming pots of coffee, platters of meat and cabbage, bowls of rice and *poi* and plates of hardtack. They set them on a long table under a spreading *lichi* tree. Men began coming down the green slope of the lawn and Van noted the large, loafing dignity of the older Hawaiians and the graceful ease of the young. They crowded up to the table, helping themselves, then sat down on the grass to eat. Small bluish, spotted dogs with wise little faces and pointed ears like foxes' watched for scraps. The garden was bright and flowers stirred a little in the increasing sunlight.

He entered the kitchen and Kai-ko lifted his head.

"Fine morning, Van."

"Wonderful."

He seated himself at the long table covered with a red and white checked cloth and the Japanese women served him. Dudie came running in.

"Do you want to ride with me, Kai-ko? I told Nuhi to saddle up Forty Dollars. Mother wants me to look up two of her Holstein cows in the lower pasture. They are going to calve."

"Bet your boots, Dudie, I'll go."

She danced out, swooped on one of the dogs, kissed it and vanished in the direction of the barns. Presently Van saw Ku-lani coming down past the tanks. She halted, squatted to examine one of the dog's paws, then entered the kitchen. Going to the back of the stove she brought out a large cardboard box and set it down on the floor beside her chair, spread a newspaper on her lap and commenced carefully feeding two half-fledged squabs with spoonfuls of grain softened in water. Her rough fingers gently pried their bills open and they squeaked greedily and quivered their wings.

"Aren't they hideous little brutes?" she asked, looking at Van, but her voice was affectionate. "Their mother and father got blown away by a big wind so I adopted them."

"Have they names?" Van asked and was intensely aware

of her personality and the peculiar timbre of her voice which invested the simplest words with a subtle charm.

"Tom and Jerry."

She got up and replaced the box carefully near the stove.

"Don't forget by and by to put them out in the sun, Otero."

The woman nodded and rolled her eyes.

Ku-lani seated herself at the head of the table and began eating but before she had half finished Pia called her and she went out. Through the open door Van saw a Hawaiian woman on horseback holding a very sick-looking child in her arm. Ku-lani went to her and she passed the child down apathetically, dismounted and followed Ku-lani to a small cottage which Van suspected was the office.

Presently Pia returned.

"Joe," he said to the Hawaiian boy who was helping the cook with the dishes, "Ku-lani speak make one more cot. Lily's baby got fever and Ku-lani going to keep here one or two days."

Van strolled out.

He watched Ku-lani carry the child to a cot under the bamboos, place it inside the covers, instruct the mother further, then mount the horse Pia led up for her, followed by four men and seven dogs. And Van remembered her unfinished breakfast. . . . This girl gave of herself recklessly, but probably for her to withhold would be to perish.

Kai-ko came out and laid a friendly hand on his shoulder.

"Well, what are you going to be about?"

LAVA

"I think I'll stroll up the hill. It's rather nice coming to a place in the dark, there are so many surprises."

"Well, before you do, take a look around here at the stallions and bulls. They are in corrals by that grove of eucalyptus and the pigs are just over that ridge. I'm off for a while with Dudie."

Van watched them mount. Dudie held the old buckskin mare and Kai-ko mounted with surprising ease, then the child scrambled up in front and picked up the reins. The mare moved off slowly and carefully as though feeling the responsibility of her double burden. Kai-ko waved good-by but Dudie was entirely occupied with the business of guiding the mare. Her little golden head just about reached Kai-ko's heart.

Van got his hat and walked off in the direction of the grove of eucalyptus. At its foot were sturdy pens built of heavy timber. Inside the first a mammoth Percheron stood. His quarters flashed light when he moved. He eyed Van, then walked up to the fence and stuck his head over the top rail. Van scratched his jaw, marveling at the docility of the massive creature. Some distance beyond, inside a second enclosure a golden thoroughbred was pacing around and around, with the strength and lithe grace of a young tiger. When Van approached its eyes glinted and its delicate ears lay back. He spoke to it and it shook its head and sprang into the air. He stood appreciating its beauty and vitality; even its hoofs, small and round, seemed charged with life. He watched a purple flash of light run through the gold of its coat when it moved, sharply.

LAVA

"Gorgeous," he thought and went on slowly. The ground was rough and slightly moist under the heavy shade of the tall, ranked trees. The air was filled with their clean strong smell. In a small strongly fenced pasture an immense red Hereford bull paced with slow ponderous dignity wrinkling its nose and sniffing the warm air a little. Beyond, in a detached pen a black and white Holstein stood stamping at flies and beyond again, a small Golden Guernsey, delicate as a deer and beautiful in a masculine way. It tossed its head at him and switched its tail warningly. Van smiled, he had no intention of going into the pasture.

He stared at the sweep of the island northward to the Kohala mountains and marveled at the blueness of the sea. A flock of wild Hawaiian geese circled overhead uttering wild cries. They swooped onto the lawn and walked across it, stretching out their long sinuous necks, then rose again and settled about a water trough at the foot of the hill. He saw pigs rooting among the weeds and rocks, a sow prostrate suckling her offspring; two boars almost the size of ponies with wide faces and ridiculously turned-up noses. Sighting him they crowded up to the fence hopefully, grunting. He watched them for a while, then strolled back to the barns. He noted the huge tanks that collected water from every roof and estimated that there must be more than a million gallons in storage. Evidently the ranch depended upon rain for its water supply.

He wandered on, inspecting sheds and out-buildings and saw higher on the slope of the hill long milking sheds. Above them calves dozed contentedly in a precipitous pasture just touched with the sun which had cleared the tangled

LAVA

trees of the hilltop. He saw men loading bags onto mules and asked what the sacks contained.

"Grass seed."

Farther on a truck was being filled with boxes of seedlings that were evidently to be set out somewhere.

"These acres will remember Ku-lani when she is gone," he thought.

As he mounted the hill the land fell away and he looked back on massed trees with roofs showing between them. Gray, desolate reaches empty of all human habitation, stretched away on all sides. Frozen flows, somber old forests of *ohia* with a new greener growth thrusting up through them, wild slopes, verdant openings among the trees in which specks of grazing cattle showed. An occasional stone wall wound its way across the country and there was a surprising send to ridges and folds giving mute testimony to the once fluid state of the island.

He startled a bunch of sleek workhorses and they went off snorting with lifted heads and tails. A wild peacock flew up with a resentful, startled screech; turkeys gobbled from every hollow. He saw the rootings of wild pigs and watched a band of sheep bobbing through the brush.

When he finally gained the summit he saw the dark, lava-blighted slope of Hualalai and to the south Mauna Loa, splendidly simple, and in the east the impressive outline of Mauna Kea, blue and aloof.

He sat down on a log and pulled his hat over his eyes. The day was absolutely still and he had a feeling of distances being impelled—outward. He felt rather than heard the sigh and thud of the sea breaking against distant lava promontories. Were the people who lived on Hawaii madmen or heroes? He looked thoughtfully about him. Kilo-hana was a place of incredible beauty and violence set in the spectacular workshop of an island still in the making. The work of a lifetime might easily be wiped out in a night.

A scurry of wind came from nowhere and died in a damp hollow of fern. From below came voices, faint and clear and he saw the speck of the buckskin mare making her way across a path winding through the green meadow formed by silt washed from the hill.

For the first time in his life he felt as though he were utterly unreal. He thought about the sick child in the cot under the bamboos, of the fledglings behind the stove, of Thelma who had fled to Kilo-hana to escape from the curious and unpitying eyes of the world. Somewhere in those desolate reaches Ku-lani was riding with her men; dogs were scaring up cattle which must be shipped to provide the money necessary to keep the ranch going and meet payments. Yes, even the dogs had a place and a minute part to contribute. . . .

Restlessness filled him and he stood up. The empty spaces about made his head swim. There grew in him as he stood on that high hill-top a sense of incompleteness, of futility. . . . For the first time in his life he wondered if he had fed himself on illusions. He had always been convinced that he had cleverly side-stepped life, cheated it. Now he wondered if life had not, perhaps, cheated him by leaving him completely out of it.

CHAPTER V

About three Van saw the dust of returning riders on the thread of road leading through the dark *ohia* forest which gave on to the vivid green meadow. Picking up his hat he started down to meet them, his face grave and thoughtful, his eyes concerned.

Sighting him, Ku-lani waved and the gesture brought a sensation of warmth, strangely pleasant. He waited for her to come up. The horses looked dusty and tired coming through the long, cool grass. When they got to where he stood Ku-lani halted but the cowboys rode on.

"Well," she said, leaning down a little from her saddle, "how has it been today, fairly quiet?"

"I feel," Van said with one of his faint, lighted smiles, "as though I'd failed you, somehow. One chimney is half down and two of the water tanks have tipped over. Thelma phoned for Dr. Arlen to come over."

"What does she think he can do, stop the island shaking?" she asked with a laugh but her eyes were worried. "Glad that held." She stared at the cracked ridge. "I knew there had been some fairly hard shakes because I saw stones rolled out into the road just below here. Well, it's all in a lifetime but perhaps it's just as well to get the volcanologist over. I must get to my milking. I'd offer you a ride but my horse is hot and you'd soil your breeches."

LAVA

She spurred up the long incline and Van watched her disappear around a curve of the hill. Then he started back slowly. His eyes went to the dark slopes of Hualalai, its summit was jealously hidden in cloud but there was a suggestion of treachery in the leaden forests and flowing contours of the land. Solitude brooded upon the vast reaches and the sea was so still it seemed dead.

As he walked the long narrow tree-shaded road he glanced up at the swell of the hill rising impressively above the houses and meadow. It looked savage and stealthy and steep and seemed to be staring at some terrible future which it would not, or could not share with the rest of the island.

He hastened his stride until he reached the garden. Birds sang in the trees, tired dogs lay in the sun. He saw Kai-ko lying on the grass but when he heard approaching steps he sat up.

"Van?"

"Yes."

"Ku-lani asked me to take you up to the barn. She's milking and she wants you to see her registered Holsteins and Guernseys."

Van stooped and Kai-ko got up and took hold of his arm. He helped the old man to make his difficult way up the steep incline, past horses being unsaddled and men skinning sheep. Two sweat-stained mules stood with drooping heads under some mulberry trees and a man was oiling a tractor in an untidy shed, piled with bags spilling corn, pipe-laying tools and broken crates.

He guided Kai-ko through a steep corral where cows

LAVA

like vast shiny black and white dominos lay contentedly chewing their cuds. Kai-ko halted and stared at the frowning hill and his fingers tightened on Van's arm.

"Where's that crack?"

"Directly above us, Kai-ko."

"I'm afraid that Ku-lani's in for a bad time," the old man said, sighing like a tired child. "It's rotten luck that there should be all this humbug just when she's got her title to the place. It's hard enough going, without extra expenses."

He started on, patient, slow-moving, devoted. At the sound of their voices Ku-lani stuck her head out of the door, waved, and disappeared. They entered the long shed filled with dusty sunshine and the sound of cattle busily eating. The warm air was sweet and milky. Kai-ko made his way to the feed room and sat down on some sacks and Van leaned against the door looking at the long line of glossy backs and switching tails. On the upper side of the barn, built on the hillside, calves with mild eyes watched eagerly for the food which Ku-lani and Pia were preparing.

They worked systematically and without wasted effort. A dozen dishpans were on the floor of the feed room, filled with mixed grain on top of which Ku-lani heaped two scoopfuls of powdered milk. Pia mixed, his huge body doubled over and his arms white to the elbow. Ku-lani went and began bailing up calves.

"Come! Come! Come!" she urged, thrusting them into their places. Occasionally she pushed against them with hurried affection in order to expedite the work. Pia carried out the heaping pans and began shoveling scoopfuls of the mixture into the narrow feeding trough.

When the bailing was finished Ku-lani helped him carry the heavy pans and set them down at intervals.

"Let me do that," Van offered.

She glanced at him and laughed. "You'd ruin your white flannels," she said good-naturedly and passed on, gray with dust from the powdered milk which Pia was spilling into the feed box. Van felt thrust aside, an intruder in a busy world which had no place for onlookers.

"Why," Van turned to Kai-ko, "are these calves fed powdered milk?"

"Every cow here is shipped to the leading dairy in Honolulu and when their calves are old enough they are sent back here until they are matured. Then Ku-lani breeds them to one of her prize bulls and they and their offspring are re-shipped to the dairy, which is owned by the ranch. The cows here only supply milk for the place and others have the younger calves put to them until they are old enough to eat the meal."

Ku-lani halted for a moment thrusting aside with a floury wrist a lock of hair which had escaped from the red handkerchief bound about her head. Then her arm went down to her side as though it were, all at once, tired.

"I've been wondering," she said, looking up at Van, "if it wouldn't be just as wise to let most of the water out of the two big tanks. I hate to waste it but if these darn earthquakes are going to keep up they will loosen the foundations and they may go over or burst and damage the houses."

Her face was attentive, without color and thoughtful, and it gave Van an unpleasant feeling of his own lack of experience, of his inability to help or advise this valiant girl, trying to guard the place she loved from titanic forces.

"Perhaps it would be wise," he agreed finally and his eyes went to the ranked tanks hiding the houses. Then, impulsively, he took a hurdle. "Could I attend to it for you?"

"Would you? Two of my cows have calved and as soon as the milking is over Pia and I have to drive them up from the hayfield and milk them out."

The galvanized-iron roof rattled noisily as the island gave a convulsive start. The cows and calves stopped eating for a moment and their eyes grew wide and alarmed. Kai-ko got to his feet and faced the hill instinctively and Ku-lani and Pia watched it through a small window. Then as the ground quieted they picked up buckets and milking stools and started down the line of cows.

Another long shudder ran through the earth and Ku-lani paused in her milking.

"Van."

"What can I do for you, Ku-lani?"

"Spray the calves. The sooner I get them all out of here the better. The gun is in the feed room and the mixture in a tin by the bran bags." Then she laid her head against the warm flank of the cow and went on with the milking.

LAVA

He went into the little room and Kai-ko groped down, found the tin of spray and handed it to him. He found the gun, filled it up with the mixture, and started down the line of little animals licking up the meal with coral pink tongues.

"When you've finished, unbail them, will you, Van?" Ku-lani called out.

He nodded. He worked clumsily and was unpleasantly aware of his complete inexperience with any kind of work, but a curious pleasure went through him as he pressed in among the warm bodies that showed no fear of his presence and he appreciated, in a diluted way, how Ku-lani must love these creatures so utterly dependent upon her for care.

He was sufficiently reflective and realized with a sort of dismay, which he tried to stifle, that for the first time he was doubting, questioning, the wisdom of the attitude to which he had adhered. It had safeguarded him from hurt but was, perhaps, robbing him of some vital experience. He looked through the slats of the lower wall at the crude, splendid, forceful reaches of the island. The air was filled with the rich, soft sound of milk going into pails. Like two rhythmic machines Pia and Ku-lani worked without speaking. Studying the girl's intent, thoughtful profile Van wondered what she was thinking about, her menaced holdings or some immediate task which must be attended to before the next claimed another atom of her.

Pia rose and passed behind her going to the next cow and his eyes went down with a sort of respectful, impersonal admiration, the admiration that one man has for another skilled fellow worker.

Van noticed him for the first time. He walked slowly as though harnessing the strength housed in his great body. Above his red sweater his neck showed like polished brown satin and his hair curled gaily and youthfully over his forehead. He had an intelligent face which Van suspected might become mulish at times, and a disarming smile which would win instant forgiveness for any misconduct of which he might be guilty.

A succession of quivers passed through the ground and Ku-lani picked up her stool and bucket and set them aside. She began unbailing the cows. With vast deliberation they went through the open doorway into the sunshine. When the last one was out Ku-lani stood in the door watching them going down the rocky trail that led to the meadow. The expression of her face baffled Van. After an instant she turned.

"Find Nuhi, Van, and tell him to see to the two big tanks. Pia and I have to get those cows and attend to them." She fished in her pocket. "Give this key to Joe and tell him to open the store and give Kondo whatever he needs for dinner. Kai-ko."

"Yes, Sister-dear."

"Go with Joe and tell him to make the entries correctly. Sometimes he's careless."

The old man got to his feet, nodded and began finding his way out. Van walked beside him. When they reached the store Kai-ko found the steps and sat down.

L A V A

"I'll send Joe up," Van said.

"Might come back when you've seen Nuhi and give me a hand."

"All right."

He passed groups of men winding up the day's work, saw the two Japanese yardmen, Shiba and Sigaki, picking up the bricks of the half-broken chimney and wheeling them away. Thelma was seated at the table under the *lichi* trees leaning her arms listlessly before her. She glanced at him, then detached herself utterly from him and all he represented. He entered the kitchen and the cook glanced up.

"You like some kind?" he asked, snatching a roast out of the oven and slamming it on top of the stove.

"Miss Garland told me to give Joe the key to open the store for you."

"Better you give, more quick, Joe little slow. Better we go now, I got plenty work, too many fellas to feed. Thirty."

Van started back and the cook walked beside him, a wiry aproned figure with bristling black hair. Kai-ko got up and Van unlocked the door and they entered.

It was a store of fascinating smells and shelves that went from ceiling to floor. Shelves stacked with canned goods, soap, medicines for horses and men. Rolls of leather, bags of flour and sugar, boxes of crackers, rain coats, bootlaces, kegs of salt salmon, tins and sacks of coffee littered the floor.

Kai-ko made his way carefully to the counter. Fishing

out a soiled ledger he handed it to Van. The cook selected what he needed and went off. Several of the men came in and waited with hanging arms. Kai-ko spoke to them in Hawaiian.

"Van, these men work for Ku-lani but live down on the bluffs, give them what they want and charge it against them."

Van found their names and made the entries.

Ku-lani and Pia passed, driving the two cows and the girl called out something in Hawaiian and the waiting men laughed.

Kai-ko pushed a scale across the counter and Van filled it with sugar and one of the men made an aside to his fellows. Kai-ko laughed.

"Well, Van," he said, "these men say Ku-lani has a new hand."

Van smiled. He worked quickly thinking about the tanks which must be emptied.

"Where is Nuhi?" he asked, looking up.

"I'm Nuhi," a young Hawaiian said, hitching around a knife strapped to his hip.

"Miss Garland asked me to tell you to open the two big tanks and let out most of the water. She's afraid they may go over."

"I think more better, too. I fix now."

Van watched him go out; his body was vital and radiated suppressed energy. The store shook fiercely and protestingly every minute or two and the men exchanged remarks.

LAVA

"I'm afraid we are in for a bad night," Kai-ko said. "Here, Ikaki, take your stuff."

The man came forward, picked up half a sack of flour and a dripping side of salmon and went out.

Van closed the ledger.

"Let's get out," Kai-ko said and waited on the steps while Van locked the door.

The sun had set and the island seemed to have been dipped into a sudden inky twilight. Mynah birds were settling noisily to roost, wild geese cried overhead, dogs lay hopefully outside the kitchen door. The woman, Lily, sat beside her sick child watching for Ku-lani to come down from the barns. Thelma was still sitting at the table under the *lichi* and orange trees. Kai-ko joined her but Van strolled down to the lawn below the long, glassed-in front of the house. The diamond-shaped panes burned dully in the afterglow like dying coals. The silence of the evening was profound and the island seemed to be waiting with immense patience for some event on its way.

Formerly in silence and solitude Van had been able to think clearly and sometimes profoundly. He did not have the common deceptions of hope, happiness and a just all-wise God watching over individuals, ready to shoulder burdens, punishing or rewarding according to merits. He knew such beliefs were soporifics for those who seek sleep instead of understanding. His father had maintained that all action was harmful, in that it brought unlooked-for results and he had molded his life accordingly, armoring himself against it by an inflexible negation of effort.

LAVA

He paced to and fro in the perfumed island dusk, a meditative ghost in white flannels. Disquieting thoughts prodded him, a natural reluctance to abandon his old attitude struggling with a new desire, projected into him from vital volcanic surroundings and observance of a fellow human being's perfect accord with her environment. He was tempted to experiment, to associate himself with life, but if he did so, even temporarily, it might have incalculable consequences. He might find he could not disassociate himself from it. He would be abandoning old safe pastures to venture into new unknown ones. Restlessness filled his heretofore untroubled being. Sounds penetrated his consciousness, the incessant rattling of shaken windows, water running out of tanks. He saw the lights of a car coming up the road and horsemen streaking across the twilight-blurred meadow heading toward high bluffs some four miles below and to the right.

The garden seemed haunted by an uneasy presence which was unable to assert itself. He sat down on the grass in his favorite attitude, with crossed arms laid upon his knees. He felt the island toiling beneath him, strange resentful jerks, desperate wrenches and occasionally a succession of earthquakes that fled, as though terrified, from the mountain top down to the sea. He got up and paced the lawn. A car roared past and vanished behind the mass of the building. The volcanologist probably. He started back.

Under the orange trees Ku-lani sat on a bench unlacing her boots and talking to a heavy-shouldered, hawk-faced man. Pia leaned against a tree-trunk in the shadows and

Kai-ko sat, his arms resting on the table. When Van approached Ku-lani glanced up.

"Van, meet Dr. Arlen—the Volcano doctor."

They shook hands, then the scientist sat down and resumed what he had been saying.

"It certainly looks that way, Ku-lani, much as I hate to say it. I established a seismograph in South Kona today on the slope of Mauna Loa and when we've set up the one I brought here, I can tell better. The big one at the Volcano registered only a few shocks today but you say—"

"We've had over three hundred since we got home last night."

The man frowned and looked in the direction of Hualalai hidden from the long ridge. Van fancied that Ku-lani paled; she stopped unlacing her boot and glanced at Thelma sitting somewhat withdrawn. The girl's small white face was clenched and her eyes dilated as though she felt the nearness of death breathing upon them; her thin fingers, laced tightly together, looked like thin amber sticks of bamboo.

"Perhaps," Ku-lani said, "I'd better send Dudie and Thelma to Kona for a while."

"It would be a wise precaution and relieve you of extra responsibilities—you have enough."

Ku-lani smiled and resumed the deliberate unlacing of her boot.

The island expanded and contracted quickly beneath them.

LAVA

"Frankly," Dr. Arlen said, "I wish you'd get out yourself."

"That's out of the question. I'm shipping tomorrow. Father's just agreed to let me finish buying Kilo-hana," Van heard the affection in her voice, "and if I left—well, I won't."

The scientist gave her a glance of admiration which she did not even see.

"What about Thelma?"

"Pia can take her and Dudie over tomorrow night after we get back from shipping. Some of the men's wives are uneasy and want to leave."

Thelma made a violent, negative gesture and walked away into the shaken dusk. Van felt an immense compassion for her and made as though he would follow. Ku-lani's eyes said, "Yes," and he started after her.

"Thelma," he said kindly when he caught up.

She darted a hating look at him.

"I won't go back—to Kona!" she said fiercely.

"Ku-lani doesn't want to make you. She only—"

"Can't you see that I can't? They don't understand. Only Ku-lani can and does."

"Then compose yourself," Van urged gently. "Don't make things more difficult for her. She has enough."

"To think of without me? You don't know her," and the girl's voice implied that not knowing her he had been unfairly robbed. "She's selfless. People wonder about her because she lives here with only Japs and Hawaiians, gossip, but she's so big she doesn't pay any attention but just goes on her appointed way. She told me to come and live with her, said if I surrendered to what people think of me that I would become what they think me. Over here," she looked around then burst out, "Oh, if this place is spoilt, if God lets it be spoilt—"

Van took hold of her shaking arm.

"I'm sure it won't be, Thelma."

"Tell Ku-lani," the girl said in stifled tones, "that I'll be back in a little while."

Van watched her enter the long cottage where the office was and, probably, extra guest rooms.

"Poor Thelma," Ku-lani said when Van delivered her message. "This is pretty tough for her."

On the table beside her stood a glass of weak whisky and water; a succession of tremors made it splash over and she said, "Hold that, Van, will you?"

She drew off her boot and laid it on the grass, then a thought seemed to occur to her.

"Otero," she called out, "bring the pigeons out here, maybe some kind fall on top."

The woman brought the box out and placed it near by.

Van sat down on one of the benches and guarded the glass with his hand, staring at a jagged crimson crack showing in the dark heavy clouds piled above the horizon. It looked like a long wound in the sky and emphasized the peculiar quality of the evening and the mass of the island, steel gray against the quick-silver of the sea.

Kai-ko leaned on his elbows, his gray head thrust forward

LAVA

as he listened with awful concentration to the words being exchanged between Ku-lani and the volcanologist.

"I think," Arlen said, "that an eruption can be looked for within thirty-six to forty-eight hours. The seismic disturbance has been almost constant since I got here. The question is whether it will be from Mauna Loa or Hualalai. Everything points to the latter. From the look of things the lava column must have shifted from under one mountain to the other. Because of the hill and the ridge to the left the position of this place is a bit precarious. You could be almost surrounded by lava before you knew it unless you keep a lookout posted on the hill."

Ku-lani smiled. "I know I couldn't keep awake and my men work as hard as I do, so I could hardly ask any of them to stay up. I don't suppose that you could possibly tell where an outbreak might occur if Hualalai did erupt."

"There are two main rifts, faults, in Hualalai. One between here and Kona running down a long ridge where the 1801 flow came out, and the other back of here between Hualalai and Mauna Loa where the 1843 flow came from Mauna Loa between here and Waimea."

Ku-lani drew in her cheek and began unlacing her second boot.

"Jolly," she observed.

"Dinner ready," the cook announced from the kitchen door. "Better eat quick, too many *oni-onis* and I like put fire out."

"Just a minute, Kondo," Ku-lani said, pulling off her boot. "Pia, help Dr. Arlen to put this shock recorder."

She pointed to a small coffin-like box lying in the shadows. "Where do you want it put, Tom?"

"That back veranda is level with the ground, isn't it?"

"Yes, and it's on a concrete foundation."

"Excellent."

"Joe," Ku-lani called and the boy came. "Help Pia to carry this thing onto the veranda."

"What this kind?" he demanded.

"It keeps a record of the *oni-onis*."

"Pele no like white fellas try to find out what kind she doing down below. Sure if use some damn kind thing happen."

Ku-lani laughed.

"Well, you can kill a pig and some of the chickens tomorrow and make your apologies to the old lady."

"Please, Ku-lani, I no like touch."

"Very well," she smiled. "Kondo—"

"Let me help Pia," Van said, bending down and taking hold of one end of the box. They carried it into the house and Van heard Ku-lani teasing Joe.

It was installed under the scientist's supervision and then he set it going.

"I'll get my coat out of the car and bring Kai-ko in," Arlen said, vanishing into the sudden tropical night.

By an overhead electric light suspended from the ceiling by a long cord Van watched the infinitesimal white line the delicate arm had started to trace and he heard the ticking of the clock inside the recorder. The telephone rang and Ku-lani answered it but just as she started to speak the house

LAVA

suddenly and savagely humped upward. Furniture bounced off the floor and tipped over and with a crash the kitchen chimney fell upon the roof. The house began jerking back and forth and Van grasped Ku-lani's arm and started for the garden but she pulled him back.

Deluges of bricks rolled over the gutter smashing on the concrete walk in front of them. Her face was unmoved but she breathed hurriedly. The bricks continued spilling noisily down the roof and from within the house came sounds of dishes shattering and of saucepans shooting off the stove in rowdy avalanches. Van embraced a post with one arm and held onto Ku-lani with the other. Bookcases pitched over, prostrate furniture danced foolishly, walls cracked and from the garden came terrified voices.

"Long one," Van said, smiling, and her valiant answering smile unlocked something inside him. The house continued to swing back and forth and the second chimney went down with a roar on the roof.

"Hard one," Ku-lani panted. "I hope someone is with Dudie. Listen to those poor devils of dogs howling. What's that funny sound—the new one?"

Van strained his ears. The world was filled with noise, bricks rattling down the roof, water hissing as it was tossed back and forth in tanks, the extraordinary sound of trees violently shaken, not by wind. Peacocks shrieked indignantly, stock stamped back and forth in their enclosures; then he heard an enormous gathering sound—from the hill.

"That ridge," Ku-lani said and her face became bleak. "Oh, my calves!"

🌿 🌿 L A V A 🌿 🌿

Even in the confusion and terror of the moment Van thought, "How many things have a place in her heart," and he experienced an instant of indistinct, confused tenderness toward her. He saw a pulse throbbing in the side of her throat but her eyes were clear and her face had an intent listening expression as though her mind were registering and recording every detail transpiring in her shaken world in order that she might cope with it the better.

The house staggered to a stop.

They paused for an instant longer, two more bricks fell over the gutter and they dashed out.

The garden was filled with stammering, terrified people crowding about Ku-lani. She thrust them off.

"Be still!" she commanded and her face twitched. "Guess it just got started—"

A vague enormous rustling filled the night.

"Mother, stop that ugly noise, I don't like it!" Dudie said, tearing herself out of Sizu's arms and running over.

"Be quiet, Dudie, it'll stop in an instant. Listen! *Listen!*"

From the hill came a monstrous, smothered tearing that gradually lessened.

Ku-lani strained into the night and Van watched her. She was bare-footed, with the legs of her breeches unbuttoned but subtly she was injecting her courage into those about her. Their cries diminished, stilled, the dogs stopped howling and only gave an occasional whimper.

"It's—*pau*," she announced finally. "Pia, Nuhi, drive

LAVA

the calves out of the hill pasture. Kondo, put out the fire. Where's Thelma?"

"I no know, I no care," Joe cried. "What I tell you? Better break that damn box."

"I'm here with Kai-ko," Thelma said in a flat, shaking voice.

"Hurry, boys, open the gates and come right back."

Ku-lani stood as though her mind were occupied with a thousand matters.

Kondo vanished and through the lighted windows Van could see him staring at the débris-strewn floor.

"Van, help me to get the cars out of the garage. Kai-ko, stay with Thelma and Dudie. Bill Nakagowa and Frank go and see if the stallions and bulls are all right. There Lily, don't be scared. All finish."

Ku-lani disengaged herself from the weeping clinging woman who had abandoned her child whimpering from its cot.

"I'll have Pia drive you all down to the bluffs when he comes back from turning out the calves."

"I think it might be just as well for us all to camp there tonight," Arlen said.

Ku-lani nodded and started for the barns. Van followed.

"Get the Packard and head it out, Van, well down the road. I'm going for the truck."

She hurried on and darkness engulfed her.

Van tried the garage door, then lurched all his weight against it; it was jammed. It gave all at once. The aged dishonorable car resisted his efforts to start it for a while, then yielded and quivered to life. He backed it out and stopped below the house. Thelma rushed over.

"I wish Ku-lani would hurry; it's so dark, even the stars seem dimmer."

Her voice caught.

"Ku-lani has lots to think of before going," Van said gently and Thelma nodded distractedly.

"Perhaps I can get you some coffee presently," Van said after an instant. "I'm afraid there's no dinner."

Thelma shook her head violently and got into the car but Van went to the kitchen and saw the cook wading through over-turned saucepans, vegetables and stewed meat, roasts, broken sauce bottles and shattered dishes. Great crocks lay on their sides slowly spilling sticky masses of *poi* onto the littered floor.

"Gar-damn, too much humbug!" Kondo said, his black hair sticking up stiffly as he poured buckets of water into the stove sending up dark, hissing clouds of steam and ashes. "Gar-damn, dinner all spoil!"

He whistled and the dogs came in looking guilty, then began eating wolfishly and hurriedly. Van watched them for an instant then went out. Ku-lani was just climbing down from one truck and Nuhi from the other and Pia was driving the calves down the road. Their little hoofs rattled like noisy rain on the hard rocky road.

"I sorry, dinner all stop on top floor," Kondo said as Ku-lani came over. "You like I make more? Can build fire outside."

LAVA

"Never mind," Ku-lani said, and her voice sounded tired. "Pia, take the Packard and drive Thelma and Dudie and the women to the bluffs; they can stay with some of the boys and their wives tonight. Then come back—"

"Sweetheart, no stop here, go now!" Otero begged.

Ku-lani placed her dry hand on the woman's shoulder.

"Little more I come, some kind must look see first. Boys, put the cots onto the big truck just as they are. Don't wait to undo them, the other I'm afraid has no light."

Pia tried them.

"No more," he announced.

The telephone began ringing and Ku-lani went instinctively to answer it. Van looked after her anxiously.

"Father? Yes, Tom got here. They are coming in flocks. Had one just now that nearly shook our teeth out. You got it too? I'm just getting the kids and women out of here for the night. I'm afraid the road may get blocked, the hill slipped a little. Think I hear another one coming. Good night."

She came out laughing a little unnaturally.

"Choked him off, haven't time to waste—talking. Pia, ready? Otero, Sizu, Lily, in you get. Thelma?"

The girl slipped out of the car.

"I want to wait for you."

Ku-lani hesitated then said: "All right. Kai-ko?"

"Yes, Sister-dear."

He came forward reluctantly and Ku-lani grasped his arm, kissed his gray cheek hastily and gratefully and put him into the car. She placed Dudie on his lap and Van heard hurried, indistinct whispers then, clearly, the last.

". . . you—keep Dudie."

The old man nodded and the car went off like a huge wary beast followed more clumsily by the truck. Ku-lani stood taut until she saw the headlights crossing the hayfield, clear of the hill, then she sat down on the grass.

"Get me a smoke, Van," she said in an emptied voice.

Thelma went to her in a rush and put an unsteady arm about her rigid shoulder.

"You didn't mind my waiting? I'm only brave when I'm with you."

Ku-lani nodded absent-mindedly, then she turned her head slightly. From the direction of the eucalyptus grove came sounds of hammering. Her eyes went up to Van's.

"Lucky I sent the boys to see the stallions and bulls. Evidently some of the fences were wrenched. If they got out—"

She broke off and something in her face hurt Van, perhaps the intensity with which she regarded the big house. It looked debauched. Betrayed. Abandoned. He could see her long throat working above the still arms clasping her knees and he felt sick somewhere in the region of his stomach. He asked Kondo for cigarettes and matches and gave them to her.

"Thanks."

She had recovered her self-possession. Her eyes went up to his, grateful, friendly. Van stood above her more moved than he had ever been in his life. Wretched, unthinkable, that she should be so tried, that this place which she loved, that was sacred to her should be so menaced. He regretted that he had no refuge to which he could transport her and Kilo-hana, no haven where he could snatch up this warm, infinitely cool and valiant handful of ashes threatened from above by avalanches and from below by lava. His impulse was to place his hand on her head or to take her fingers into his but instead of doing either of these obvious and natural things he sat down upon the grass beside her.

The look she accorded him was like a quick, secret touch on the heart. For a moment he was unable to free his captured gaze for he knew that she appreciated that he had allied himself with her, temporarily, and would give her his entire support.

The light from the windows, which were like blinded staring eyes, fell on her face, calm and absolutely white, and the minute her gaze left his, she became still and secret and he appreciated that no one could correctly estimate this girl, her greatness, her fidelity to that which, for want of a better name, was called—life.

"I'm going to turn off the tanks, then I suppose"—she looked at the people about her, waiting for her—"we'd better get out—for tonight."

"It's wisest," Arlen said.

Her eyes, filled with darkness, went to the house and a tremor passed through it as though it were as profoundly moved as she was. Her deep-cut lips tightened and she took a fortifying breath. Van read her thought as she gazed at the abandoned building and brick-strewed garden. "If it were only me, I would not go."

Then she unclasped her arms from her knees and looked around. A bitch crawled up and licked her hand and she touched its head briefly, glanced around, saw the box with the two fledglings in it and gestured with her head.

"Kondo, push that box back into the middle of the table till we are ready to go."

The men came back and laid their hammers on the table.

"Pens all fix up," they announced.

A vast, peculiar shiver passed through the air as though death stalked past; then the island began writhing appallingly beneath them. The ground humped, heaved, tilted sidewise, straightened out and swung violently back and forth. Then the whole island seemed to fling seawards. The buildings were plunged into sudden astounding darkness rent by the roars of landslides ripping out the forested sides of the hill, by trees lashing about as though shaken by terrible whirlwinds. Muffled detonations, dreadful roarings, sounded deep in the earth. Birds rose shrieking into the air, stock careened around in their shaken pastures, dogs howled, wood cracked, concrete split, tortured houses swung back and forth. Again the island flung seaward. Crashes, smashes, enormous hollow thuds jerked the darkness as tank after tank was thrown over, and beyond and above was the sound of solid old lava beds breaking up like melting ice floes and the gigantic grinding of miles and miles of stone walls being shaken flat.

And still, like a behemothian beast in torment, the island

retched, strained, fought, labored to rid itself of the lava tearing out its vitals. Van heard a thunderous roar of passing hoofs and glanced up. The Percheron stallion went by looking wildly to right and left. There was a great rent across its chest where it had evidently crashed against the solid rails of its pen breaking them down. He heard the crunching and cracking of wood being wrenched this way and that and presently the thoroughbred went by like a streak, ears laid back, eyes staring. By the dimmed light of frightened stars he saw Ku-lani lying face downwards grasping the turf with both hands as though she sought, by main force, to hold onto the soil and locality she loved. She lifted her head as the chestnut stallion streaked by on the heels of the Percheron and her face whitened.

Then with long, exhausted shudders the island abandoned its futile efforts to bring forth. Little by little it steadied but the crashing of splintered forest trees and the rattling of rocks sliding down gashed hillsides continued. Water rushed away into the dark, whimpering dogs crawled nearer, birds screamed as they circled overhead reluctant to settle down on the still trembling boughs.

"Anybody hurt?" Ku-lani asked, sitting up.

They all answered.

"Lucky no one was in the cellar," she observed.

The hurried falling of rock walls which continued to cave in filled the immediate night. Van heard someone being violently ill behind a bush. Then the noises gradually died away into a silence even more terrible.

Ku-lani sat very still, then she looked about her and took

a long steadying breath. Van read in her face a sort of horror which left her in complete possession of her faculties, more difficult to endure for that reason.

She got up, mechanically picked up the two pigeons and replaced them in their box which had been thrown upon the grass, then she stood beside the table as though she had been confronted by a specter.

"My cattle—and horses, will all be—mixed up," she said. Then she laughed unnaturally but there was a sob under the laugh for a great work—halted.

The ground twitched and Arlen said:

"Ku-lani, the sooner you get out of here the better. That last shock was about as hard a one as a person would care to experience."

"It's wrecked the lighting system completely and about everything else too, I suppose. Kondo, have we any candles?"

"Got, but too nice, long red kind for parties."

"Where are they?"

"Inside pantry drawer. I get." The man passed her. "No use you go inside, house all crack."

"Lucky it was a frame building, if it had been concrete or rock it would have been demolished," Arlen said. "As soon as we get lights I must look at the seismograph."

"Bill."

"Yes, Ku-lani?"

"Start the truck." Then a thought occurred to her and she ran off down the road. Presently she returned. "We can't get out, the road's—blocked."

Kondo returned holding two long red lighted tapers in his hands. The flickering uncertain light fell on his lined, angry face and showed a glimpse of Thelma huddled on the grass. Van assisted her to her feet. Her face was livid and remorseful and he divined her thought. Had it not been for her they could have ridden. Then he smiled. Horses! He could still hear them, faintly, racing away across the rocks.

"Let's get the tractor, Bill, and see what we can do. Frank—"

"Yes?"

"Go and see if the bulls got out—too."

She took a candle from Kondo. The bitch which had whined crept up to Ku-lani and followed at her heels as she and Bill went off in the direction of the barns.

CHAPTER VI

The hours of that night were, to Van, divorced from all reality. Two slender vermilion tapers, destined to grace some festive board, burned like valiant hearts between them and a world of darkness. By their feeble, flickering light the tractor was found and got down to the road blocked by splintered and uprooted trees, rocks and tons of earth. While Ku-lani and the men were maneuvering with the unwieldy machine Nuhi materialized suddenly out of the dark, announcing calmly that he had abandoned the truck when the great shock came as he wanted to come back and help. But the vast, continued trembling of the cracked and shaken hill, a sort of immense silent jarring, forced them, finally, to abandon the work.

Like a huge disappointed beast the tractor thrashed noisily back into the garden.

Van had an unpleasant moment when they crested the rise. Behind the house was a glow, flames leaping upward devouring the black pit of the night. Then he saw the silhouette of Kondo's figure squatting before it, busy with pots and pans. Ku-lani's fingers closed upon his wrist with a brief, fierce pressure.

"It's things like that," she said, "that illustrate what I told you about everyone being in and essential to," she laughed, "the—snowball."

LAVA

A pain like a fine hot wire burned in Van and dulled out.

"All these people," she indicated the shadowy figures following them and Bill descending from the truck, "need me and I need all of them. So does Kilo-hana, and it goes beyond and beyond, like waves spreading outwards."

"I got coffee," Kondo announced, straightening up when they appeared, "and bacon and hardtack. Eggs all broke."

"Kondo, you're all right." Ku-lani sat down in the glowing circle of firelight and the men came up, sturdy untidy figures. Steaming cups were passed around and plates piled with ship's biscuit and strips of bacon. Dogs, gorged with roasts and stew, dozed on the edge of the lighted space and like a huge sick beast, exhausted with futile efforts, the island rested beneath, gathering strength to wrestle with its next awful pang.

Ku-lani talked with her workers and the scientist, and Van lay on his elbow watching the ring of faces, Arlen's keen, with watching eyes, Ku-lani's intent. With her hair thrust off her forehead she looked like a careworn child with something on its mind. She was figuring a plan of campaign, Van knew, while she attended to the moment. Kondo stood slowly eating a piece of bacon; there was a smear of grease on his yellow cheek and his eyes looked indignant. Thelma sat listless somewhat behind Ku-lani and Joe squatted as though poised for flight. Nuhi stood drinking coffee and talking to Bill and Frank, and other men, whose names Van did not know, conversed together in lowered voices.

LAVA

In the lighted circle Van saw bricks and leaves littering the lawn, the concrete walk had cracked, benches overturned and the house looked dissolute. Presently up the dark slope of the garden he saw Pia's hulking form approaching. His eyes looked hot as though he were angry or tired.

"Where did you leave the Packard?" Ku-lani asked as he joined them.

"In the hayfield. You no see the lights?"

He seemed aggrieved.

She shook her head.

"What time is it?"

"After ten o'clock," Bill Nakagowa said, pulling out his watch. Van studied him covertly. In his curiously serene face there was a queer mingling of Hawaiian and Japanese. His skin was the rich diluted brown of a Polynesian but his eyes slanted a trifle lending his face an elusive quality. His mind seemed to be fastened on abstruse matters but Van suspected he was an efficient workman.

"We'd better take blankets and get what sleep we can. We will have to milk at three, then go down and ship the steers. Bill—"

Ku-lani turned.

"Yes?" he said.

"Tomorrow first thing you and Frank go and round up those stallions or they'll kill each other if they haven't done it already."

The man nodded and looked at his confederate, a heavy

LAVA

Portuguese with a three days' growth of sooty beard upon his chin.

"I want to stay here for a couple of days," Arlen said, "and if you can spare a horse tomorrow I'll go up Hualalai and try to find out where the center of disturbance is."

"Of course you can have a horse and a boy. Joe—"

"I not like go up mountain," the boy said, hanging his curly head.

"Scared?"

"No scare," he said indignantly and his mates laughed.

"Well, Sonny, you take the Doctor."

A small fellow with a withered hand and engaging smile nodded and lighted a cigarette.

Ku-lani fished for one, then sat silent for a moment. Thelma went off in the direction of the cottage and when she was out of ear-shot Ku-lani turned to Arlen.

"I suppose tomorrow we'd better pitch a sort of camp on the bluffs for a few days. We could get out of here on horseback or on foot if we had to but Thelma can't and she won't leave me."

Arlen nodded and Van sat up.

"I'll do whatever I can to help you tomorrow, Ku-lani," he said.

"You can help Nuhi and the yard boys to pitch camp. I need all the other men, some for shipping, some to fix up the stallions and bulls—how about the bulls, Frank?"

"All gone," the man said, "but I sorry so I never been telling you."

"They'll be fighting too," Ku-lani said, "but we can't

LAVA

do anything until daylight so it's no use worrying about it. Nuhi, you drive the truck tomorrow while Van and Kondo and Shiba and Sigaki get the stuff for camp, and, Sonny, you report on the mountain tanks while Tom gives the mountain the once-over. Pia, get a cot and put it up for Thelma, she can't sleep on the ground." Then she frowned. "How are we to get the stuff out? I'd forgotten about the road, it'll take several days and a gang of men to clear it—"

"When I come up, I look," Pia interrupted, "one place below the third pepper tree can cut the wires and go through if Nuhi drive easy."

"Show him before we leave tomorrow."

"What time the boat coming?"

"About ten."

"Then better all man sleep now."

Kondo threw logs on the fire, sending up showers of sparks, then one by one they prostrated themselves and pulled blankets about them.

For a while Van lay with his arms clasped under his head. He heard an occasional rustle in the foliage overhead, and animals, everywhere, moving restlessly. Turkeys gobbled, pigs grunted and every so often a cock pheasant cried stridently and it was always followed by an infinitesimal shudder of the earth. About him people sighed and grunted in the heavy sleep of physical exhaustion. Finally he dozed off. He was awakened by the sound of a dog whining and lowered voices. Raising himself a little he saw two wrinkled, empty sets of blankets and the dark

LAVA

outlines of Ku-lani and Pia carrying something away. They disappeared in the direction of the bamboos and he heard them moving about. After a while they returned and crawled back into their covers.

"Is anything the matter?" Van asked in a whisper.

"Mene-hune is having her puppies," Ku-lani said. "We made her a nest under the bamboos so the other dogs won't disturb her and because," her eyes went to Thelma, "it might affect her." Then with a long sigh she settled herself afresh.

Van lay wide-eyed staring at the stars. He realized with dismay that the last twenty-four hours had affected him sufficiently to make him abandon, for the time being, his rôle of being an unconcerned spectator. According to the rules he had laid down for himself and adhered to, up until now, it was time for him to go. He had often wondered in what way, by what trick, life would try to get hold of him. It seemed that it had, temporarily, by flocks of earthquakes. Ridiculous, unreal supposition. He thought of his father's statement, "He who forms a tie is lost." He had not actually formed a tie but he had permitted a human being to depend upon him, a little, and virtually it amounted to the same thing. He drew a deep breath. He would help pitch the camp and go, before he became too deeply involved in this extraordinary slice of life. He could leave, with decency, still, but if he lingered it would become more and more difficult to extract himself from Kilohana and the people of Kilo-hana. He would wake up some morning and find himself hopelessly entangled, and he moved in his blankets as though to free himself of folds, wrapping him.

Ku-lani sighed in her sleep and buried her head deeper in her arms. The dog whimpered from the bamboos and she sat up quietly in order not to disturb other sleepers. She listened, heard another low whine and got up and stalked off into the dark toward the massed, graceful heads swaying a little against the stars. After a bit she came back and Van sat up.

"Did you see where Kondo put the candles?" she whispered.

"On the table, I think."

"Mene-hune is having a bad time and I want to give her a shot of pituitrin."

"Is there anything I can do to help you?"

"Could you go to my office and look in the medicine closet and get the hypo and pituitrin. I'll go back to her."

Van got up and took a candle.

"Don't light it until you get to the cottage; everyone is dead tired and tomorrow will be a long day."

"Of course you aren't tired," Van said in a low voice and she smiled at him.

He went off, found the cottage door and entered, and closed it after him. Striking a match he touched it to the taper and it shone on a small room, on a desk strewn with papers, piled with letters under long shelves of books dealing with the care and feeding of stock, breeding and diseases. He opened a small closet filled with bottles of medicine, rolls of cotton wadding, bandages and instru-

LAVA

ments. Finally he found the hypodermic and tiny phials of drugs. Searching through them he found the one Ku-lani wanted, slipped it into his pocket and extinguishing the candle went out.

Across the fire he saw the pointed flame of a candle against the yellow-stemmed bamboos and Ku-lani on one knee bending over a box. He walked across the grass, damp with dew, and joined her. She looked up, stretched out a grateful hand and took the articles from him.

"Now a cup of water."

He got it from the fire.

She dissolved a tablet in the cup while he held the candle. From within the straw-filled box came sounds of straining.

Ku-lani worked quickly, speaking alternately to the bitch and to Van.

"She had one pup about two hours ago and the second should have followed in about forty-five minutes." She glanced at the watch strapped to her able wrist. "All right, girl, in a minute. Hold the candle higher, Van. Now, Mene-hune, I'm not going to hurt you."

Deftly she inserted the needle in a fold of loose skin and shot home the plunger and jerked the needle out. The dog squirmed then licked her hand.

Van looked down at Ku-lani's intent face, the little dog's dilated eyes were fixed upon her, grateful, trusting. A muscle quivered inside and Van felt the island stir as though in response.

"Thanks ever so much." She held up the hypodermic and the drug phial. "Put these on the table for me and leave the candle and matches. I'll have to wait a bit and see how things progress. Sometimes you have to give a second dose."

She blew out the candle.

Van stood, astounded by the sudden dark. He felt Ku-lani sitting somewhere near his feet but could not see her and heard the bitch stirring about in the straw.

"This isn't—real," he thought.

He had observed extraordinary happenings but never expected anything in his subsequent life to equal this incident. Here he was, helping a girl to be mid-wife to a dog, valiantly trying to discharge her obligations under the shadow of a wrecked hill and upon an island racked with earthquakes. Useless to argue with facts, as profitless as trying to argue with thin air. It was real!

"Go back to bed, Van. There's absolutely nothing for you to do and no reason why you should lose your sleep."

"I haven't slept and I'm more awake than I've ever been in my life."

He felt her looking up at him and without thinking seated himself upon an overturned nail keg he had seen. They talked in lowered voices and once in a while Ku-lani struck a match to see how things were going. Presently he heard a squeak.

"That's another," Ku-lani said. "Don't strike a light, it'll disturb her."

He felt her groping about in the box and heard the rough quick rasp of a dog's tongue on her hand, then mi-

LAVA

nute stirrings. Ku-lani leaned back embracing her knees and pressing her shoulders against the keg.

"I'm afraid I've got you into more than you bargained for when I invited you to Kilo-hana," she whispered, "but it was entirely unforeseen."

"This experience is something I will never forget."

"Don't feel you have to stay, just because things are in a mess. It's been nice having you and I would have been fearfully uneasy yesterday while I was gone, about Dudie and Thelma and Kai-ko, if there hadn't been some white person around in case of an emergency."

Van felt a pang, realizing that of them all he would have been the most unfitted to take a lead.

"When did you say your passage to the Orient was engaged?"

"I still have ten days."

"Eight, you'll have to catch the boat to Honolulu two days earlier."

Van did not answer.

Silence brooded over the island, a silence that seemed charged with fatal issues like the silence of intense thought. Van was dimly aware that something definite must come out of these events building toward a gigantic culmination. The highly colored fabric of life being woven under such unusual circumstances must show some distinct new design, if not for these others, for himself.

Ku-lani sat perfectly still and the thought came to him that he had never met another woman who could sit still without moving or speaking. The fact seemed to endow her with a special charm. She sat as though waiting for life to come to her, but to her way of thinking that was impossible for she was already in it, part of it, an essential cog in a magnificent whole.

"I'm afraid," he said as though answering his own thoughts, "that meeting you, coming here, is going to affect, alter, my whole conception and philosophy of life."

"You mean things I've said, feel, believe, make you—wonder?"

"Exactly—and what I've seen."

"Don't you want to?"

Ku-lani felt rather than saw his denial.

"Why?"

The single, whispered word was intimate and affected him subtly. Yet he knew she was not conscious of the charm of her voice coming out of the dark.

"That is difficult to explain."

"But you can always—go."

"That is the greatest wonder," he said gravely. "I'm not sure that I want to."

Dawn broke blood red, staining the east like a streaming crimson vein. Van rolled over in his blankets and lay for a minute with his head pillowed on his arms.

Fragments of the night returned, impressions, left-over thoughts. Then he became aware of some immense change in his surroundings, a change which he felt rather than saw. For a moment he was puzzled, then he glimpsed the hill. Its gashed sides, bleeding red earth, were somehow unpleasantly suggestive of the torn flanks of a gigantic beast, maimed, helpless and un-understanding.

He sat up and saw everyone had gone except Kondo, who was working about the fire.

"You like coffee?" the man called out.

"In a few minutes."

He sat up and looked about. The world had changed overnight. He saw the brick and leaf strewn garden and the house which looked, for some reason, as though it were recovering from a debauch. Thelma came out of the cottage and called out:

"Lazy bones!"

And for the first time he felt her friendliness.

"Dr. Arlen's gone up the mountain with Sonny, Ku-lani and the boys left for Kiholo an hour ago."

Van got up.

"What did you do last night after we all went to sleep?" He started to reply but she laughed. "Ku-lani told me. When you've had breakfast look at the puppies. They are beauties."

The leaves of the trees became violently agitated for an instant and Van realized an earth wave was passing under Kilo-hana toward the sea. He shook out his blankets and folded them up. Kondo set a cup of coffee on the table and Thelma sat down on the bench. She looked happier than Van had ever seen her.

"You know," she said, "last night I felt, and you did too, that I ought to have gone with Kai-ko and the others. If I weren't here Ku-lani wouldn't leave but because of me she feels she has to. The extra trouble I cause her I am repaying by keeping her out of danger. Dr. Arlen told me this morning before he went up Hualalai that it isn't safe for anyone to be here at night. It would be"—Thelma looked across the jagged, rocky miles—"a Hell of a place to get out of—quickly. Kondo, bring me more coffee. I'm going to have a second breakfast with you, Van."

When they had finished Van started toward the house to dress and Kondo called out from where he was washing dishes:

"No stop inside too long, sure more shake come by and by."

Van had an odd impression which did not leave him all day, that overnight these folk at Kilo-hana had recognized him as one of their number. They no longer thought of him as that *Ha-ole* but simply as *Ha-ole*.

When he came out, Nuhi, eager and enthusiastic, waited.

"Already Shiba and Sigaki and me fix new road, better load truck, plenty kind to take down. Have to go four or five times, maybe more."

"Let's start then," Van laughed, "I'm afraid I'm not much help, Nuhi."

"Never mind, Ha-ole," the man tossed his curly head like a frisky young bull, "I show you."

Tents, ropes, sheets of corrugated iron were collected and stowed into the truck. Van assisted with the loading and Thelma sat on the grass and watched. Occasionally the ground shook fiercely as though to say, "I know what you are doing!" and the scarred sides of the great slope smoked with dust. When the truck was loaded to capacity Nuhi scratched his head.

"I think more better you and Sigaki stop here and get more things and Shiba and me take load down and dump, then no waste time."

"All right, Nuhi."

Van watched the truck lurching through the green slope that went down to meet the hayfield; it left a swath of crushed grass in its wake and when it reached the road it gathered speed and smoked off into the forest.

With Kondo and Sigaki's assistance Van collected all the necessary items. The truck returned and departed a second time. About one Van and Thelma sat down to a sketchy meal under the trees. Nuhi and Shiba returned and departed with a third load and rejoined them about the time they finished lunch.

"I think," the young Hawaiian said as he stirred quantities of sugar into his coffee, "that this time better you and Thelma go down, then you and Shiba can start to make camp and Sigaki and me come back for last load. Plenty kind still to bring."

Kondo set down a platter of mutton and wiped his hands on his apron.

"Me stop here until Ku-lani and boys come back from Kiholo. Sure tired after ship cattle and I make some coffee then all man can go down and eat dinner at camp." He grinned at Van. "You know how to cook?"

"A little," Van said, buttering a piece of bread.

LAVA

The man looked pleased and surprised. "I think maybe you no can. Never mind, Otero stop there and she make good chop suey tonight. Next time you try."

They departed about two loaded to capacity. Thelma sat in front holding the box with the fledglings, Sigaki and Van on the load holding Mene-hune and the puppies. Van put his arm about the little bitch and held her as they swayed down the two wheel ruts that served for a road. She looked up at him and wagged her tail and he passed his long fingers gently over her back, staring at the wrecked hill with trees nestling at its foot. Between the slender spears of two Italian cypresses the red roof of the big house showed, and clinging to the lower buttresses of the fluted hill, sheds and barns and overturned water tanks.

Already cows were making their slow way toward the milking shed and calves were collected, hopefully, once more, in the steep pasture above the barn. Van had a strange sensation looking back, as though he had left some part of himself behind there. Possibly a shed skin or a cocoon he had crawled out of. . .

When camp was finally pitched in a grassy swale of the high old mud flow that commanded a view of all three mountains, it was dusk. Nuhi moved briskly about looking into every tent to assure himself that nothing had been forgotten. Groups of sympathetic Hawaiian women and children, and innumerable dogs, loitered about offering assistance. Kai-ko sat on a barrel conversing with them but Van knew from the expression of his face that his mind was occupied with other matters. Shiba and Sigaki commandeered some old posts piled by the roadside and began breaking them up for a fire while Sizu and Otero made up cots with monogrammed linen sheets. In the purple twilight the three mountains were magnified to titanic proportions and the sea seemed hypnotized by the stillness of the sky to an equal stillness. Thelma sat by the box of puppies looking at them and Dudie ran about talking to the various large-eyed Hawaiian children who stood shyly about.

A yellow star burned a hole through the soft sky and hung in the west a hand's space from the pale new moon and a strange gust of wind passed over the island and died into the silence. On a rise a little church reared its steeple against the east. Van felt the presence of Hawaiian homes hidden by undulations in the old flow and lost in forests of blue cactus. Occasionally he heard a dog bark in the distance. Kai-ko got up and stood with his hands locked behind him facing the fire. His heavy figure looked tired and tense. He was waiting for Ku-lani. They all were.

The two women went about their task of getting dinner and the men stacked canned goods in a hastily constructed shelter of corrugated iron, but every so often one or another of them would pause and stare at the long dark rise of the land that went toward the fluted hill, diminished to the proportions of an ant heap against the flank of Hualalai.

An occasional horseman passed and women and children detached themselves and started toward their little houses. Van walked to a cactus-grown rise and stood with his hands in his pockets facing the mountain. Finally he saw the lights of a car leaving the ranch. Behind him, in the hollow, firelight gleamed on tents and he saw figures passing and repassing the fire. He watched the car making its way through the desolate slopes hidden by darkness. Now and then the lights were swallowed up by a hollow, then they reappeared. He saw them pass through the gate, then lost them completely under the high shoulder of the mud flow but he could hear the engine stealthily purring as the car made its way carefully along the cracked and boulder- and tree-strewn road leading up the bluff.

He started back.

Before he regained camp he saw the lights flash into view, the long beams cutting the dark like searchlights. When he got to camp Ku-lani was warming herself at the fire and he saw Dr. Arlen's shadow moving around inside one of the tents. Ku-lani stood with folded arms as though she were alone, but under her expression of almost vacant unconcern the perils and emotions she had experienced during the last thirty-six hours were evident in the tense whiteness of her face and in the thoughtfulness of her eyes. Some obscure instinct prompted Van to place his hand on her shoulder. She looked around and smiled.

"I'm—tired," she said. "We had a bad time shipping, the sea was funny, the waves running in all directions. We lost one steer and the horses were so exhausted from swimming out to the boat and dragging the cattle through that rough water that we had to rest them for two hours before we could drive them home. Have Frank and Bill gone by yet?" she asked, turning to Kai-ko.

LAVA

"No, Sister-dear."

"I wonder if they got the stallions and bulls, they hadn't turned up when we left the ranch."

She walked over and inspected the box of puppies and felt the crops of the young pigeons to make sure that they had been fed, then washed up at a basin set on a box.

"Dinner," Kondo called.

They had hardly seated themselves when the two missing men rode up to the fire and dismounted. Ku-lani called out to them in Hawaiian and they made some reply.

"Did they get them?" Van asked.

"Only the bulls," Ku-lani replied, frowning and staring at the vast, velvet sweep of the night. She sat very still but in her face was passionate determination somehow to cope with the problems confronting her. After some consultation with Nuhi and Pia, Frank and Bill mounted and Van watched their jaunty outlines jogging out of the lighted circle.

"Well, Tom," Kai-ko said, leaning on the table, "what have you to report?"

"It's extraordinary, Kai-ko," Arlen said, "but the higher up Hualalai Sonny and I went the quieter it got. At the summit I found no fresh cracks, saw no signs of heat and felt no earthquakes. Yet tonight when we got back to the ranch the shock recorder on the veranda registered five hundred and forty-one shakes of varying intensity which seems to indicate that this threatened outbreak will be low on the flank of the mountain."

Kai-ko thrust his hands through his sparse gray hair and Thelma moved sharply.

"I think, Ku-lani," Arlen said, "that if you'll let me have one of the trucks I'll go back and sleep at the ranch tonight."

Thelma gestured protestingly.

"Volcanoes are my—business," Arlen said, smiling, "I'm paid to study them."

"I fully expect one of these days we'll see you riding down a lava flow sitting on a white-hot boulder," Kai-ko laughed.

"Do as you please, Tom," Ku-lani said. "You can have the Packard. Would you like to have one of the boys stay with you?"

He shook his head.

When dinner was finished Arlen went into his tent, collected some articles he needed and departed. Ku-lani watched him drive off, then walked to the fire, kicked over a bucket and seated herself upon it. Dudie sat down on the grass beside her and Ku-lani placed an absent-minded arm about her and stared into the hot heart of the fire. Thelma fetched a blanket and wrapped herself in it and lay down on the grass and Kai-ko stood facing the semicircle of mountains.

Van watched the men and women clustered about the table eating and laughing. Once Ku-lani moved impatiently and he glanced at her but it was impossible to divine the thoughts veiled by her steady brown eyes. Her silence was baffling because her mind was entirely occupied with thoughts wide as the world, that in a measure embraced a world, her shaken world of Kilo-hana and all that pertained to it. There was a grave nobility to her face in the firelight.

Van listened to a breath of wind passing over the island as though the air gave a long, tired sigh and the night lurking outside seemed to be trying to obtrude itself into the glowing circle. By the faint light of stars he could dimly make out the mazes of fantastic cactus below the long gradual fall of the bluffs seaward.

Otero came and took Dudie to bed and Thelma moved over by Ku-lani. She hurled the butt of the cigarette she had been smoking into the fire, lighted another and placed her arm about Thelma's slight shoulders. Van longed to be able to talk to her but hesitated to invade her occupied silence.

Then the dark was torn by a terrible cry that stirred the hair on Van's scalp. Kai-ko wheeled around and Ku-lani leaped to her feet. It came again, weird, prolonged, charged with anguish, rage and terror.

"Stallions—fighting!" Ku-lani said, white to the lips. It came again, a livid cry out of the heart of darkness. "Pia! Nuhi!" she cried as the men ran toward her. "Saddle horses, get ropes and follow me. Van—"

She ran to one of the trucks and scrambled onto it and Van seated himself beside her. The engine jerked to life and she swung its wheel around and drove madly across the grassy hollow and down two dim, dusty ruts that led into the forest of cactus. Van felt her shaking beside him as she deftly tore at the wheel dodging through openings, avoiding boulders. Weeds thrashed the fenders, rocks struck the running board as she drove, peering ahead, listening intently. The headlights sent long spectral beams into the seas of bluish cactus that opened and closed around them. The blood-chilling cry came strongly from a rough hill to their left. She swung the car around so the headlights shone into the tangled mass of vegetation and got out. Van followed. Ku-lani darted through the labyrinth of prickly trees, stumbled over loose fragments of lava, dodged branches. The screaming of straining wires set Van's teeth on edge. He heard enormous, frantic plungings and the sharp short impact of hoofs against ribs, then horrible sounds of rending.

They rushed up a long rise and came on a level clearing and Van saw, dimly, a huge floundering mass with a smaller one darting venomously about it.

Ku-lani stooped, picked up a stone and hurled it with accurate aim at the thoroughbred. Van heard the smart whack of rock against firm flesh and the smaller horse dashed away, then swooped back for its victim hopelessly entangled in the wire fence surrounding a small cornfield belonging to a homesteader. The chestnut stallion ran in, bit savagely at the Percheron's shoulder and dodged away again.

"Rock him, Van! Rock him!" Ku-lani cried, rushing toward the plunging mammoth of a horse maddened with pain and terror and rage, wrenching to get itself free that it might attack its tormentor. Van planted a stone

LAVA

between the thoroughbred's eyes and it wavered for an instant.

"Good boy!" Ku-lani shouted.

But the thoroughbred recovered and rushed back with bared teeth, feinting at the man, then veering for the Percheron. Van threw another rock at it and Ku-lani waved her arms and shouted, but the animal passed her, swung back and Van heard its teeth snatching at flesh.

"There's a rail gate below here—" Ku-lani gasped, hurling another stone at the dancing stallion. It snorted, lashed out with its heels but she side-stepped it. Van rushed along following the shrieking wires, found a slip rail and ran back. He heard galloping hoofs coming through the cactus below, then swung with all his strength at the thoroughbred as it passed. The rail glanced off its quarters and it kicked out, but he charged it again and it shied away. Even in the anxiety and excitement he had to smile a little to himself, remembering his unruffled past life. "I feel," he thought, "like Don Quixote tilting at windmills."

There was a crash, a sound of tearing and he saw the Percheron go over, taking the fence with it. Pia and Nuhi raced up.

"Rope him!" Ku-lani shouted and they took after the routed horse.

The immediate night was filled with labored breathing and vast, futile, exhausted struggles. Ku-lani ran in but the great head began thrashing against the ground with hollow thuds.

"Ivan!" she cried and the beast ceased struggling for an instant. "Strike a match, Van!"

He took the box her trembling fingers thrust into his. The flame flared up and in the pool of darkness at their feet Van saw the black Percheron lying on its side, its great heaving flanks drenched with sweat and gore. The fine volcanic dust beneath it was black with blood and he saw an artery spurting out between its huge legs. Muscles hung like bloody hams; he saw the dull bluish white of exposed bone and sinews like silver strings severed in two.

Ku-lani bent down, caught her breath sharply.

"He's done," she said in a flat voice. "His thigh is almost cut through. Oh, I hope Pia brought his gun."

The horse lurched, got its forefeet out in front and sat up like a dog. It looked around, then began swaying back and forth in agony, mouth open, dripping saliva, eyes staring.

"Pia!" Ku-lani called and her voice went out through the dark. The man came galloping back.

"Shoot him—quick!" the girl ordered through clenched teeth.

The man took a revolver out of a holster strapped to his saddle, dismounted and his horse watched with pricked ears.

Van took hold of Ku-lani's arm, shaking a little with both hands, and Pia went up to the swaying horse.

"Aim straight!" the girl cried sharply.

There was a quick report and the great beast sank down humbly into its own blood, gave a convulsive twitch and relaxed.

"*Pau!*" Pia announced.

LAVA

Ku-lani looked around, took a deep breath and sat down. There was a sort of horror in her still face, not of death, for she was accustomed to it, but at a world overturned. Pia ejected the shell and replaced the revolver in the holster and Van stood beside Ku-lani. Pia lighted another match and examined the dead horse and seeing the marks of the other stallion's bites, swore.

Nuhi rode up.

"No can catch, too dark," he said, then seeing the limp mass, he dismounted.

"Hell, *maki!*" he exclaimed as though he could not believe it.

"Just now I shoot, little more cut in half," Pia said.

Nuhi examined the carcass, then straightened up.

"Bad luck, Ivan cost too much money. *Poho!* all these *oni-onis!*"

Ku-lani got up. "Send someone down first thing tomorrow morning and burn him. I don't want the wild pigs to get him."

Her dark eyes rested on the Percheron and Van read her thought, an atom of Kilo-hana snatched from her before it had fulfilled its time. She looked desolate and bereft against the uneven wastes of cactus roughly etched against the starry heavens.

"I burn Ivan for you, Ku-lani, my own self," Nuhi said and she nodded her thanks and Van, for no reason, thought of Allan White who had wanted to know what had become of Ku-lani, how life was dealing with her. Ku-lani whom he had known as a child and a young girl and whom he could not forget. Could anyone, Van wondered, glancing at her, even knowing her briefly, forget her? The men mounted and rode off and Ku-lani started back slowly for the car. Van walked beside her but did not attempt to speak. What consolation could he, anyone, offer her? A shiver roughened his skin. He stared at the distant outlines of the circling mountains crouched under the stars, wondering if Kilo-hana would be snatched from Ku-lani before its time was fulfilled. Also . . .

She climbed onto the truck and laid her hand on the wheel.

"Thank God," she said in a voice that was almost a whisper, "we found—him, else he would have bled to death while that devil of a thoroughbred beat Hell out of him."

Her voice caught, then she took a deep breath and straightened her body.

"Silly—to mind so fearfully. Tonight," her dark eyes went to Van's, "I wish I were like you. Detached."

"It's incredible," Van said, "but I mind—too."

CHAPTER VII

"Ku-lani's late tonight, isn't she?" Arlen asked as he walked over to the fire where Kai-ko and Van were seated. Kai-ko nodded.

"I want to show her my report to the Hawaiian Volcano Research Association," and he indicated some typewritten sheets he held in his big, brown hand. Seating himself upon an empty *shoyu* keg he hunched his shoulders and stared into the flames. In the crude light the lines in his face looked like scars dug in with a brutal knife. He went through his papers thoughtfully, then stared at the lava-spilled slopes of Hualalai, black in the red sullen sunset.

Van moved uneasily but Kai-ko sat as still as Rodin's "Thinker" and in the afterglow bulked as large.

"It's absolutely necessary for me to return to the Observatory tomorrow. I've been away ten days but I'd like to get Ku-lani to promise to remain camped here a while longer. The day I went up Hualalai, as I told you, I found no fresh cracks, no signs of heat and felt no earthquakes, while at the ranch the seismograph recorded over five hundred."

He paced back and forth, his hands clasping the papers, his face intent, thoughtful, concerned.

"Can't either or both of you persuade or influence her to reconsider her decision of this morning? The splitting jerks have been less these last three days, perhaps because the mountain fissures are more open and the earth crust in tension, but a lava outbreak is still likely."

Kai-ko raised his head. "I'm afraid, Tom, no one can talk her into remaining here. In Ku-lani you find all you look for in a man and hope to find in a woman and she's magnificent in the singleness of her purpose. Tom, I'd like to have you read me the meat of your report. You know that this is the first time in Island history when a threatened eruption has not been made the cause for a Roman holiday. I hear all reservations at hotels have been canceled and that there is practically no one coming over on the Inter-island boats except on business."

"That's a fact. When I went over to Hilo last Monday I heard it from reputable sources and also," Arlen laughed, "that people have threatened the Editor of the paper that if he so much as mentions the word earthquake again in his paper he'll be shot."

"Bosh!" Kai-ko exclaimed indignantly. "Ridiculous to suppress facts that belong to history merely because they are afraid of losing a little tourist trade."

"Well, my data is on record for the Section of Volcanology in the U. S. Geological Survey," Arlen said.

"Let's have it, Tom," Kai-ko said, leaning forward as he heard papers being gone through.

Arlen cleared his throat.

"Volcano Letter. A Weekly News Leaflet of the Hawaiian Volcano Research Association. Numerous tremors beginning at Puu-waa-waa—"

LAVA

Van moved and Arlen said without looking up:

"Puu-waa-waa is the Hawaiian name of the hill at the back of the ranch." Then he went on reading. "Puu-waa-waa is seven miles north of the summit of Hualalai Volcano, a mountain 8,269 feet high on the west side of the island of Hawaii. These tremors inaugurated a seismic crisis. This has gone on increasing and implies a new movement of the Hawaiian lava column.

"At Puu-waa-waa the tremors became shock groups in continuing series. The spasms were at first separated by several hours, later they lengthened so that the intervals of quiet were only for an hour or so. A shock recorder of magnifying power 25 was set up on the veranda at the ranch and registered a total of 2,095 individual quakes, small and great, in five days.

"A summary of the situation to date, October 6th, is that a period of tremor produced two damaging shocks of Grade IX felt in all the islands of the group. . . . The populace nearest the mountain is sleeping in the open air, stone walls have been thrown down with noticeable fracturing away from the mountain and the stronger shocks have been of the quality to displace furniture, throw down and overturn loose objects, move buildings, crack masonry and produce slides on steep hillsides.

"The outstanding event of the first week of October was a very strong earthquake on October 5th which was more disastrous even than that of September 26. There is good reason to believe that it was more intense, as its effects in cracking road fills and overthrowing embank-

LAVA

ments introduced new phenomena. Its effects extended the damage to water tanks and usually with a maximum fling down the mountain slopes in a seaward direction. A few of this series of tremors varied in length from two to seventeen minutes.

"In the quality of growing to a maximum from tremors to bumping shocks and from bumping shocks to oscillations of longer period this seismic crisis in Hawaii is unlike anything in San Francisco or Tokio. These latter are called tectonic and began with a terrific damaging shock, thereafter declining. Therefore it seems probable that the present Hawaiian crisis is volcanic and marks the shift of magma from the Mauna Loa center toward Hualalai.

"There is no question of this epicenter. The local damage shows it, the perceptibility records show it, the instrumental frequency shows it and the instrumental measures show it at the three recording stations now established.

"Puu-waa-waa has received all along the brunt of the disturbance. Unbraced foundation posts went out, the masonry of the main house was thrown down, boulder fences were prostrated, tanks burst or were flung off their foundations, new avalanches fell in the gulches of the hill. . . . The effects suggest Grade IX Rossi-Forel. Lava outbreak is expectable."

Kai-ko got to his feet and went to the fire, his broad frame bulking huge and solid and thoughtful. An old gray sweater, unbuttoned, disclosed his powerful chest and his eyes, dark and fierce, strained against the darkness that enveloped him. Van was conscious of his devotion, his solidity and force. He was kin to the island beneath his feet, one of the tie-ribs of Ku-lani's world, shaken but unshaken.

"Give that report to her, Tom, *after* she's had her dinner."

Van saw the headlights of a car making its way along the fragment of road that clung valiantly to the torn shoulder of the old mud flow and went out to meet it. Ku-lani got out followed by her devoted men and innumerable dogs, which raced with wagging tails toward the improvised kitchen. Kondo climbed down from the truck which stopped on the Packard's heels, and hurried by, carrying a steaming sauce pan in one hand and a flour sack of ship's biscuits in the other. Nuhi and Pia passed, each with a sheep flung across his shoulder.

"You're late," Van said to Ku-lani as they walked toward the group about the fire.

"One of those beastly shakes this afternoon cracked another of the tanks we set up and we had to fix it before we left so we wouldn't lose all the water. Lucky we've had showers lately or we'd be in a fix."

Kai-ko kissed her as she came up.

"Sister-dear, I was getting anxious," he said.

She smiled, hugged him and ducked into the tent, returning with Thelma and Dudie. They all went to dinner.

A gusty mountain wind tore at the flames and rattled the galvanized iron of the rude shelter under which they were sitting. Van watched the Japanese women and Kondo working about the fire while the cowboys dressed the sheep and the two yard boys fetched canned goods from the truck and stacked them in boxes placed one upon the other to imitate shelves.

When the meal was over they moved away and the men and women swarmed about the table taking their places. Ku-lani pulled an empty cracker box up to the fire and seated herself on it. Kai-ko laid his hand on her head.

"Sister-dear, I want you to read Tom's report."

She put out her hand and took it and Van watched her face, intent, thoughtful, and its strong beauty moved him.

The past ten days seemed like a dream invading reality, pushing it out. Eerie nights divided between sleep and sudden wakings, the gleam of firelight through tents, horses greedily tearing up lush grass, pigs, freed by temblores from rock-walled enclosures, roaming and rooting at large. Sudden, enraged sallies by Kondo driving prowling dogs from the stores. The screech of cock-pheasants disturbed in their slumbers by the incessant shaking of the earth. Dogs barking defiantly at the three mountains looming monstrously against the stars. A waxing moon drenching the island in mellow honey-colored light. Paling stars, a lemon light in the east, dawn breaking solemnly throwing the violent mountain masses into relief. A clear hail from Ku-lani, men rousing themselves, piling into trucks and cars. Ku-lani leading the way back to the ranch crouched under the cracked hill. Still sea and stiller island waiting— for what?

One or another of the women was usually left to guard camp, but frequently they all went back to the ranch and

LAVA

the day's unreal round was resumed. Otero and Sizu ironing the week's wash—monogrammed linens and cowboy dungarees—at the table under the *lichi* and orange trees. Cows milked, calves fed, wheelbarrows rattling along cracked walks and the sharper, more sinister rattling of stones sliding down scarred hillsides. Men repairing the damage of thousands of earthquakes, packing valuables in case of a hasty exit. . . . He glanced at Ku-lani's profile, and realized, again, that she had a gift for silence. She scanned the written pages closely, making no comment, experiencing God only knew what sensations.

There was a line between her eyebrows and the finely chiseled corners of her mouth were tense. He looked at the men and women sitting at the long table, at dogs devouring bones that had been thrown to them, at saddles stacked carefully under trucks to keep them dry from the dew, and realized that a Saga of Hawaii was in progress.

A booted and breeched girl directing the work of a ranch set in a semi-circle of volcanoes; whites, Hawaiians and Japanese working together, carrying on amid chaos and over seas of surging lava in order that people on unmenaced islands might have cream in their coffee and meat on their tables, in order to obtain the necessary money which afforded this devoted folk and Ku-lani their daily bread. Bumps, bangs, fierce angry shudderings, twitches, interrupting their labors as imprisoned forces thrust and pushed against the crust of the earth. The lowing of cattle roaming uneasily in shaken pastures, grazing off herbage growing out of disintegrating lava. . . .

Ku-lani looked up at Arlen and Van saw the controlled emotion of some final decision in her face.

"I wanted you to read that, Ku-lani," Arlen said, "hoping that it might induce you to change your decision of this morning."

"You don't understand, Tom," she said, feeling for a cigarette. "I'm compelled to take advantage of this comparative lull. Every stone wall is flat, my cattle are all mixed up, Guernseys, Holsteins, Herefords. I won't be able to register a calf for a year, unless," she smiled briefly, "I start a new breed—Earthquake Cattle." Then her face grew serious. "Every tank at the ranch is either cracked, off its foundations or tipped over and every one on the mountain is down. All the houses are off their foundations. This running back and forth carting food and water wastes hours of precious time."

"I realize that, Ku-lani, and I wouldn't ask you to do this if I weren't convinced that it's risky staying at the ranch at night. It's a bad place—to get out of."

"I appreciate your concern and you've been a peach staying as long as you have. I've talked to the boys and they are as keen as I am to move back. This rushing back and forth is the straw that will break all our backs. At night in my dreams I rebuild walls, jack up houses and tanks."

She laughed and walked to the fire and stared over it at the outline of Hualalai and the thought came to Van that the mountain was like a beautiful headstrong woman that went on having its way. Ku-lani thrust her hands

LAVA

into her pockets and straightened her shoulders but in the glow of the firelight her hair looked dull and her face tired, gray, hard as concrete and entirely moving.

Van knew that for over a week she and her workers had slept in their clothes, saving every possible instant and he realized that he was always aware of her. She was entirely unconscious of the fact. A torch held aloft to light the way for others, belonging no longer to herself but to posterity.

He studied her colorless face, care-worn and magnificent. It was not to be thought that he, that anyone, had a right to ask her or to try to persuade her to abandon her course.

Arlen looked obdurate and unhappy.

"I have to return to the Observatory tomorrow, Ku-lani; there's work I have to attend to—"

"I understand perfectly, Tom," the girl said, and Van detected in her voice the consideration and respect one worker has for another and he folded his arms tightly across his chest.

"You can't be persuaded?"

She shook her head as though she were sorry not to be able to oblige him.

"If I left Kilo-hana, even temporarily, even at your request, Father would be quite capable of finding that a pretext to cancel my deed. I came to the conclusion this afternoon that if I can raise the money, which will be exceedingly difficult to do now because of the possibility of having the ranch ruined by lava, I'll mortgage it and pay

Father in full. The damages now are somewhere in the neighborhood of eighty thousand dollars." She made a wry face. "But with even a little luck and sufficient time we can pull out of the hole. It's a gamble but worth trying—to me."

Her eyes rested on the night-hidden reaches with an awful affection.

"You know," she said as the earth wrenched beneath them, "I'm sorry for this poor damn island, it's having a fearful time."

"So are you," Arlen said.

She smiled, called Otero to put Dudie to bed and straightened her shoulders again. Thelma rose, kissed her and vanished into her tent. Kai-ko raised his head.

"Sister-dear, there is only one request I have to make."

"I know what it is and I *want* you to stay."

The old man's eyes dimmed and getting up he laid a grateful hand on her head, then walked out of the circle of firelight and stood with his hands clenched behind him facing the mountains dominating the island as though he could not conceive that they could possibly betray his lifelong affection for them. Then he went heavily into his tent.

Arlen glanced at Ku-lani and drew out his pipe.

"If you will only stay here a few days longer I will rush through what I have to do and return at the end of the week."

She silenced him with a slight gesture.

"I must," he spoke without looking at her, "make you realize fully—"

"I do, Tom," she said in an emotionless voice.

Arlen lifted his eyes and there was something tender and respectful in their depths.

"Well, I will keep in daily touch with you," he said, getting up and going to his tent.

Ku-lani folded her arms tightly and stared into the fire, averting her face. For the first time her valiant youth seemed weighted.

"Ku-lani," Van said.

"I'm listening."

"I've told you on more than one occasion that I determined never to take an active part in life."

She nodded.

"When I canceled my booking to the Orient and stayed over, I departed, deliberately and in the full knowledge of what I was doing, from my rôle of unconcerned spectator."

Her eyes met his.

"How old are you, Ku-lani?"

"Twenty-six."

"And I'm nearly ten years older. You've lived, practically, all your life on this island and I've been in almost every country in the world, but I'm inclined to feel that you know far more about life than I do. Its purpose, its reality, its epic proportions. Since I've known you, since I've been at Kilo-hana I've become a disarmed man. You've made me want to have a small part, place, in something tremendous, something I confess that I don't fully understand but from which, my instinct tells me, I have been completely divorced by my father's teachings."

Her intelligent eyes were fixed upon his face.

"You've made me begin to feel that people like me, who try to evade life, to vibrate separately from it, rather than with it, thereby helping it forward whatever the cost, are as you expressed it the night David left, simply—slackers. In some it's a form of cowardice, in others laziness."

Ku-lani unfolded her arms and laid one hand on his and Van noted the nails, grimed still with dirt, despite washing, and on the once beautiful fingers, somehow more beautiful now, abrasions from handling tools. She attempted to reply, swallowed and looked away. His hand closed over hers.

"Ku-lani, I'm being awakened, painfully, into life. I've never struck a man or loved a woman, not even in my sleep, not even in my imagination. I've never worked, never felt. I've been a sleep-walker and—content. But since I've been here—"

He felt her profound gaze and the immense bodily fatigue emanating from her body but through it he was conscious of her youth, tired, but burning on, valiant and undaunted.

"It was inevitable," he said, "that such a human being as you, combined with this environment, should prove stronger than my father's teachings, should beat them. Being here with you has made me feel as though I looked at something fine and beautiful from which I am excluded."

LAVA

She moved protestingly.

"I was gladder than you'll ever know when you said you wanted to stay on."

"I was aware of that and the feeling I have is no fault of yours. But I want to be able to do something, if you will let me, that will rivet in my mind, forever, that I, that my being here, contributed something definite toward the—snowball." He finished with a hint of playfulness to cover a deeper emotion.

He felt her eyes upon him, brown as the troubled soil beneath them. Fine, plucky, mistress of herself and her destiny, from love, from necessity and the rare caliber of her soul, she faced him.

"You," Van said, "can help me."

Ku-lani regarded him, puzzled, interested and compassionate.

"You, your youth, your strength, are being ground between two stones. If I know you or have got to know you a little through the past ten days—"

"It's in trouble that people really do get to know each other, Van," she said softly and his fingers tightened over hers as he looked at her forehead, bare, courageous as a conqueror's.

"It's anxiety lest your father—"

She gave a quick nod and he saw the agitation of a vein in the side of her throat.

"Every day," she said in low hurried tones, "I'm scared that he'll arrive, because of this mess of earthquakes and the way everyone rings up trying to get me to leave. They undoubtedly talk to him too. Can't you hear them saying, 'It's criminal of you, John, to permit that girl to stay there.' Every car that comes up the bluff stops my heart. All these flocks of earthquakes and the anxiety they bring with them wouldn't make me feel so tired and scared," her lips spurned the words disdainfully, "if it weren't for that sword hanging over my head."

"If you will permit it I can take that one away."

"You mean?" she began in steady enough accents.

"That I will and can advance you whatever you need to possess yourself of Kilo-hana outright. You may borrow it in the form of a mortgage or accept it as a gift. I have, thanks to my father, more money than I need." He paused, "And I know you are sufficiently intelligent to realize the motive that moves me to make you this offer."

"You do it," she spoke slowly, "a little for me but mostly for yourself?"

"Exactly, Ku-lani."

"Van."

He weighed her face in the dying firelight and saw reflected in the pupils of her eyes, tents filled with sleeping people, dogs stretched in the warmth, tethered horses, trees, and the ancient lava-spilled acres of Kilo-hana, supporting the registered stock which were her care.

"Yes, Ku-lani?"

She got to her feet and he rose and stood beside her. She was tall for a woman but in that moment he towered above her. She caught hold of his arm with both hands and pressed her cheek against it like a child overcome with gratitude which it cannot express. His hand went out and clasped her head against him for an instant, then he disengaged himself gently.

"Then you will let me do this—Ku-lani?"

She shook her head.

"But your wish to, and the impulse which is responsible for it touches me to the heart."

Van looked away. He had been struck a blow right over his.

"Is there no way in which or by which I could persuade you to accept this gift—the first gift I've ever made to life?"

"Oh, Van, I know it's given with both hands."

"Then be generous enough to accept it in the spirit in which it is given."

She seized him by the shoulders and he was amazed by her strength.

"What is it? What is the matter?" he asked mechanically.

"You've been kinder to me than anyone ever has; you realize all that Kilo-hana means to me, how I love it"; he detected a break in her voice which she instantly steadied. "I know you believe me when I say if it's going to be blown up it would be easier—to go with it."

He nodded and his hands went to her shoulders returning her grasp automatically, then as his fingers tightened down he appreciated how deeply she was affected. He had a peculiar, vivid impression that there was only so much emotion in the world and they were, equally, sharing it,

LAVA

because he was fitted or able to appreciate the quality of her affection for Kilo-hana and her terror lest it be wrested from her, the essence, the very pivot of her world. A world rimmed by volcanoes, formed by volcanoes.

He felt the shaking of her body and her agitation was transmitted to him through his hands upon her shoulders. It invaded his body, bewildering his heretofore always clear mind.

"Calm yourself, Ku-lani," he said.

"It isn't that I'm—scared," she said. "It's only," and her voice caught, "that I've never known anyone like you, and never expect to again, for living as I do, here, cut off from the outside world, it's not likely that I shall ever have another opportunity. Your kindness, your gentleness, your courtesy, your appreciation of—of—everything, unlocks a door in me which has been closed ever since I came back from school. You've done what Kilo-hana has for me. Differently. Most people think I'm a sort of a plow horse—"

"I recognized the instant I met you sitting on the steps with Kai-ko, that you represented something fine, very fine, and beautiful. Something that has made me stop and think, against my will. Meeting you, being here with you has, I'm afraid," his voice sounded amused and regretful, "has changed my whole slant on life. Forever."

"If it hadn't been me, Kilo-hana," she said in a husky whisper, "it would have been something else. You can, sometimes, postpone your moments but—they await you."

LAVA

He looked into her upturned face, serious, gilded with firelight.

"Your wisdom is amazing, but it could have only been someone like you, as real as you, who could have shown me my—delusion." He took her face between his brown, intelligent hands. "And I wish that you would let me—"

Her fingers left his shoulders and closed on his wrists.

"I will," she said in a fierce whisper, "I will, if Father attempts—"

"Thank you, Ku-lani." His hands left her face and found her fingers, locking them.

"I must go to bed now or I won't be fit for work tomorrow."

"Do, you look shockingly tired. And I have Kai-ko's request to make."

She looked into his eyes.

"It's granted. I want, I'd like to have you stay—too."

He watched her enter her tent, then sat down on the *shoyu* keg and stared into the red heart of the fire. He had no regret, to his amazement. Twice, and he realized it to the full, twice in the last ten days he had departed from his life long determination to keep out of life. Once, temporarily, when he had stayed over, now he had definitely allied himself with the fortunes of an individual.

He realized that interest in Ku-lani had deepened into admiration, then into a stronger feeling; not love in the accepted sense of the word, but something finer and stronger. Reverence or worship or a combination of both.

LAVA

For her strength which was beauty and for her beauty which was strength and for her youth.

He got up and walked beyond the firelight and stared at the sleeping mountains which had despoiled vast portions of the island, mountains harboring no one knew what further horrors in their breasts, and he felt acutely that this island, so strong, so lawlessly beautiful was a world still in the process of creation.

He started back to his tent and paused beside Ku-lani's. She had pulled her cot outside and turned it so she faced Kilo-hana even in her sleep. A faithful sentry always on duty. On the ground beside her was a lantern, turned low, and an alarm clock and over the side of her bed one hand hung and it looked the tiredest thing in the world. Van bent down and put it reverently inside the blankets and lifted the flap of the tent he shared with Arlen and Kai-ko.

"And I, the son of my father," he thought, sitting down on his cot, "have been caught by life, like the veriest fish of them all and with the oldest bait—a woman."

CHAPTER VIII

"Ku-lani," Arlen said next morning when he was ready to leave, "I'm going back to the Observatory by way of Kona to check up on the seismograph I set up there. Is there any message I can take to your father?"

"Tell him I'm—all right."

"I shall tell him something else too," Arlen said with a smile.

"What?"

"That you're magnificent."

She grinned like a derisive boy and climbed up on the truck.

"Expect me back about the end of the week," Arlen said, buckling up his brief case.

She nodded.

"Leave the tents and cook house, Van—just for luck," she called out. "But bring everything else. Nuhi will be back for the first load in about an hour."

"I'll have it ready," Van said, watching her drive away with her men and dogs.

"Well, Tom, I hate to see you go," Kai-ku said, placing his hand on the scientist's shoulder.

"I dislike leaving just now but I'll be back shortly."

Arlen handed his case to Sonny and he put it into the Packard and waited.

LAVA

"Anything I can do for you in Kona, Kai-ko?" Arlen asked as he got into the car. "Sonny's just taking me as far as Garland's and I shall rent a car from there. He ought to be back by one."

"I don't think so, Tom, thanks," Kai-ko said, stepping back as the engine started.

Nuhi returned about eight and took everyone but Van and the two yardmen back. They stayed and broke camp but a great vagueness enveloped Van while he worked. He had a sensation of having cut a cable and being adrift, rudderless, on a horizonless sea, without a compass to guide him or a wheel by which to steer a course. When the last article was stowed into the truck it was after five. Van's body ached pleasantly from fatigue but he was conscious of an inner ache, the ache of emptiness. He had definitely abandoned his old attitude toward life but had not yet adjusted to the new.

He looked back at the deserted tents as they drove away.

"Am I lost or found?" he wondered as Nuhi turned down the road leading along the shoulder of the bluffs. On one hand were shattered hillsides, dislodged boulders weighing tons, uprooted trees and on the other gaping cracks overhanging cactus-grown, rock-strewn slopes.

A sullen, sulphurous sunset burned in the west and the grim gray slopes of Hualalai looked tired and old.

Nuhi drove carefully until they reached the flat ground below the gate, then speeded up. Occasionally he made a remark but a waiting silence pervaded the locality and strange, lonely shadows lay on the sea. An immense pres-

LAVA

ence seemed to lurk below the ash-gray horizon and in the struggling trees of the forest through which the laden truck labored painfully.

Van folded his arms and stared at the long slopes of the mountain. A door which his father had closed had been opened by Ku-lani and he stood on its strange threshold not knowing whether to enter or step back. He was hanging between two worlds, belonging to neither. For fifteen years he had drifted, literally, body and soul, like a detached leaf blowing among the stately trees of a forest, going on and on, never catching up with, or on to, anything. It had been his defense against life and now, in the full realization of what he was doing he had surrendered. . . . He was unarmed, defenseless and too ignorant to know how to help himself or what to do with the key that had been put into his hand, that had unlocked the door . . . to let him through . . . to what lay beyond . . . an undiscovered world waiting for him to take his place in it.

When they drove into the littered garden Kai-ko was waiting.

"Van, Garland wants you to call him up," he said, scratching his head until the sparse gray hair stood up like the antennæ of a distracted beetle.

"Did he say what he wanted?" Van asked, getting out and lifting down the box of puppies.

"No, but I fancy he expects you to go back."

Van carried the box to the shelter of the bamboos and Mene-hune followed wagging her tail. Van put down the box, thinking here was a chance to retreat if he wanted

LAVA

to. . . . Kai-ko waited and Van felt the old man's liking.

"All Kona is up in arms because Ku-lani has returned here. The phone has been going all day. I'm glad Kulani's riding the pipe line. People are going to and have always made things difficult for her."

Van straightened up and they walked to the house together. It was almost dark. Pia was kneeling over the seismograph changing a record. He glanced up, nodded, then went to the railing and poured a strong-smelling varnish over the disc, fixing the smoke smudge.

Van took up the receiver and called his number. Presently he heard Garland's voice on the line and he was conscious of Kai-ko waiting behind him.

"Yes, Kai-ko and I have elected to stay here, indefinitely, anyway until conditions subside or something blows up." It was done—irrevocably. "Thanks, kind of you but please don't be concerned about my safety. Things have been fairly quiet these last two days. Yes, we are back at the ranch. Please remember me to your wife. I'm enjoying myself immensely. Good-by."

Kai-ko sat down in a rocker and stuck his large bare feet out in front of him. Pia picked up a lantern, lighted it and disappeared in the direction of the kitchen.

"I'm afraid," Kai-ko said, "that we are going to have most of Kona about our ears before long," and he sighed like a tired child. "Ku-lani is unfortunate in that by the very force of her personality she attracts the spotlight and focuses it upon herself without meaning to. . . . There is certainly not another woman and probably not many men who would have stuck to their guns as she has under the circumstances. The weak have an instinctive jealousy or resentment for the strong."

Van inclined his head.

"If she had fled she would have had everyone's sympathy; because she did not people criticize her judgment and discuss her. I'll wager that she is the main topic of conversation in every home on Hawaii. It's a pity that Ku-lani and her father do not get on. They are both unusually strong characters but are diametrically opposed in disposition and temperament. I still hope that something will turn up some day to bring them together and enable them to recognize each other's fine qualities. Ku-lani has her father's strength without his desire to domineer. As a child she was, of course, a captive but she never surrendered. Her body obeyed his commands because he was an adult but her spirit stood apart—always. Being the only daughter, John wished her to be an ornament to his home, but Ku-lani was rich, even then, in the energies of the earth and craved something bigger, something constructive. As a child, as a girl, she groped—trying to find an outlet for the forces within. She always had a sort of passionate aliveness. The day she began to earn her own bread she made the real discovery; it was not love, not even maternity, but by work that she discovered the world and since then she has spent herself without calculation."

Kai-ko leaned down and scratched his bare foot.

"People say she is too occupied with the rough facts of life, that she is hard, she is obliged to be hard—but it's vivifying! The part of herself, the best part was born *after* she came to Kilo-hana. They deplore the fact that she is 'wasting' her life here but it is only those who see what she is doing here, what she does here every day, who are able to judge whether she's wasting it or not. But people who do not understand circumstances never surrender their right to pass judgment."

Van nodded and stared thoughtfully at the dismantled house.

"I hope," he said after a moment's pause, "that my staying on here—"

"Has not afforded an added topic of gossip?" Kai-ko asked.

"Yes."

"Doubtless it has, but what of it, as Ku-lani would say?" Kai-ko chuckled.

"Yes—what of it?" Van thought, staring at the seismograph and for no reason felt suddenly lonely. Then he heard her coming down past the tanks talking to some of her men and he turned in his chair so he could see her.

"Is that you, Sister-dear?" Kai-ko called.

"I'll be with you in a minute," she called back and disappeared in the direction of the office. Presently Nuhi appeared.

"Ku-lani like you two come to her office."

Kai-ko heaved himself out of his chair and took Van's arm and they went along the cracked walk past spicy geraniums and large, juicy-leaved bananas that looked like green ghosts in the firelight flickering across the lawn. Kondo

LAVA

was squatting before the blaze peering into the various tins and saucepans on the grill which one of the men had made. An odor of cooking reached Van's nostrils as he and Kai-ko passed. Ahead through the opened door Van saw Ku-lani bending over her desk but at sight of them she straightened up and tipped back her swivel chair. Pia was seated in a corner and Nuhi and Sonny stood at the door. Kai-ko and Van entered and seated themselves on a long trunk.

"This looks like a council of war," Van said.

Ku-lani gave him a quick, warm glance.

"It is," she said, leaning forward to scribble down a memorandum, then pushing her chair back until it touched the medicine chest.

A lantern filled the little room with a hot yellow light that exaggerated everything. Ku-lani did not speak for a moment and Van studied her intent profile. The strong modeling of her brow was almost contradicted by the softness of her eyes which had a liquid quality when she was thoughtful or moved, but he had seen them flash fire the night that David had gone. The fall of her shoulders, the fine line of her arm and the curve of her fingers still holding the pencil had all the essence of unstudied art and there was that in the proportions of her body that suggested a reduction from heroic size.

"Thelma tells me," Ku-lani said, "that a lot of people have called up today about our coming back."

Kai-ko nodded.

"Who?"

He ran through a list of names.

Ku-lani tapped the arm of her chair with the pencil.

"I suppose," she said, "they asked Tom and he told them. I wonder what they expect me to do, leave things in this mess and sit around waiting for the earthquakes to stop? If anyone rings up and talks to me I'm going to tell them that if they are prepared to pay all the boys' salaries and me what the ranch brings in on an average a day I'll consider going," and she smiled and Van knew she never would.

"I'm afraid," Kai-ko said, "that your father and possibly others may come over."

"I hope they do," Ku-lani said, grinning like a boy. "And I hope we have a flock of earthquakes that will scare the daylights out of them."

The Hawaiians laughed.

She glanced appraisingly at Van. "You have a fine crop of sunburn," she observed.

He passed his hand over the bald and blazing top of his head and squinted at his nose.

"I forgot to wear my hat today," he said, laughing.

"Well," Ku-lani said, getting up, "I suppose I have to brace myself for the pleasure of a visit from Father. Why can't people leave me alone? I suppose that they feel that I'm leading the lot of you to slaughter." She looked at the Hawaiians. "Do you—have any of the boys said they'd like to go?"

The men shook their heads.

"You two," she glanced at Van and Kai-ko and got up and went to her desk, "expressed yourselves last night.

LAVA

That being the case I suppose we'll have to unite and withstand the siege. I can't decide whether or not to send Dudie to Loki. Thelma," a quick thought came to her and she finished, "well, it's just a question of time for her, she runs a temperature every day and as long as she prefers to be with me, while she can, it seems to me it's none of their business."

Van got up and walked to the desk.

"Nuhi, tell Kondo that when dinner's ready, we are."

The house lurched toward the sea and Van put out his hand to save a stack of books from falling, but they shot to the floor with a crash, taking a mass of papers with them. He stooped and gathered them up and put them back upon the desk; then he leaned over and examined the blanks. Ku-lani smiled.

"Those outlines of calves, I have to fill in with the markings of each individual animal." She picked up one of the sheets. "You see, they are double so you have to draw in each side, then you fill in the date of birth, breeding, etc., and send it away for registration. I draw them in first with pencil, then trace them over in ink afterwards. I have to do a lot tomorrow. Thanks to these damn earthquakes I'm way behind and I have to get some out before the end of the month."

"I could trace these in after you draw them," Van said.

"All right, you can help me tomorrow." She turned to Pia and another long shudder went through the earth. "Did you leave horses in the corral?" she asked and something passed between them.

LAVA

He nodded.

Ku-lani placed her hand on Kai-ko's shoulder.

"You know," she said, "the road to Waimea is closed and the one to Kona is just about impassable and has been ever since the first big shake. I wish the supervisors would do something. It's our only way to get out freight and bring in supplies. I have to ship six Holsteins tomorrow; the dairy wired for them this morning as they are short of milk. Wish they'd given me more notice, but people on the other islands don't—realize. I'm a bit uneasy about taking the cows in the trucks over two of the fills in the big lava flow. Sonny, you and Nuhi go easy and if you have to, unload and lead the cows across."

The man nodded.

"Sure, Ku-lani, us look sharp."

Ku-lani suppressed a smile but Van felt the profound depression of her spirit and it added to his depression, affecting him oddly. It seemed as though the world had stopped going forward. Ku-lani talked, worked, laughed, the well-equipped machine went on, functioning perfectly but for some reason her spirit was affected, touched with depression. Was it strange? Her world was, practically, in ruins.

They went into the kitchen where Thelma and Dudie were already seated at the table covered with its red and white cloth.

"Here, Mummy," Dudie said, laying her hand on the back of the chair beside her. Ku-lani pulled it out and sat down, leaning her elbows on the table.

LAVA

"Mummy, what are you thinking about so hard?" the child asked after a silence.

"You, dear."

"What about me?"

"I'm wondering if I shouldn't send you to visit Aunt Loki until these earthquakes are over."

"But I don't want to leave you, I like Kilo-hana better than Kona. Don't make me go."

"Mother's so busy, dear."

"I know, all these nasty old earthquakes. Why do they keep coming all the time?"

The child dug her spoon into some rice and *shoyu* and Van watched her. She was Ku-lani over again.

"I'm so mad with them, my play house is smashed and the dog kennel tipped over and the boys' houses look so silly sitting flat on the ground without any legs. I wish they would stop!"

Ku-lani smiled.

"So do I, Dudie." She paused for a minute. "Grandfather may be coming over; wouldn't you like to go back with him?"

"I don't like Grandfather."

Ku-lani smiled and helped Kai-ko and Van to some mutton but appeared to forget about herself. She weighed the dismantled kitchen thoughtfully, but Van knew her mind was occupied with other matters. Her face was too still, too white. She was appalled by the situation but her roused femininity faced the danger with a passionate desire to defend her own. These acres she loved, these people who were dependent upon her, the stock that was her pride and her care.

"No eat?" Kondo demanded, staring at her empty plate. "S'pose you no like mutton tonight I fix some other kind."

"This is fine, Kondo. I was—thinking."

The man scowled and went out, returning with a pot of coffee which he set down on a plate. He waited, staring at Ku-lani's plate and she put something upon it and he went away and Van marveled at the devotion that this girl evoked in everyone whose life came in contact with hers. Thelma began coughing and took off the wreath that hung about her slim neck, weighting it.

"Ku-lani," she said when the spasm was over.

"Yes?" The girl came back from some lonely distance.

"If you'd feel—better, I'll go to Kona with Dudie."

"Absolutely not! As long as there is any Kilo-hana left, you, everyone who wants to stay here is welcome."

She pushed her chair back and walked into the garden. Kai-ko turned to Van.

"Ku-lani's upset tonight."

"Shall I—do you want me to go after her?"

"Yes!" the old man said emphatically.

Van went out.

"Ku-lani?"

"I'm here."

He followed the sound of her voice and saw her facing the hill. The faint glow of a coming moonrise showed behind, magnifying its size. Her chin was lifted as though she were tipping back tears into her eyes. He went up to

LAVA

her and took hold of her hand. He did not press it, his touch was a mere contact but the feel of her dry, calloused, work-hardened fingers almost unmanned him. It was abominable that she should be so tortured, that this ordeal should be so prolonged and that he, that no one, could help her.

"You are upset," he said gently.

She nodded and he heard her swallow and bent suddenly and kissed her hand, and he felt a tremor pass through it.

"Be careful," she warned, "if you are too kind to me I may cry. I'm just on the edge of it now. You know," she lifted her magnificent eyes to his, then looked about her, "I feel as though part of me had died. I think I don't mind but I do; it's like seeing someone you love tortured," and she gestured with her free hand at the houses and hill and the silent miles about her. "I fight on—because I must. I suspect," she smiled wanly, "I'm beaten, but it doesn't seem to matter; you have to go on fighting anyway. This thing isn't over, I know it! But Kilo-hana isn't, as I told you once,—just a place to me!"

"I know," Van said. "There is a soul—in things."

She nodded vehemently and he felt the rigidity of her body transmitted through her hand that he held. "The boys, all of you, have been splendid but they feel depressed as I do—tonight. As fast as we repair things new earthquakes destroy. But you can't stop!"

"No, Ku-lani," he said, and thought she couldn't stop or be stopped but the price she was paying was terrific.

She turned to him. "I must do something quickly to shatter this feeling that has come to Kilo-hana, that doesn't belong here! Help me—Van!"

"Pray command me," he said, and she smiled.

"You said that the night Father turned David out. It sounds nice." She spoke the word as though it had been used for the first time, freshly. "Nice, like the old world which I shall probably never see. Nice—and foreign."

She stood with her eyes fixed on the hill as though she were evoking, or trying to evoke, something from the night, courage perhaps, or belief in her shaken gods.

"Don't despise me," she said after a silence.

"Despise you, Ku-lani, how could I?"

"Because for the moment I feel—checked."

"I know that nothing could check you for *more* than a moment," Van said gravely.

She turned to him and her face lighted. "You are a darling. I like you because you understand and don't—love me."

He wondered.

"I worship what you stand for, embody; youth, life, fortitude."

"That's different," she said, smiling, and her smile was a flame which enveloped them both and their surroundings.

"Go," she commanded, "and call the boys, tell them I want them—all!"

Van released her hand and walked off toward the men's quarters. The houses were all flat on the ground with now

LAVA

and then a foundation post sticking out like a broken leg.

"Pia!" he called.

The man walked out on the veranda.

"Van?"

"Ku-lani wants you all at the house."

"All right, I tell."

Van retraced his steps past the tanks which had been replaced on their foundations and through the shadowed garden. He saw packing boxes of valuables stacked on the lawn, car and trucks parked—heading out, with dogs lying beside them and he thought about the horses kept in the corral overnight. His skin roughened. Enough . . . enough . . . to daunt anyone!

The lighted kitchen windows looked like beacons to guide him and he hastened toward them. Ku-lani was quietly finishing her meal and he sat down and finished his. She looked across the table at him once, and smiled and he felt warmed. Presently he saw figures coming down the slope of the lawn. Ku-lani got up and went to the door.

"Boys, as soon as things are cleared up we are going to have a party."

"Party!"

"Yes, dance, sing, have a good time—in the big living room."

"*Maikai!*" came in a chorus.

"Help Kondo to clear up."

The men entered and helped the cook and the two women to stack dishes. Ku-lani walked through the pantry stacked with provisions taken from the wrecked cellar and piled above ground.

"Bring a lantern, Van," she called.

He picked one up and followed her. Its circle of striped light made the big, beamed room seem even loftier than it really was. Shadows like uneasy ghosts lurked in corners, shrouded furniture looked on. Through the diamond-paned windows of the veranda he could see trees dimly outlined by the moonlight. Behind him Kai-ko and Thelma and Dudie came. The old man groped his way to his chair and Thelma and Dudie curled up on a couch. Ku-lani walked straight to the piano and Van set the lantern upon the floor and helped her to turn back the top.

"Shall I put the light on a chair so you can see?" he asked. She shook her head and her fingers found the keys instinctively.

He withdrew, seating himself so he could watch her.

With her head thrown back and her eyes fixed on some distance of her own, that he, that no one might share with her, she played. The light gilded her tense profile and the echoing rafters gave back the music that her strong fingers tore out, hulas, like wild, beating, broken hearts. He had a vivid feeling that she was calling upon the strong gods of youth to uphold her. She was the very spirit of Kilo-hana. In her boots and breeches, soiled but superb, she played on, young, tortured as the racked island beneath her. The room slithered seaward and jerked back but her fingers did not falter. Her still upward gaze had something divine about it and her wide-open eyes shone from

LAVA

under the fine, dark arches of her courageous eyebrows.

The pantry door opened and men in dungarees and women in kimonos filed in. Ku-lani's face did not alter but she smiled at them. Pia carried a guitar, Sonny and Nuhi, ukuleles. Outside the seismograph ticked on and dogs, deserting the cars, lay at the door and on the veranda. Sonny and Nuhi and Pia went and stood behind her and her dark, lighted eyes swept their faces with a fierce gratitude.

"*Lei E!*" she commanded and the men began singing.

After a few verses Nuhi put his ukulele on a chair and began a hula and with a shriek of delight Otero went on the floor and began caricaturing it. The others leaned forward applauding. Joe slid out like a young snake, his supple body undulating, fluid, graceful, his liquid eyes fixed upon the ceiling as though he were hypnotized by it. Ku-lani turned her head and smiled, then signed to Pia and Sonny to keep on singing and rose. Nuhi turned his back on Otero and the Japanese woman began dancing at Joe. The boy hung his head and tried to eclipse her efforts while Ku-lani circled, enticing and repulsing Nuhi. He shifted the knife strapped to his hip and redoubled his efforts.

The house staggered and straightened out. There was a moment's pause, a round of breathless laughter and the music and dancing went on. Van studied Ku-lani. He knew from his few moments with her outside the kitchen how moved she was but . . . her face glowed faintly from her efforts, her lips were slightly parted in a smile, lips as fascinating as the words that issued from them from time to time disturbing his tranquillity. She continued to dance, moving gracefully about the dismantled room, her face looked pure and bright but there was something of the sleep-walker in her eyes, in her easy, unhurried motions. He had never seen such an expression in her face before; she seemed to be enveloped in a flame for an instant, then she pushed back her hair from her moist warm forehead and the transfiguring mood passed.

Van's locked arms tightened across his chest.

"The grit and glory of that girl," he said in a low voice and Kai-ko laid his hand on Van's knee.

"Dancing hulas over—Hell," the old man said with admiration and affection. "Nothing can beat her—even death," and his blind eyes filled.

Van watched from lowered eyelids. The light from the lantern clung to her forehead and in a hollow of her throat. Every so often the house shook remindingly and each shudder was greeted with shouts. Thelma lay on her elbow with a *lei* about her neck and Dudie watched her mother with shining eyes. Then she scrambled down.

Ku-lani held out her arms and the child ran into them.

"Mother, I want to dance with you."

"All right, sweetheart."

"You dance with me, Dudie," Nuhi urged, bending down and taking hold of her hand. The child beamed.

"I'll dance with both of you," she announced.

Van watched, marveling at the ease and grace with which the child imitated her mother's and the cowboy's movements. Her little hands opened and closed like butterflies, her eyes were fixed upon her mother's face and her cheeks a fiery rose with excitement.

"Fine! Dudie, fine!" The onlookers applauded and Van watched her tiny bare feet, as expressive as hands, moving across the furniture-grooved floor, keeping perfect time with the music. Ku-lani watched her beneath long, lowered lashes, smiling a little when the child followed her every movement perfectly. Then all at once she snatched her up off the floor and kissed her.

The music came to a stop and laughing and panting the dancers sat down.

"Now Shiba, Sigaki, Sizu, Otero," Ku-lani called, "Japanese dance, Japanese hula."

The four Japanese got off the carved teakwood chairs they had been sitting on and advanced to the middle of the floor. Ku-lani sat down on the arm of Kai-ko's chair and laid her hand on his head.

"If any of the so-called pure-minded saw this," she laughed, "they would think that we were—staging an orgy!"

Kai-ko nodded and pressed her hand to his cheek. Van watched the four stiff figures moving automatically and Kondo, leaning forward entranced. The dance old as the Orient and symbolical, did not seem out of place in the dismantled but still stately room. It seemed part of it and part of the empty, splendid reaches outside. Watching it and the circle of absorbed faces the realization dawned upon him that there was no race, no sex, on an occasion such as this, they were all just human beings united to carry life forward toward its goal and he felt a deep, inner stir realizing that he was associated with these valiant folk. . . .

Outside, the night held its breath and the lantern fought to dispel the darkness of the big room. Van straightened up and folded his arms more tightly; the average onlooker would certainly misjudge this strangely moving scene, would misjudge Ku-lani and these devoted people united with her to keep the flag of courage flying. . . .

CHAPTER IX

"Hand me that folder, Van, will you?" Ku-lani asked, stretching out her arm. "Thanks." She accepted it from him, drew out a fresh registration blank and returned it. When she finished drawing the calf she had tied up she rose, cut the curl off the end of its tail to identify it as drawn, untied it and drove it out, then selected another animal and sat down.

"We've finished eighteen since lunch," she said, smiling and looking across to where Van was sitting inking in the marking of the calves she had drawn in pencil. "This is great, having an assistant; it saves me hours of time." Then she applied herself once more to her work. Van watched, marveling at the speed and accuracy with which she drew. Occasionally she frowned, rubbed out a line and went carefully over it again.

He dipped his pen into the ink bottle and looked around. The barn was warm and sweet. Outside he heard animals moving softly about and the sound of cuds being chewed. From below men called to one another as they worked and the incessant sound of hammers being plied filled the immediate afternoon. Through the slats he saw the reaches of the island drugged with sunshine and the immense expanse of the sea.

"I don't know what to do about Dudie and Thelma,"

Ku-lani said without looking up. "I should send them away. Have you noticed, Van, that there's been a different sound to the last three earthquakes?"

"Not especially, Ku-lani, I've lost track—there are so many varieties."

"Well, the last three," Ku-lani paused to find the right word, "were ugly."

"None of them sound particularly attractive," Van said with a smile.

She laughed and straightened up for an instant and stared at nothing. "I admit that. Thelma was awfully kind to me when I was at school. You see when I went away I was engaged to Danvers and while I was gone he married Drina." She grimaced. "I was young and felt that life had dealt me a foul blow. Now I know it was for the best. Thelma's younger than I am but we've been friends ever since we were kids. When Naps and David and I were little we used to sneak over to her house. Hi-ball, her father, let us make as much noise as we wanted to. Then Puhi would come for us, terrified that Father might find out. He'd pretend to be angry and say, 'No use make like this, by and by Ha-ole Hao catch you and whip you sure,' but really he was scared and would smuggle us in while Father was in the office."

She sat lost in thought.

"After I came home, divorced, people made me feel like a leper. Loki and Thelma were the only ones who were decent, who understood. About a year ago Thelma met a dear boy, part Hawaiian, they were fearfully in love and wanted to get married. Hi-ball would have consented but people began screaming, as they always do, and it ended by them working him up into the same mood. He forbade them to marry and so—they loved each other anyway and you know the rest. I feel dreadfully sorry for Thelma, it was rotten luck he was killed roping a bull. Why can't people," she hurled the word from her, "leave each other alone!"

She desisted from drawing for a moment and he noticed her figure, supple, charged with force, but her eyes were unfathomable.

"When Thelma told me, I asked her to come to Kilohana." She got up, unfastened the calf and handed Van the finished drawing to trace. "Now all this has happened and I feel responsible, having her here."

"If she's happier with you, don't worry about her, let her stay," Van said, dipping his pen into the ink. Ku-lani did not reply and he glanced at her and realized that he was drawn to her by the force of her strong soul.

"But it isn't only her that I have to think of, Van," she said, thrusting her hand into her pocket. "There's her baby to be considered, too."

He could not reply.

"It's rotten luck that this should all happen just now." She frowned and drew a soiled scrap of paper out of her pocket and handed it to him. "Puhi sent this over last night by his son."

Van scanned the unformed writing scrawled across the little sheet, torn out of a note book. "All man go Kilo-hana tomorrow." He read it, then looked at Ku-lani marveling. She had known all day that her father was coming and had said nothing.

Without show of emotion she thrust the piece of paper back into her pocket. "I suppose 'all man' means Luke and Ben as well as Father and probably Aunt Sarah, Drina's mother. They'll have everything to say about my staying, about Thelma being kept here! Especially Aunt Sarah!"

"Did I meet her at the *luau?*"

"No, she was in Honolulu, thank God. You know, Van—"

A peculiar vicious shudder passed through the earth rattling the iron roofs. It was accompanied by a strange rushing sound.

"Did you notice that noise, Van, like water?" Ku-lani asked.

"Yes."

"Only, probably it isn't water," Ku-lani observed with an expressionless face. "Serves me right. I wished last night that they would come and have the daylights shaken out of them."

She sat down rather listlessly and resumed her drawing.

"What were you starting to say when that one came?" Van asked.

"Oh, I was talking about Aunt Sarah." She paused in her work, then her eyes met Van's. "It's odd how some people affect you, mostly by the things they think about you, rather than what they actually say. Now, Aunt Sarah always makes me feel indecent, immoral—"

LAVA

Van laughed.

"Well, unnecessary anyway and that's worse. If she comes with Father she'll make me feel as though I had, personally, wrecked everything or at any rate that I'm entirely responsible for this destruction of Kilo-hana."

"You seem devoted to her, Ku-lani," Van said, glancing at her with a smile.

"Oh—passionately! I hate people who create in you the feeling of being superfluous—because it isn't fair. No one is—entirely." She stared at a spot of sunlight, then resumed her drawing.

"Thanks, Ku-lani," Van said.

She glanced up quickly.

"For what, Van?"

"That makes me—what you said—feel better. I've felt superfluous many times since I came here."

"You mustn't feel that way."

"But I have, because I've realized that I've never contributed a thing toward life."

She went to the door, pushed her hair off her fearless forehead and stared at the cracked hill. Then she leaned against the casement as though she were tired.

"The present is an outgrowth of the past," she said thoughtfully, "and is largely determined by it but, Van— the future always remains free!"

He put down the folder and went to her. She looked up at him and there was a roaring in his ears like a breaking sea. She placed her hand upon his shoulder as she would have placed it upon a child's.

"You know those lines, Van, from 'The Light of Asia'—"

"What lines, Ku-lani?" he asked.

"*Within yourselves deliverance must be sought,*
 Each man his prison makes."

He felt her fingers tighten upon his flesh and felt as though he were awakening from a drugged sleep. He stared at the passionate, consuming sunlight blazing on the island, bewildered and dazzled. She looked at him, once, then her eyes went to the roofs and tree tops below them, and back to the hill.

"If we had a cloudburst that whole thing would come down on top of us," she observed.

Van nodded, hardly hearing what she said and she seemed to divine it.

"You are thinking of what I said a moment ago?"

"Yes."

"You'll get out of the prison of self—painfully," she said. "I—know."

He did not answer and her fingers tightened down a second time upon his shoulder and he looked at her hand.

"I've been walled in—so long."

"That doesn't matter, Van. You can get out if you want to—enough."

A calf stamped and a bee buzzed by them.

"I want to, Ku-lani. I will."

"When you have you will be—free," the girl said and

the quality of her voice disarmed him for it was as warm and strong as the sunshine pouring on the island. She smiled at him, then listened intently.

"I hear a car!" She straightened up. "Come and be thrown to the lions with me."

She picked up the folder, went through it carefully, counted the finished registration slips, arranged them in order and placed the pencils carefully inside. Van took the book from her, closed it and put it under his arm. She stood looking at the roofs below the barn, then rolled down her sleeves, slowly.

"I loathe battles," she remarked.

"Your whole life is a battle, Ku-lani, and Kilo-hana your battle ground."

"To fight for a thing you love is one thing, to be harried is another, and I'd be routed now, I'm afraid, if I didn't have that card you gave me the other night, up my sleeve to throw at Father—if I have to," and her eyes went up to his gratefully.

She spoke laughingly but he knew she was dreading the ordeal of seeing her father and it seemed outrageous, unnecessary, that she should have to endure it on top of all the rest.

They started down through the corrals and she glanced at the waiting cows.

"I suppose I'd better tell Joe to help Pia with the milking. They'll talk—hours."

The ground moved oddly beneath them, throwing them a little off their balance.

LAVA

Ku-lani grabbed Van's arm.

"Listen!"

Again he heard the peculiar rushing sound as of waves splashing underground.

"I hate that noise, it gives me gooseflesh," she said. "I suppose it's lava or gases going through subterranean passages."

Her face was awed and still but she forced her stiff lips to smile.

Van's heart cramped and his long fingers closed upon her arm. Her dark brown eyes accorded him a swift grateful look that disconcerted him. He was not worthy of such gratitude.

When they passed the sheds she called out to Joe and the men stopped their work to look at her. Doubtless they knew or suspected that her father was coming and were reluctant that she must be subjected to a difficult hour in the balance of which the fate of Kilo-hana doubtless hung.

They gained the lawn and she said suddenly:

"How rich are you, Van?"

"Rich enough," he said, smiling, and she gave him another of her rare, grateful looks.

"I shall not accept unless I'm absolutely driven to it. I've never accepted money, help, from anyone. I want to win my spurs—alone."

"It seems to me that you've done that, already, Ku-lani."

She did not answer and he glanced at her and saw with astonishment that her eyes were wet. He had never seen her cry and it moved him profoundly. It made her seem young and defenseless. She did not attempt to speak or thank him but stared at the sea.

Kai-ko came out of the kitchen.

"We're here," Ku-lani called and he moved toward them. "Where's Thelma?"

"She's gone for a walk with Dudie. She left as soon as we saw the car."

Ku-lani nodded.

"Good, there's absolutely no reason she should be subjected to this—ordeal."

Her foot tapped the grass, then she stilled it impatiently and Van saw the corners of her mouth tighten. They heard the car hesitate at the foot of the hill and she smiled.

"I guess Father's not too keen about the new road."

After a minute it started roaring in low gear and presently they saw it swaying in the ruts like a huge shining insect, the mudguards flashing light like metallic wings. It straightened into the driveway and Van saw it was completely filled with people. Garland and Luke sat in the front seat and he saw, with relief, Loki waving from the back. Ben was beside her and an elderly, sharp-faced woman. Drina sat on one of the small seats.

Ku-lani's eyes met Van's and she grimaced.

"I knew Aunt Sarah would come—she'd have to be in at the death!"

Then she stepped clear of Kai-ko and Van.

Van saw the line by her mouth that he had noticed the night David left. Her face arrested him, he had never seen such an expression upon it before, dreaminess, intense concentration and a sort of sternness. It was as though she were delivering up her person as a sacrifice but keeping back some essential part of her. Then she seemed to wake up. She took another step forward; she did not hurry nor did she hold back but waited, confronting them with the immense dignity of youth.

The car halted and Loki called out and Van went forward and opened the door for her.

Ben and Drina got out and she followed.

"Nice to see you, Van. Ah, Kai-ko, how's my old man?" Then she held out her arms for Ku-lani.

The girl kissed her and Garland got out.

"Hello, Father."

She made no false gesture nor did she pretend an affection she did not feel. He spoke to her and Luke and Ben looked about them uneasily. Drina hesitated until her mother got out ponderously.

"I'm surprised that you didn't bring Danvers too," Ku-lani remarked with a shade of scorn in her voice.

"He had to go to Hilo," Drina said.

"Aren't you going to kiss me—Ku-larni?" her aunt asked.

She did not seem to hear.

Loki stared at the house and garden and her eyes brimmed.

"Poor Kilo-hana, poor Ku-lani. Dreadful all this mess. It not seem like the old place with everything smash. And that poor hill, all broke. Look like it sore. Make me wild like Hell, all these damn *oni-onis!*"

LAVA

Ku-lani's face softened for an instant, then she said stiffly:

"Shall we go inside, Father?"

"I had no idea things were in such a state," Garland said. "I thought it was mostly talk. Why didn't you tell me?"

He turned on his daughter.

"What was the good, nothing can be done about it," Ku-lani replied.

"I don't believe that I've been presented to this young man," Drina's mother said and Van was aware that he was undergoing a keen appraisement.

"Van," Ku-lani said, "this is—Aunt Sarah."

"I'm pleased to meet you, Mr. Van Dyke," the woman said. "You've been expected back in Kona for some time."

"My original intention when I came over was just to stay a day or so," Van said in his courtly way.

The woman gave him a sharp look, started to say something, but checked herself, evidently impressed by his manner.

"I suppose," she said archly, "that the earthquakes proved too fascinating," and she looked at Ku-lani waiting with one hand thrust into her breeches pocket.

"They are incredible," he answered gravely.

Ku-lani started toward the house walking ahead of her tall father and brothers.

"Kai-ko and I come in a few minutes, Ku-lani," Loki called, "I like take a good look at all this mess."

Van suspected that she also wanted to talk to Kai-ko.

LAVA

Drina and her mother walked in with Van. The woman had a bantering tongue and, Van suspected, probably the heart of a Borgia. For no reason, all at once the garden seemed more strewn. He noticed papers blowing about the boxes of packed crockery and he thought about the boots upon the veranda.

"How perfectly awful!" Drina cried as they approached the house. "Ku-lani didn't tell us that things were in such a condition. Look, Mother, both chimneys are down and the house is all propped with beams. Aren't you terrified to be here, Mr. Van Dyke? I should think you couldn't get away fast enough."

"You get accustomed even to earthquakes," Van said.

"Are you really sleeping up here again?" the woman asked, fixing him with hard black eyes.

"We moved back yesterday."

"I really thought Tom Arlen was telling John that to make him take some step. It's two weeks since this thing started and he's done absolutely nothing!"

"What could he do?" Van asked.

"Why, insist upon Ku-larni leaving. Everyone else has left North Kona. It's ridiculous, her staying on."

"To me it seems magnificent."

"Young man, it's stupid! Only a fool would remain on under such circumstances."

"Or a hero," Van said, stepping aside to permit them to enter. The woman gave him a quick, knowing look, then smiled as though she knew some secret she did not choose to share with others. Van's skin burned faintly.

LAVA

Drina hesitated.

"Do you think it's wise to go in with the house braced like this?"

"It's a bit cracked too," Van said, concealing a smile, "but it's safe enough. We were in the living-room until midnight."

His heart tightened, recalling that intensely moving evening which the world would have undoubtedly misunderstood.

"Perhaps," he suggested as they went onto the veranda, "we'd better wait here for a few minutes. Perhaps Kulani would like to talk to her father alone."

"There is nothing to talk about; John has come over to tell her that she must leave and stay in Kona until this thing is over."

She glanced scornfully at the boots scattered on the floor, then she stopped.

"What's that?" she pointed at the shock-recorder.

"A seismograph."

Both women recoiled slightly.

"What!" Drina exclaimed.

"A seismograph to keep a record of the earthquakes. Would you like to see how it works? It's quite interesting."

Drina hung back but her mother swept forward. Van explained the mechanism and she listened with a line between her eyebrows and her mouth tightened to a crack.

"Upon my word! A seismograph on the veranda and that little idiot wants to stay. Why, it's absolutely ridiculous. I always told John no good would come of allowing her to have this place. She hasn't the brains of a mynah bird. What's that yellow stuff in the bottle behind that chair? Something to drink?"

Van restrained a smile. "It's the shellac you pour over the records to set them."

"Records?"

"I'll show you one that Pia took off last night. Arlen took the others when he left."

He got the blackened disc out of an envelope.

"You smoke this first; it's quite white before you use it. This," he pointed at a small lamp and a pair of clamps, "is the apparatus you smoke it with. The little white cross lines are earthquakes."

He held it out for them to see.

"You don't mean that all those white marks are earthquakes! It's quite impossible!" the woman exclaimed and Drina drew back.

"Yes, this record is not as interesting as some of the others Dr. Arlen took. The only real period of tremor we've had for three days was yesterday between two and five-thirty when I was helping to break camp. There were about ninety shakes in three hours."

"Why, the lava must be right under here!"

"Mother, let's go home!"

"Don't be an idiot! If Mr. Van Dyke isn't afraid, you've no call to be." The woman's hard bright eyes scanned his face. "When do you propose leaving?"

"I don't know."

"It must be a great comfort to Ku-larni having you

here," the woman said with a hint of playfulness in her voice that Van instinctively distrusted. He had an unpleasant feeling that she was trying to defer to him a little because she suspected or imagined that he was a person of consequence.

"I'm afraid I have not been particularly useful but I've enjoyed the opportunity to get to know her."

"Did she ask you to stay on?"

"No, I asked if I might and she was kind enough to say she'd be glad to have me."

"Umph! Just like Ku-larni to burden herself with guests at such a time. Where is Thelma?"

"She went for a walk."

"Ku-larni should have sent her and Dudie and Kai-ko too, for that matter, over to Kona the instant this thing started."

"She wanted to but they preferred to remain here."

"Perfectly absurd and Thelma in her condition. I'm inclined to feel that the lot of you are a pack of idiots. Why, the whole island is up in arms because John has not insisted upon her moving out."

Then she appeared to recollect something and hastened into the big room.

Van followed, feeling ill. The woman seemed to see everything at once, sheeted furniture, pictures wrapped in blankets and stacked in a corner, book-cases lying face downward, books carelessly piled, the grooves in the polished floor where the grand piano had slid back and forth and the bricks out of the fireplace.

LAVA

Van had a hasty impression of Garland seated in Kai-ko's chair and of Luke and Ben on the lounge looking pleased and uneasy.

Ku-lani leaned upon the piano facing them, her face absolutely inscrutable.

The room which had been so mellow and warm twenty-four hours before was filled with silence. Suspicion and hostility were in it and Van had a horrible sensation that some one of the seated three had just stabbed at the roots of Ku-lani's life. Her face reminded him of David's when he had staggered out of the office.

"Luke, your mind is—slimy," she said in a voice of controlled fury.

He writhed a little, like a dog trying to create an impression that it has not transgressed.

Garland snapped the elastic about his note book. There was a moment of silence, then Drina and her mother seated themselves on the two dining-room chairs that Shiba and Sigaki had used the previous evening and Van stifled a smile. He leaned his elbow on the mantel not knowing whether to go or stay. Ben and Luke glanced at him and something in their faces made him vaguely uncomfortable.

"I missed what you said, Ku-larni," her aunt said, fixing her with her darting eyes.

"I told Luke his mind was slimy," the girl repeated.

"Ku-lani!" Garland said in a great hollow voice which seemed to come out of emptiness, "that is hardly a fit term to apply to your brother."

"It's true."

LAVA

"I'm afraid, John," the woman turned to her brother, "that what I predicted has come true. Ku-larni has taken color from her environment which is—rough, to put it mildly. Do you," she addressed the girl directly, "ever wear a dress?"

"I haven't time to."

"I warned John that the advantages you've had would be wasted here, that you'd become masculine and—"

"Coarse?" the girl suggested.

She was beautiful, she was magnificent and Van felt it was a sort of blasphemy for these people even to look at her.

A curious capacious twilight began gradually filling the room and blurring the island outside. The house shook protestingly and Drina started to her feet.

"Oh, Uncle John—let's go!"

"Be quiet," snapped her mother. "If you are frightened go into the garden and wait there until we are through—"

"Crucifying," Van thought contemptuously and his face hardened. He looked at Ku-lani leaning upon the piano. It was impossible to penetrate her silence, even her words. She did not seem aware of anyone or anything except some thought that persisted in her mind, occupying it to the exclusion of everything else and Van knew instinctively that it had to do with him or something which had been said about him, perhaps in connection with her. He burned.

Garland sat, fixing his daughter with his eyes.

"All this," he gestured slightly at his sister, "is entirely aside from the matter which I came here for."

LAVA

Ku-lani waited.

"I came to tell you—"

"That I must leave?" Ku-lani asked, looking at her father from beneath her lashes.

He nodded.

"Why?" Her eyes opened. "Because of the earthquakes or because of what people have said about my remaining here?"

Her eyes were hard as stones, and veiled.

Garland's face widened with the tightening of his jaws.

"What people say and think is no concern of mine."

Ku-lani smiled her father's secret smile and for the first time, and with a faint shock, Van saw a fleeting likeness between them.

"I'm supposed to feel, then, that it's solely concern for my safety?"

"What other reason could it be?" her aunt interposed.

"I wasn't addressing you, Aunt Sarah," Ku-lani said a trifle stiffly.

"Nevertheless I shall talk to you if I wish to. I've always maintained that you had a few brains"—Ku-lani smiled doubtingly—"but since coming here today and seeing the state things are in, I've reached the conclusion that I've been entirely mistaken. Anyone as old as you"—she glanced at Van to make sure he was listening—"nearly twenty-seven! who can't see the necessity of getting out after all these warnings—"

"Warning?" Ku-lani asked.

"Why these earthquakes are warnings from God!"

LAVA

Ku-lani smiled. "Why drag God into it, why should he shake a whole island to pieces to warn one person, and what have I done that could possibly offend Him?"

"Well, for one thing you live like a man."

"I live," Ku-lani spoke thoughtfully, "as women ought to."

"Sister-dear, you—win!"

Van looked around, Kai-ko filled the door and a pace in front of him stood Loki.

"Now what kind foolish you all making in here?" she demanded, crossing the room. "Fighting with Ku-lani? She not got enough trouble with all these damn *oni-onis* breaking her house and busting the ranch?" She waited an instant as though to give them a chance to defend themselves.

Garland looked coldly at his wife.

"That will do, Loki."

She snorted. "You think I sit back and hold my tongue and let all you fellas jump on one girl. Shame! Ku-lani white, she more than twenty-one, this her place and if she no want to leave that her business. Make me sick the way people never minding their own business!"

She looked like a mountain ripe to erupt. Garland hunched his shoulders uneasily, looking first at his wife and then at his sister and Van realized, like other strong men he had known, Garland was almost putty where it concerned the women of his household. He looked pulled this way and that.

"My concern for Ku-lani's safety—"

"Oh, Father, don't lie!" the girl cried in exasperated tones. "It isn't my being here that really bothers you; it's what people are saying about your allowing me to remain."

"We won't discuss that point, the gist of the matter is that I insist upon your leaving."

Ku-lani regarded him with immense scorn.

"Suppose I refuse?"

"I shall compel you to go."

"Oh, John, shut your face!" Loki cried in exasperation, but he did not hear her.

"You can't put me out, I'm half-owner and—I *won't* go!" Ku-lani cried, banging the top of the piano with her clenched fist. The sound filled the room with shocked silence.

"I'm your father," Garland said loftily.

"Only in body."

She leaned her elbows on the piano and stared at him and Kai-ko made a dissenting gesture which she did not see.

"I shall compel you to go," Garland repeated.

"By force?"

He did not answer.

"Now, John," Loki said, "I tell you ten thousand times you smart but you no got good sense! What for you carry on like this making big fuss and damn fool of yourself? Better we go. Never can tell, maybe soon we catch some bad earthquakes. If you not making that sacrifice soon for your mill I make my own self and stop all these *oni-onis*. If you not doing pretty soon sure lava come out."

LAVA

Drina glanced furtively at the door as did Luke and Ben.

"Van, isn't it about time for you to set the seismograph?" Kai-ko asked.

Van appeared to consult his watch. "There are ten minutes to go."

Luke writhed a little on the couch and Van saw him staring at the windows along the front of the house. Outside a purple twilight was slowly claiming the island and gathering up the sea but a break in the leaden clouds hanging over the horizon showed like an open angry furnace, glowing hotly.

"For this—disobedience," Garland's face got grayer, "I shall not permit you to finish buying Kilo-hana."

"You can't go back on your witnessed deed."

"I shall find some way to."

"If I could," Ku-lani paused effectively, "pay you in full now—this instant—"

"You haven't the money."

"I'm not saying I have, but suppose I had—"

"I should think," Garland's sister broke in, "that you'd be delighted to wash your hands of her and the place. You'll never have a moment's peace as long as Ku-larni is half-owner."

"How about me, if father is half-owner?" the girl asked disdainfully.

Luke and Ben consulted together in whispers and Garland appeared not to be listening. Van's long hand hanging limply over the mantel shook slightly and he thrust it into his pocket.

LAVA

Garland measured his daughter.

"If you could," he emphasized the word, "pay me in full, now, feeling as I do at this moment, I would be glad to wash my hands entirely of you and Kilo-hana," but Van saw the instant that Garland spoke the words he regretted them.

Ku-lani straightened up and looked around. "You are all," she spoke as though she had difficulty managing her voice, "witnesses?"

Garland watched Ku-lani's white face with a sort of remorse.

"Yes, Sister-dear," Kai-ko said, but his eyes had an inward look as though he were bound and compelled to watch someone he loved being tortured.

Ku-lani passed her hand across her forehead and to Van it looked the cleanest thing in the world. Her eyes came to his, met them, looked into them and he felt as though life had opened its arms to him, accepted and embraced him.

"Van."

"Yes?"

"Will you go to my office. I'll wait—here."

She spoke in a husky voice and with an effort, he saw beads of moisture on her lip but her face did not alter, it was a bleak white mask giving nothing away. As he started hastily across the room she called out:

"The deed and mortgage on Kilo-hana are in my right-hand desk drawer."

He nodded and went out and was astonished to realize

LAVA

he felt nothing. He borrowed a lantern from Kondo and saw Otero going toward the big room with another. Under the *lichi* and orange trees groups of men stood unhappily wondering, doubtless, if Kilo-hana and Ku-lani were to be taken from them.

He set the candle on the desk. Pia or someone had put the folder down carelessly spilling out the registration slips and he picked them up. Then he took out his check book. His hand grew chilly and shook slightly.

"How much?" he wondered impatiently, "I don't know how much." Then he signed his name and left the check blank. He took the deed and mortgage out of the drawer and hurried back, for he had an unpleasant impression that he had left Ku-lani holding a pack at bay. Wretched that there should be such misunderstanding between father and daughter.

He was conscious of everyone's eyes upon him as he entered but saw only Ku-lani. She leaned upon the piano as though she were tired. Van walked quickly to her and handed her the check and his pen. Placing the slip of paper on the polished piano top she began filling it out and Van watched her dark bent head.

When it was filled out she took the papers from Van and crossed the room to her father. He took them from her, then glanced at the check. His eyes seemed to get yellow and his skin tighter as he looked at Van.

"This means?" he asked in iced tones.

Drina and Luke and Ben exchanged pleased glances and Aunt Sarah fixed Ku-lani with her eyes.

LAVA

"It means, Mr. Garland," Van said, "that I wish to buy a half interest in Kilo-hana and Ku-lani has agreed to mortgage your share to me."

Garland weighed the check between his long dry fingers and Luke peered across his brother at it.

"It's," Van spoke stiffly, "a Bank of England check."

Garland looked at it a third time, folded the papers he had in his left hand about it and thrust them into his coat pocket.

"I will have the papers fixed up and send them back to you, Ku-lani," he said without looking at her.

"Now, John, that *pau*," Loki said, "better we get going. I no like to travel over that broke road in the dark. Why those damn supervisors not been fixing it yet I don't know. Just little something for now. I shame for them!"

Loki addressed her husband but her great dark eyes were fixed upon Van.

Garland rose and started out followed by his sons, and Ku-lani looked after them with an odd expression on her face. Drina's mother rose, fixing Ku-lani with her eyes and Drina stared at her cousin as though she cherished a morsel to recount to Danvers when she got home. She opened her mouth to say something but the words were never uttered. There was a roar, a lurch and the house began shaking savagely as though it wanted to get rid of them. Drina screamed and Van thought, "A terrified woman's scream is a revolting sound." She grabbed for him, missed and clutched the teakwood table.

LAVA

Loki grasped Kai-ko's arm as though to steady herself and her eyes went to Van's, cool, courageous and approving. Drina and her mother rushed unsteadily toward the door. The house continued to jerk back and forth and beneath was a rushing, hissing sound.

"Rose!" Sarah called from the door.

"I come when the ground stop shaking," Loki called back. Then taking Van's face between her hands, she kissed him with brimming eyes.

"Van, you good man, I happy you coming to Kona." Then she laughed and wiped her eyes. "Sha! Silly, always I cry when I glad."

She kissed him again.

Kai-ko stood digging moisture resentfully out of his eyes like an overcome child, then his hand fell on Van's arm gripping it. Loki glanced at Ku-lani, who was staring out of the windows at the glaring gap in the clouds.

Loki rolled her eyes roguishly.

"By and by, after we gone, you tell her I glad for her." Then in a huge whisper, "And soon I sneak back again to see all you fellas, but better I go—now. Everyone angry but soon forget and everything be all right again. You see. I telling you true."

Van glanced at Ku-lani and knew she wanted to be left alone, so accompanied Loki to the car. When they left he started back slowly to the house. He saw Ku-lani at the telephone and after a minute she came out looking gleeful. She placed her hand on Van's shoulder and shook herself like a young colt freeing itself of fetters.

"Where's Kai-ko? I've just been talking to David, he's coming over in a couple of days. Oh, Van!"

And Van thought as he had that night outside Garland's office, youth leagued against age and the despotism of age, but this time youth was triumphant.

CHAPTER X

"Ku-lani."

"Danvers!"

Van, lying sleepless, saw her sit up in her cot, frowning incredulously and peering at a dark figure standing at the edge of the lighted circle filled with sleeping people and dogs.

She got out of her blankets quietly and stood for a moment looking about her as though to assure herself that everyone was sleeping, then she went forward with swift, silent strides. Danvers started toward her but she signed to him and he halted.

"What on earth are you doing here?" she asked in an exasperated whisper. "Drina said this afternoon that you'd gone to Hilo."

"I didn't go," he said, grasping her hands. "I've come to ask you, to beg you," he lowered his voice and spoke earnestly but Ku-lani shook her head.

"I won't, Danvers, and I'm too tired to talk to you for long. Father was over today."

"I know," he spoke in a smothered voice, "you have to—go."

"I bought Kilo-hana today."

"Bought it?"

"Well, Father was bought out."

"By whom? By that Dutchman?" he asked fiercely and suspiciously.

Van lay very still and his skin burned.

"Yes, Van bought in." The girl spoke in low, moved accents, looking at the braced house.

Danvers weighed his surroundings, then observed:

"A fine investment—you."

"That's beastly."

"It's true!"

Ku-lani's head went up indignantly, then her face became thoughtful.

"Yes, I suppose that's what everyone thinks but they'll never understand his—niceness."

The inflection of her voice upon the last word went to Van's heart. Ku-lani was unique, a being apart from her fellow humans yet whole-heartedly one of them.

Danvers moved impatiently.

"It isn't hard for a person to be nice to you."

"You," Ku-lani smiled, "couldn't even be true."

"Good God!"

"Not so loud."

"Come down to the house, I must talk to you."

"We'll talk here."

"You know very well I was tricked into marrying Drina —by your father!"

"We were both tricked, but it's too late to think about that now."

"Ku-lani, go with me!"

"Where?"

LAVA

"Away from Hawaii."

She looked at him, then thoughtfully about her.

"Danvers, there's not a man who could mean to me what Kilo-hana does, not one for whom I'd leave it."

He stared at her.

"You think that and yet that's what he expects, hopes—"

She shook her head.

"The rotten part of life is that when a person gives—beautifully, without an ulterior motive, the world—people in general—can't understand or misunderstands. But," her face lighted, "that doesn't really affect or alter the quality of the gift."

Her face was transfigured for an instant and there was a sort of gallantry about her wide forehead touched by the firelight.

"I know that's what you—and Kona are thinking, that he stays because of me, but it's something bigger than an individual."

Van wondered if there could be anything bigger than Ku-lani.

Danvers laughed.

Ku-lani stared at him, then smiled a lonely amused smile.

"Must life always boil down to—people?"

"Yes. But you are and always have been a dreamer."

"Me a dreamer?" she asked scornfully. "I'm a plow horse but I love my plow," and she looked about her and seemed to glow.

"Ku-lani," Danvers grasped her hands a second time,

LAVA

"I've got to talk to you, really, I never have since before you went to school."

"Danvers, there's nothing to be said."

"I don't believe," he said fiercely, "that you ever loved me!"

"You know I did, as a girl loves, but I'm a woman now and my values are different, and my gods," she paused, "are strong gods and they will not forsake me."

Danvers gazed down into her lighted face and gestured unhappily.

"Ku-lani, you live in a world of your own that others can't get into."

Van moved a little in his cot. So Danvers realized that too!

"But you're beautiful!"

"I?"

"Yes, but you are sacrificing your womanhood and wasting yourself—here."

"By leading the life I do? Danvers," she accused, "you are thinking other people's thoughts!"

He did not answer.

"It was nice of you to come, but if it's found out it will make things more difficult—"

"You've had," Danvers' voice sounded remorseful, "and are having a dreadful time. I've been almost mad thinking about you here, practically alone."

"I'm not alone, everyone here is *with* me and you may not believe it, can't perhaps, but it's beautiful in a way, too."

LAVA

Danvers moved as though he were thrusting something away.

"And then you try to tell me, make me believe—"
She stopped him.

"Oh, I didn't mean that, I'm convinced he wants to marry you; neither of you are that—sort."

"Sometimes," Ku-lani spoke slowly and there was a catch in her voice, "even the people you love make life very difficult. Soil it by their thoughts. Earth thoughts!"

A log broke in two sending up a shower of golden sparks, a dog rose, turned around twice, and lay down with a sigh nearer to the fire. The dark roof of the house lowered upwards eclipsing fields of stars. Danvers glanced at the cots pulled together under the trees.

"Yes," Ku-lani said as though in answer to his unspoken thought, "I suppose it does look funny to one—coming in, all of us, whites, Hawaiians, Japanese and dogs sleeping together."

Danvers moved impatiently.

"The whole situation is—"

Ku-lani stopped him with a slight gesture of her hand.

"The cord between us is cut, Danvers, not by your marriage or mine, which was just an incident, an experience from which I learned, but because now we think in different directions."

"What do you mean?"

"You think inwards and I—outwards."

"I suppose," Danvers said in a shaking voice after a moment of silence, "that—Dutchman thinks outwards too?"

"Yes—he does," Ku-lani replied and appeared to be listening to music Danvers could not hear. He looked at her indignantly, dropped her hands and strode off. Ku-lani watched the night swallow him up, then sat down on the grass supporting her chin on her hand.

Van lay watching her, then pushed back his blankets. She sat staring into darkness, still, lonely, intent, outcast with herself for the moment, perhaps. Van could not endure the supposition and put his legs over the side of his cot. She was so intent upon her thoughts that she did not hear him coming until he stood over her.

"Ku-lani, I was awake, I heard."

She took a deep breath as though tearing herself free of something. Her face was absolutely white, all the blood in her body seemed to have congealed about her heart. Then she shivered violently.

"People," she said in a vehement whisper, "make me—sick with rage."

She stared into the dark detaching herself from the moment, from her surroundings and Van wondered to what or to whom she was committing herself so irrevocably.

"Would you mind if I sat down by you?"

"No. Why did he, why does anyone come! I hate beautiful things to be spoiled."

"Nothing has been spoiled, Ku-lani."

"It has been for me, for a while."

Van sat in silence beside her, then finally said in his gentle voice:

"The moment is over—Ku-lani."

LAVA

She turned to him and her face lighted.

"Oh, you're nice, always!" she said and the quality of her voice made the words shine, illuminating the darkness about them. Then she shivered again.

"Let me get you a sweater."

She nodded and he fetched his from the crotch of the tree where he had left it. She took it from him and put it about her shoulders. He felt undercurrents and sat silent. The bloom of the great star-studded night had gone, leaving only a great emptiness filled with cold.

"I wish," Ku-lani said, taking a deep breath, "that there were a gate to shut out the world. Most people's minds are grubby and—grubbiness hurts."

"You are—immune," Van said, looking at her.

Her eyes went up to his and he received a smile that dizzied him and made him feel as though he had been transported into another world. Then he looked at her absorbed face and appreciated that Ku-lani had an individuality which excited and—escaped. In her eyes, soft in the firelight, was an unreadable appeal but he suspected that a man would come out of her arms, even out of her embraces feeling baffled. Beyond anything or anybody she belonged to herself.

"Ku-lani—"

"I know what you are going to say."

"I wonder, do you."

She glanced at him and waited.

"Here," he spoke quietly, "I've been permitted to touch the heart of beauty."

Her face broke.

"Oh, why did you say that!" she gulped, "it makes me feel beastly."

He took her hand.

"This is an experience which, even I in my ignorance know, is not granted to many. I am fortunate to be so privileged and it is something which I shall never forget."

He thought that there were tears in her eyes but they did not fall so he never knew, but he had a vivid impression that this girl was of no particular race or age; she was a being, spacious, brave, belonging to something tremendous.

"You know what I thought you were going to say, Van?" she asked after a silence.

"I haven't the slightest idea," he said gravely.

"I was afraid you'd regretted that your moment had come, that you wished that you could have escaped it,—what you did this afternoon."

"That is impossible. I appreciate, now, that when life is ready to use a person, or a person is ripe for life to use, it puts out its hand and draws him into itself. It was written that my hour should sound here; these earthquakes, and being with you, knowing you, have shaken me out of myself. For some, evidently, the call does not come until life is half over, for you, I fancy, it sounded at the moment of birth. I confess I have been slightly appalled," he smiled at her, "realizing that I loosed an act upon the world today and no one can ever tell what the consequences of an act may be."

LAVA

She smiled at him.

"That act—freed me."

"I wonder? Perhaps it will bind you still tighter to—"

"Kilo-hana?"

"Oh, I don't know, Ku-lani!" he said. "I feel as though I were groping in darkness."

"We all are."

He nodded and picked up her hand and looked at it. The island stretched beneath them.

"I wonder," he said when the earth stilled, "what will be the outcome of this—experience."

She did not answer.

"I suppose this—awakening came to my father," Van said. "It must have. I think he should have told me."

"Maybe it didn't," Ku-lani said. "Some people are in life but are never conscious of the fact, really. Never in contact."

Van studied her intent profile. It had a perfect immobility. Again she detached herself from him completely.

"I wonder how I could have ever deluded myself," Van said after a silence.

"How, Van?"

"Deluded myself with the thought that I didn't want to be in contact with life. Perhaps I'd lived too long within myself, watching the play of shadows," then he smiled, "but I was the shadow and the rest was—real."

"Van."

He looked into the dark enchantment of her eyes.

LAVA

"Yes?"

"Don't look—lost!"

"I'm found," he said, but he thought, "I'm lost—forever because—" but he did not finish his thought and looked away to the stars burning steadily above them. "I wonder," he said after a moment, "if I will ever be able to take my place properly."

He stared into the dark and Ku-lani laid her hand upon his two, clasped about his knees. He smiled, mechanically, for his mind was occupied with other matters.

"Of course you will, but it'll take time to adjust."

He looked at her shadowed eyes filled with memories of her own adjustments.

"I shall always be proud, Ku-lani, that I came in contact with life through a person like you. I thought the other night when we talked at camp and I shall say it to you now, that you are a sort of a torch to light the way for others."

"No one can show you the way," the girl said, "you have to find it yourself."

He did not seem to hear her.

"I have a curious feeling about you, Ku-lani, it seems to me—"

"I'm a very ordinary girl," she interrupted, smiling.

"You're extraordinary. I feel that you have been and always will be in life. I cannot imagine it without you or believe it will ever be entirely without. You are in everything and everything in you."

"And in you and in everyone," she whispered. He felt

her dark, clear eyes looking into his and saw her forehead, clean, valiant as a boy's.

"Then don't let what was said, thought, spoil the rest of this incredible experience."

"I won't," she whispered fiercely. "It must, it shall be kept perfect."

He kissed her hand.

"Tomorrow, Ku-lani, things will be back where they were before your father and the others came over."

She shook her head. "Life can't go back, it has to go forward."

Her fingers closed on his with a quick strong pressure and she got to her feet looking enchanted. He stood beside her, tall and quiet.

"Well, then—forward," he said with one of his faint lighted smiles and looked down at her but she had gone from him again and he thought with a pang, "Forward—to what?"

Van slept late and when he woke the sun was touching the roof of the house. He heard Kondo working about the fire. A dog yawned and stretched beside his cot and he put out his hand and touched it and felt the quick rasp of its tongue on his wrist. About him the sounds of morning rose like a voice triumphant out of pain.

He sat up and looked about him. Kondo nodded as he passed into the kitchen carrying a steaming saucepan in his hand. He came to the door after a moment tying on a clean apron.

LAVA

"Ku-lani speak you buy Ha-ole Hao out."
Van nodded.

"You number one good man, Mr. Van. Ku-lani happy now so all man happy too. Tomorrow Mr. David come. Good, he can help Ku-lani. She work too hard. I got coffee, everykind ready for you."

Van nodded, went into the house and dressed slowly. Already his act was spreading its waves outward, traveling toward unknown shores. The morning was boundless and he felt the heart of the island beating. When he came out he stared at the torn sides of the hill, which seemed to drowse a little, relaxing in the sun. When he entered the kitchen, Otero halted him.

"You my sweetheart too," she announced and took three steps of a hula. "Tonight make party for you, Ku-lani and the boys gone to catch pigs."

Van managed a smile but his chest hurt him. He was aware of a deep inner stir. The obedience of these people to their instincts was amazing, that of children. They were happy for and with Ku-lani. Earthquakes could not halt the work in which they were all equally engaged, but evidently it could and had been halted for a day to salute joy.

He sat down to his meal thoughtfully. For some reason his mind picked up from somewhere Kai-ko's words the first afternoon he had talked to him. They had been about Ku-lani but Van felt that they applied also to himself. "You cannot hasten your tides." He moved uneasily. His tide was coming in. . . . The first wave had broken on the beach—yesterday. He did not regret what he had done, far from it, but he was in awe of its consequences. Perhaps he ought not to have stepped in, separating father and daughter. By his act he had set fire to the bridges that held them together, despite the fact that they did not get on. He moved uneasily. Ku-lani had declared that his act had set her free but in freeing her had he not also bound her faster?

Kai-ko appeared in the door filling the opening, a huge, lovable, untidy old figure.

"Well, you've had a hair cut," Van observed, pulling out a chair for him.

"Kondo barbered me. I felt like a shaggy old bear all at once." He curled his gray mustaches until they stood up triumphantly. "All bets are off for the day. There's to be a *luau* tonight in your honor."

Van felt unworthy and invested in warmth. According to these people's way of thinking he had, it seemed, become a sort of demi-god who had given this world of Kilo-hana into the keeping of those who loved it.

"And that check," he thought with humbleness, "is my entrance fee into the hearts of these people and into life. Too horribly little."

Kai-ko leaned his elbows upon the table. He started to say something, then stopped and called out to Kondo to bring him coffee.

The hours of that day seemed invested with a strange quality, a day outwardly, singularly like its predecessors but detached from all the days that had preceded it or that would ever follow it. Van spent the forenoon with Thelma and Kai-ko lying on the warm lawn. Thelma sat silent for the most part, playing with one of the puppies but Van had a strange impression when he glanced at her small face that her mind was brooding on something. She looked as though her whole soul were listening. The day was curiously hot and seemed to have halted, hoarding its beauty. In it were secrets of the hillsides and songs of the forests and empty miles about, and the distant placid blue sea, dreaming about the shores of the island.

"I wonder," Kai-ko said, placing his hands on his knees and leaning a little forward, "how Garland feels with himself today?"

Van did not answer.

"You know, Van, Garland is an extraordinary fellow. He's imprisoned within himself. I think, in my own heart, he wants to get out but he doesn't know how. I've known him ever since he came to Kona, penniless. From a worldly standpoint he's been tremendously successful but his ancestors got between him and the land he elected to live in. He fights Hawaii because it's a lawless, extravagant land but in his heart he loves it, or wants to love it if he knew how. That is the great tragedy of some men and women —they want to love and they don't know how."

Van started, made a slight movement like somebody pounced upon from an ambush. He felt Thelma's dark eyes upon him and changed his position as though he were trying to free himself from her scrutiny. His instinct told him she was wondering about him.

LAVA

"Garland has everything and nothing! In his youth he set secret idols up in his heart, power and wealth, and he can't free himself of them. He has lived for himself always, but his buried self with which he was born lives in Ku-lani. He imagines that he disapproves of his three youngest children, Naps and David and Ku-lani, but in reality he longs to possess them. He swings like a pendulum between two shores, the one he is on and the one he would get to if he could. I know. When he first came to Kona he had nothing; gradually he got possession of all the land, mine too. Bad years came, blight took hold of the coffee. I went under and he advanced me money, I knew at the time, with the ultimate intention of getting hold of my land, but later when through an accident in his mill I lost my eyesight, he canceled the mortgage and insisted upon my living with him and Loki. I accepted conditionally, that I would try it for a year, and I've been with him ever since. At the time of my accident, or just after it, Danvers married, and I knew it was wiser not to attempt to live with them. It never works out."

Kai-ko stared ahead.

"I thought of old John all last night. I know, though he would never admit it even to himself, he regrets frightfully that he's lost Ku-lani. I still hope," the old man straightened up, "that something will bring them together. It's unthinkable that he and Ku-lani, who is by far the finest of all his children, should misunderstand, be unable to recognize each other's fine qualities. If some disaster should overtake her, or this place," Kai-ko stopped, then spurred himself on, "she would never go to him and he would never come to her—now. But perhaps I misjudge him."

"Do you think I shouldn't have done what I did yesterday, Kai-ko?"

"It was written," the old man said, laying his hand fondly on Van's knee.

He got to his feet and faced the sweep of the island, then walked heavily away. Van laid his crossed arms upon his knees and watched a flock of wild geese swoop down.

He felt wedded to misery. He appreciated as he sat in the sunshine that the worth, the quality of events alter, inconceivably and suddenly, when apprehended differently by different minds, or even by the same mind at different times. He stared at the magnificent island spread out before him. It seemed empty of life, despite the life about him, as some still, dead, splendid star. A shining loneliness, a shining silence invested the day and walled it in, sealing it to something.

Thelma made a swift unexpected gesture that startled, almost angered him, then laid her hand on his arm.

"Van."

"Yes," he said without looking at her.

"Ku-lani said Danvers came here last night."

He inclined his head slightly, and waited. She did not speak for a moment and he looked at her. Her face was like a white mask in the sunlight and her eyes were possessed by thoughts torturing her. He felt the trend of her thought alter.

LAVA

"You look unhappy, Van," she said at length. "Why?"

"I don't know, Ku-lani." The name came to his lips unconsciously and he realized it was because she occupied his mind incessantly, then he corrected himself, "Thelma."

She gave him a deep look.

"I know how you feel," she said gently. "You did something generous and fine yesterday and today you are feeling as though you'd paid in counterfeit money."

He looked at her amazed.

"When I—" she began and Van moved as though to stop her tearing a garment away.

"I know what you are going to say, Thelma, but what I did and what you did can't be compared."

"You're wrong, Van, and right. But you gave expecting, wanting nothing back while I—"

Something in his face or eyes halted her.

"Do you love Ku-lani?" she asked, looking astounded.

"I worship her. I would do anything for her, but I am wondering about the wisdom of the impulse that moved me yesterday, wondering what it's leading to. Nothing probably." He realized he was tired from the crowded days and restless nights that lay behind and that still hovered over him. Days and nights in utter opposition to all the other days and nights he had ever known.

The day seemed to stop dead and wait.

He stared at the graceful heads of bamboo thickets motionless in the sun. All his life had missed fire, he thought bitterly, and now he had been seized by a great ground swell that he was not fitted to wrestle with successfully. Thelma watched him as though she could not credit his last words, as though he were something entirely foreign, incomprehensible and strange to her. He folded his arms across his chest as though to control his thoughts. He felt smothered. Body and soul experienced a nervous reaction from tenderness. Mad, completely mad of him to have come to Kilo-hana. What had he to offer Ku-lani? He had heard her declare that no man could ever mean to her or be to her what Kilo-hana was, and beyond everything he had felt uncounted times that she belonged to herself! Who was he to try to intrude himself into her life, filled to the brim and spilling over? And what had he done when he put the knife into her hand that made it possible for her to cut the last tie that bound her to her father? And yet—he recalled Kai-ko's words. It had been written that it should come to pass.

He moved as though trying to free himself from a net of his own weaving in which he had become entangled. Thelma got up with a strange expression on her face, kissed him and walked away.

"Despite everything," Van thought with fury and disgust, "I remain—walled up!"

He got to his feet. Idiotic of him to feel so torn. Profitless. He must go . . . on. Each man must be his own redeemer.

About two o'clock Ku-lani rode in with Pia and Nuhi, followed by Sonny leading two mules laden with sheep and hogs. She dismounted and walked to the table under the orange trees where Thelma and Kai-ko and Van were sitting. She sat down, dusty and radiant, and the day opened up again, and started to go forward.

"Kondo, bring me some lunch," she called.

"I nearly woke you up this morning, Van, to ask you if you didn't want to come and hunt with us."

She reached for the plate Kondo brought and drew it up in front of her.

"I'm sorry that you didn't."

"Never mind, next time Sonny goes out, which will be in three days, you can go with him. Many earthquakes today while I was gone?"

"The usual daily dozen," Kai-ko said, folding his arms across his great chest as though he were hugging himself contentedly.

Thelma tossed out a wreath she was making and Van heard Dudie squealing with delight as Nuhi made passes at her with a dead pig. When Ku-lani finished eating she went to the office, returned, entered the kitchen and instructed Kondo about something. Then she came up, and joined the three sitting about the table. Van looked at her; she was the abundance of the earth, sane, sound, radiating warmth like a lesser sun.

"Now," she announced, "the boys are going to get the pigs ready and I'm going to wash my head."

They adjourned to where the outdoor stove was and sat down upon the grass. Otero and Sizu and Thelma began braiding wreaths while the men scalded pigs and scraped them. Ku-lani filled a bucket from the kerosene tins steaming on the fire and took down her hair. She shook it out and Van was surprised at its length and gloss.

"Get me that box, Van," she said, and he fetched it and placed the bucket upon it for her. She dipped in her head and he thought, "She is entirely unaware of herself as an individual."

In her riding breeches with her workers grouped about her she soaped and rinsed the brown lengths of her hair, talking and laughing. He had never seen anything like her and knew he never would again. The green garden dozed, butterflies swarmed and undulated over the flower beds, dogs looked on. Ku-lani's depression and exhaustion of the previous evening had fallen from her, leaving her cloaked in radiant youth, lighted from within and investing her face and body with freshness.

When she had soaped her hair sufficiently Pia fetched buckets of fresh water and poured it over her head. With her face turned sideways she looked like a child. When her hair was rinsed to her satisfaction she picked up a towel spread on a rose bush and rubbed and tossed it out.

"And tomorrow David'll be here!" she almost chanted. "Wish it were tonight so he could be at the *luau* but it can't be put off as it might be bad luck."

Pia straightened up from his scraping of his pig. "Tonight real *luau;* not like that one you have at Ha-ole Hao's."

Van smiled and Kai-ko heaved a sigh of content.

"I've a hunch," he said, "that tonight will linger long in our memories," and he placed a large, affectionate hand

LAVA

on Van's shoulder. He felt freed to enjoy the moment. Ku-lani tossed back an armful of hair.

"Sometimes life surprises you with its niceness when you least expect it. All day I've felt like a bird let out of a cage."

Nuhi grinned and nodded emphatically as he dipped his bloody hand into a bucket of water to cleanse it.

"I think you never forget Kilo-hana, Van, when you go away."

Van nodded and thought, "Yes, like a ghost I've come into their lives and like a ghost I shall probably go, leaving a shadowy memory behind."

And suddenly he felt as though all life was emptying out through a gap in the trees, like water going out of a bathtub leaving him behind. He watched the group on the lawn, Sizu and Otero with their heads together gossiping, Nuhi and Pia busy about the hogs as only Polynesians can be, working with a sort of delight mixed with anticipation, moving their hands as though engaged in a sacred rite. Kai-ko sitting in the sun, invested with force despite blindness, and Ku-lani drying her hair.

These people were like the green warm forests swathing the slopes of Kona; they did not think but went on fulfilling their laws. The great hulking men had the soft clumsy grace of young animals, clothing force that was directly absorbed from the island beneath them which Van divined, rather than actually felt, toiling on. . . .

Thelma desisted from the work of weaving a garland of roses and the half-finished wreath splashed her lap with color. Her brilliant eyes had a strange expression in them as though she were listening for a summons; then she thrust back a lock of her fine curling hair and picked up another flower.

He watched men, directed by Kondo, laying a long tablecloth on the grass under the trees, covering canvas with glossy banana leaves and purple sprays of bougainvillea. Ku-lani strolled over and inspected their work.

"We didn't have time to go and get fern," she said when she rejoined the group on the lawn, "but it doesn't look bad. Pia, is the *imu* ready? It's five and the pigs ought to go into the ground; as it is, we won't be able to eat much before ten."

"No matter, got all night," the man answered, pouring a bucket of scalding water over the glistening carcass of the pig he was dressing, silvery white in the leveling rays of sun.

The rhythmic sound of a horse jogging up the dusty road made them look around and they saw Puhi approaching. Dismounting he secured his horse to a tree and came over looking happy and invested with importance. Nuhi spoke to him in Hawaiian but he walked up to Ku-lani and reached into his breeches pocket.

"Ha-ole Hao have papers all fix up this morning and speak I give to you."

"Thanks, Puhi," Ku-lani said, then aside to Van, "Speedy work; he's mad."

She began going through them.

"*Luau* tonight?" Puhi asked, glancing hopefully at the pigs.

LAVA

Ku-lani nodded.

"For what?"

"Because of these," Ku-lani said, lifting the papers, "because Kilo-hana is mine."

"I glad for you, Ku-lani," the old man said squatting on his haunches and watching Nuhi and Pia washing off the pigs. He took his pipe out and filled the bowl with cheap tobacco, his knotted brown fingers working lovingly about the bowl. He looked about him and smiled like a happy child, then stared at the houses and hill, in all likelihood trying to estimate the cost of the damage. Van listened to the three men conversing in Hawaiian and was aware of a lassitude of soul creeping over him, outgrowth of his thoughts and emotions of that day or perhaps because of approaching evening. He thought over the two weeks he had been on Hawaii. From being a dreamy spectator, he had become a participant of the world's agitation, almost overnight. Subtly the desire to act had got hold of him at Kilo-hana and his very inexperience had given him the necessary audacity only to find that that same inexperience hampered him from knowing what road to take.

His behavior, reviewed calmly, was inexplicable. First he had stayed over, then he had stayed on. Voluntarily he had taken part in the extra work entailed by the earthquakes, appreciating, deliberately facing the possibility that his temporarily altered attitude toward life might develop unlookedfor results. Fragments of conversation snatched between earthquakes with Ku-lani and Kai-ko had been largely responsible for setting him to thinking on different lines. Observation of these people of different races and inheritances now one in a single purpose had contributed toward his remaining. The spectacle of a girl uniting, through the force and magnetism of her personality, everything about her into a solid whole, amazed him. He had hesitated a little, then deliberately set his shoulder against a door that his father had locked against him, overcome by a desire to experience, to know. . . .

He had voluntarily after two nights and a day of thinking offered Ku-lani the money necessary to enable her to get clear title to the place. The fact that it would be, eventually, repaid him did not alter or in any way affect the motive which had pushed him to lend it. Repayment was incidental, but the act affected the roots of his life carefully constructed upon other lines. Where, to what, would it eventually lead? It must affect in some profound and subtle manner all the rest of his life. These days at Kilohana would show, for him at any rate, some new, distinct pattern.

He got up and strolled away.

He felt unhappy but it was an exalted sort of unhappiness. "At any rate," he thought, "I've done something definite. I've associated myself with life and the fortunes of individuals who are products of a unique environment but who are fundamentally linked to others whose lives wash against theirs."

His heretofore instinctive mistrust of life had been replaced by a dim appreciation of the immense significance of the world about him.

LAVA

He stared at a tired twilight dying solemnly on the sea and felt as though gods, his old gods, had been shaken on their thrones. He went to his room and studied his reflection. His features were unchanged and he realized, with a smile, that he had rather expected them to be different, for he had become different. His eyes were a little tired and his skin browned but the expression of his face was unchanged. It was meditative, remote.

"Am I," he wondered with a touch of sadness, as he removed his tie, "to be always just a long Dutch ghost?"

When he had changed he went out. Lighted lanterns suspended from boughs shone on the green and purple table spread on the grass. Kai-ko was seated in a rocker which had been placed for him and Ku-lani sat on the grass, her elbow upon his knees. She was in a gay-colored kimono and her hair, freshly brushed, and secured with a ribbon was hanging over her shoulders. He started toward them and heard an earthquake rushing down the mountain. It passed beneath them, giving the ground a fierce shake and fled, as though appalled, for the sea. Neither Kai-ko nor Ku-lani appeared to have felt it and he wondered what they were conversing about so earnestly.

Seeing him, Ku-lani looked up.

"I suppose I should start dressing," she observed, getting to her feet.

Van leaned against the tree and folded his arms, watching her go toward the cottage to which she and Thelma had removed their belongings since the wrecking of the main house. She appeared all at once to have become invested with the quality of a trusting child, to be off her guard, and the supposition filled him with uneasiness.

"Van, you're quiet?" Kai-ko said.

"More so than usual?" he asked with a touch of playfulness in his voice.

"Not actually, but I've had an impression all day that something has been bothering you."

Van laughed. "Many things have been bothering me, Kai-ko."

Kai-ko, being a man, did not ask what but nodded his head.

"You're a fine fellow, Van, and it's been a pleasure knowing you."

Van moved uneasily, for he had an impression that the stream of events was gathering speed, hurrying down a long hill.

"Until I came here I hadn't a single care or real interest," Van said. "Now, though I haven't, actually, a care, I shall have a very real interest in this place and these people."

"Until I lost my eyesight I was an active man, since then, except when I'm at Kilo-hana I feel as though a veil hung between me and life."

"Until I came here, there was always a veil between me and life," Van said, "but being here for the time being has torn the veil away."

A snatch of music came from behind the barn and again Van hid a disturbing feeling of events streaming on, gathering impetus.

LAVA

"I wish," Kai-ko said, "that it had been possible for you to be here when things were normal. The Sundays are superb. People flock to see Ku-lani from all over the island, bringing gifts of flowers and food. They spend the day hunting, discussing local problems, and go home loaded with presents. I think that this is the only island in the group where the old atmosphere and customs which used to make Hawaii so loved, remain."

"I think I prefer this experience."

"You'll never duplicate it," Kai-ko observed.

The angry roar of an approaching earthquake shook the ground fiercely.

"They've been pretty frequent this last hour," Kai-ko remarked, grasping the arms of the rocker.

Van nodded, watching legs and lanterns coming past the tanks and the barns. He heard music and a curious constriction tightened the muscles around his heart. Ku-lani came out of the cottage dressed in white breeches and shirt. Her eyes went to Van's as though she knew some joke which she did not choose to divulge.

Thelma walked up and placed a wreath about Van's neck and he was singularly moved, perhaps because of her original animosity.

"Thanks, Thelma."

She kissed him with tears in her eyes and sat down.

Otero and Sizu, resplendent in kimonos and *obis* instead of *holokus*, appeared carrying garlands which they put about Van's neck. The various Hawaiians, freshly scrubbed and in starched shirts, followed suit. Van realized with

LAVA

dismay that he was robbed of the ability to speak. The older men were shy and solemn, the younger merry and mischievous. Kondo came out of the kitchen with a *lei*, which he had evidently made himself from its appearance. It was greeted with shouts of mirth by Otero and a round of laughter from the Hawaiians.

"What for laugh?" Kondo demanded with affected anger. "This number one good *lei*. Japan style!"

Otero gave him a smack and he flourished his apron at her and she ran away with a delighted shriek. Kondo held up his offering and Van bent his head for it.

"Number one, aloha, Mr. Van," he muttered and departed.

Ku-lani came up last with a wreath of fine yellow flowers. She placed it upon his head and kissed him simply on one cheek but her eyes were wet.

"I feel"—Van managed his voice with difficulty—"like a dissolute Roman senator."

His fingers closed on her wrist for an instant and he looked at her through misted lashes.

"Never," he thought, "never shall I come into contact with anything like this again in my life."

Ku-lani stepped back and the men picked up their instruments and began simultaneously singing a reckless hula. Ku-lani and the Japanese-Hawaiian, Bill Nakagowa began dancing a hula and Ruby, his Hawaiian wife who had come up for the occasion from their little homestead on the bluffs, seized Joe and they started. The two Japanese women appeared carrying trays filled with glasses and bottles of *sake* for the Japanese and *okolehao* for the Hawaiians. The song came to an abrupt gusty stop that left the air vibrating.

The men crowded about the table helping themselves and Van watched the scene thoughtfully. An earthquake rushed seaward and Van passed his hand meditatively across his forehead. A week ago, anywhere else, such a shock would have halted life for a moment at any rate; now these people, he himself, simply disregarded it. He looked at the boughs arching overhead; they were still trembling. Then he felt Ku-lani at his elbow.

"Will you have either, any?" she asked, gesturing at the glasses.

"I think, don't you, seeing the occasion is in honor of Kilo-hana, that I should have a drink of each."

The men applauded and Nuhi said with an air of satisfied virtue:

"Me, I never drink, but tonight I take one glass for good luck."

Ku-lani handed Van a tumbler of each kind of liquor and her eyes swept the circle until they found Kai-ko. She called out and he shook his head.

"I drink with you in spirit, Sister-dear."

"To Kilo-hana," Van said, looking from one glass to the other as though he could not make up his mind which to drink from first. "And to all of you!" and, he thought, I should add, "Hail and farewell."

Pia stepped forward.

"Drink this one first," he touched the glass in Van's right hand, "that *okolehao* for Hawaii, then *sake* for Japan."

LAVA

Van raised the glass and realized, with horror, that he could not swallow. As though Ku-lani realized how deeply he was affected, she raised her glass above her head and above her clean white shirt her face was flushed.

"To Van!"

He came out of a sea which for a moment had closed over his head.

When the toast was drunk he finished both glasses and set them on the table. Then one by one he divested himself of his wreaths, placing them about the necks of the assembled company, save the one which Ku-lani had given him and it poised like a rakish halo, encircling the burnt baldness of his head.

"That good kind," Pia said. "We give out aloha to you and you give back to us." He smelt the wreath Van had placed upon him, giving him a quick friendly look, then everyone busied himself putting food on the table.

Kai-ko seated himself at one end and Ku-lani told Van to sit at the other. Looking down the long table in the dim light Van thought that no one could have distinguished the old man from a Hawaiian. He ate with the same gusto and talked in sonorous Hawaiian, making wide embracing gestures with his arms. In the overhead light of lanterns suspended from the trees his strong features were bronzed, emphasized, and the wreath about his neck added to the illusion. He seemed to be invested with a phantom of the vigor and enthusiasm of days left on the farther side of darkness.

Old Puhi sat, radiating joy. Occasionally his eyes went

to Ku-lani and he smiled beatifically, then thrust his wrinkled brown hand into a bowl of *poi*. Ku-lani sat midway down the table, opposite Thelma. Once Van saw her eyes darken and go to Ku-lani's, then she resumed her eating. Pia reached back and took his guitar off the table and Sonny got his ukulele. They sat cross-legged, singing, while the others ate on, laughing, talking, pausing to join in some verse of the song. The ground gave a peculiar vicious twist which no one heeded and Van felt restless. Their utter disregard seemed a challenge to the gods of the mountain. Another wrench came and Nuhi looked up:

"I think Pele like come and have some *luau*," he observed, his dark, bright eyes laughing.

Thelma's hand paused in mid-air and she stared slightly with a white, bleak look on her face. Presently she rose and walked away. Dudie looked at her mother.

"Mummy, Thelma is sick," she announced.

Ku-lani rose without a word, overtook her and Van saw her bend and ask the girl a question. She nodded and Ku-lani called back for Otero and the woman rose with a wise look and hastened away.

After a while Ku-lani returned, spoke to Kai-ko and Van heard through the pause in the conversation, the girl's low, carrying voice.

"Yes, she says since this afternoon when I was washing my head."

A peculiar chill went over Van again and he had a disconcerting sensation that life was hurrying forward with indecent haste.

CHAPTER XI

The feast broke up about midnight. Ku-lani had summoned Sizu and excused herself and they vanished into the lighted cottage. The men lingered about the table, sitting and lying in groups. Kai-ko asked for a chair and Van brought one and placed it near the fire, then got a blanket and spread it on the grass for himself.

Beyond the fire on the green slope of lawn he saw Hawaiians and Japanese, heard them talking and laughing together but there was a waiting tenseness about their figures —which he felt in his own body—that was directly connected with what was going on in the cottage behind them. Kai-ko sat, his body sagging forward and his eyes closed but Van knew he was not sleeping. Once he muttered in his mustache:

"The gameness of that girl!"

And Van knew he was thinking about Thelma, who had kept what she knew to herself as long as possible lest it mar the evening and he felt abashed, for it had been to celebrate what he had done. . . . So horribly little. . . . It was not to be thought that he, that any man, deserved such consideration. Shadows flitted across the lighted windows, voices reached him, indistinguishable, but upsetting. Directions given and obeyed. Kondo came at intervals and carried kerosene tins of hot water to the office door and one or the other of the Japanese women took them and brought back others which he refilled.

Puhi sat smoking his pipe and talking to Pia in lowered tones, a faithful old figure, pathetic and appealing.

About two Pia rose, went to the office and called to Kulani. She came to the door, shook her head and disappeared. Van threw a corner of the blanket over his legs and leaned his elbow on the grass, staring into the flames. His body, his mind, felt drugged. Pia spoke to Kai-ko in Hawaiian, rejoined his mates and Van heard them going off toward their quarters and others departing on horseback for the bluffs.

He felt the island slip from beneath him, then it heaved up sharply and he got a strange, disquieting impression that it was trying to rise out of the sea. The houses rattled and he saw Otero's shadow on the cottage window holding up a lantern lest it be overturned. It was abominable that those workers and the valiant girl they were helping should be so unnecessarily tormented.

He heard Kai-ko give a long sigh and glanced up and saw he was sleeping. Van laid his head on his arms and closed his eyes. Surely by morning Thelma's ordeal would be over. The unbelievable agony women endured in a world closed to men! Women, undefeatable, the strong warriors and standard-bearers of the race! Weariness weighted him and he relaxed, trying to sleep, but he was aware even when he dozed of voices in the cottage, long since shaken off its foundation and sitting flat on the ground. A log broke in two and flames and sparks streamed upward.

LAVA

He closed his eyes tighter and pulled the blanket over his head. Once he heard, or thought he heard, a cry, quickly stifled, and his skin got uncomfortably rough. Once Kulani came to the steps and smoked a cigarette. There was a tense, debating expression upon her face and before her smoke was half finished she threw the cigarette away and went in.

Van sat up, filled with restlessness and was subtly aware of some enormous catastrophe on its way toward them. After a little he lay down again. The night was oppressively hot and still. He dozed off and woke with a start. Pia hurried past and something about the way he carried himself gave Van an unpleasant tightening sensation through the chest.

"Pia!" he said but the man ran by and Van threw off the blanket and sat up. Then the muscles about his heart cramped.

Behind the black loom of the hill was the sullen glare of volcanic light and somewhere in the distance behind it a vast pillar of smoke was poking and thrusting higher and higher. The reflection from it had changed the night to a bowl of bronze and threw its dull, gigantic reflection across the sea. For an instant Van sat frozen. Behind him, in the cottage, a delicate girl was trying to give birth to her child and above a mountain was preparing to overwhelm an island with lava.

In the terribly lighted garden he saw the familiar shapes of trees huddled together as though appalled at the fate in store for them and their fellows on the mountainside.

"Kai-ko!" he said and did not recognize his voice.

The old man grunted and sank back into his sleep. Van got to his feet and realized, with disgust, that the blood in his legs felt as though it had been watered. Ku-lani rushed out of the door and stood on the steps facing the mountain hidden by the hill, one hand against the door jamb, as though for support.

Her face, like her white shirt and breeches, was a fiery rose color from the growing red light. Pia stood behind her, his features outraged, incredulous, impotent. After an instant Ku-lani turned and grasped his arm.

"Wake everyone," she said in a breathless whisper. "But don't let them come here! I've just given Thelma some chloroform and will give her more. *She mustn't know!*"

Otero and Sizu came out, looked, threw their aprons over their heads and sank upon the ground uttering stifled cries. Ku-lani went back into the house and Pia ran off through the terribly illuminated garden. Van shook Kai-ko roughly. He looked bewildered for a second, then his senses, sharpened by blindness, grasped something from the night. His arms stiffened pushing him up out of the chair.

Ku-lani came out and went to him in a rush.

"Kai-ko," she choked, "Hualalai has erupted!"

His hands went up to his eyes as though he would tear them open. Ku-lani swallowed, her throat muscles jerking convulsively.

"Thelma—can't—be—moved! Pia!" Her voice went out across the night. "Pia! Oh, Otero, stop that crying. I can't think!"

LAVA

The man appeared running with great strides and the garden was filled with hurrying figures making for the fire and Ku-lani with desperation was waving them away.

"Fire! Fire! Mountain broke!" Otero screamed, clutching Shiba about the neck, but her husband thrust her off and faced the dreadful light, his stiff gray hair standing up like the bristles of an aged, angry boar.

"Get the cars," Ku-lani ordered. "Otero, stop that crying! Pia!"

The man stood like a mule.

"Pia! Don't stand like a jackass. Take them!"

"And you?" he demanded and his eyes were terrible.

"I must stay—Thelma," she choked and said something in Hawaiian.

The man looked appalled.

Old Puhi's head writhed unhappily toward his right shoulder and his arms hung as though tired; then he directed a strange look at Ku-lani and vanished into the dark.

"Hurry, Pia, hurry!" Ku-lani snatched up Dudie, kissed her and thrust her into the Hawaiian's arms.

Van heard the Packard roaring out of the barn and it came tearing down the slope of the lawn, Nuhi at the wheel.

"Good boy!" Ku-lani cried and people began piling into the car.

"That's enough. Pia, get the truck to take the rest."

Dogs began to leap in and were pushed out. Ku-lani stamped her foot.

LAVA

"Let them in!" she cried in an unnatural voice.

Mene-hune waited by the bamboos, wagging her tail.

"Van, while Pia's getting the truck run up on the ridge and see which way the lava is heading."

He sped past the cottage and through the groves of trees that stood like a ranked army doomed to be overwhelmed. Behind him he heard cries, voices with the ugly note of fear in them and the enraged squealing of a pig. His heart beat so it nauseated him. He was forced to stop for an instant, then rushed on. Gaining the ridge he crested it and stood transfixed.

Hualalai looked like the funeral pyre of the world. With deliberate ferocity the fearful light cloud was pushing upward as though it were bent upon demolishing the stars which showed blanched and diminished in corners of the sky which had not, as yet, been obscured. Beneath the rolling diseased smoke columns, lava, crimson, liquid as water, spouted into the sky and fell back upon the mountain bathing it with gore. In the cruel, fierce light Van saw the specks of fleeing cattle and horses racing through openings in the forest. Wild pigs and sheep passed, birds consulted noisily in the trees. An enormous rending sound filled the night as two searing streams began breaking down the sides of the mountain.

Van thought with amazement, "I don't feel, I'm beyond feeling."

Even his brain seemed numbed and his limbs paralyzed but he could hear the loud, uneven concussions of his heart above the greater noises of the night. He tried, angrily,

LAVA

to rally his scattered forces. He must observe, estimate correctly. The stream to the right was about three miles away on the Kona side, making for the sea, the one starting on the left was rushing down behind the hill and heading toward Mauna Kea.

He rushed back, dodging among the trees, stubbing his toes against broken pieces of lava. He sped through the garden and saw Ku-lani leaning into the truck loaded with terrified, huddled figures and shivering dogs. Pia was at the wheel.

"Two streams," he said, and realized his lungs were straining. "One to the right, heading for the sea and as well as I can judge about two or three miles away and the other starting down behind the hill."

Ku-lani nodded distractedly.

"The rifts Tom spoke of." Then she caught her breath. "Pia, if you don't think it's wise to try to get— out, drive down as far as you can to Kiholo and go on foot. There are canoes there."

"I keep sharp watch." He jammed in the clutch. "No use try to go Waimea side, road all bust and if go on foot maybe lava catch."

He pulled in the gear.

People cried out.

"Ku-lani! Ku-lani! Hawaii finish, all burn up. Come! Never mind Thelma, she die anyhow."

Dudie hung onto her mother's neck.

"Mummy, I don't want you to stay, the world is all red and ugly, I'm scared."

LAVA

Ku-lani thrust the child back into the seat.

"Mother can't go, Dudie! I'll come by and by. Kai-ko, Kondo, Van!"

"I stop!" Kondo announced, looking truculent.

Ku-lani seized him by the shoulders and thrust him into the truck.

"Kai-ko, hurry up."

"Sister-dear, you said you wanted me to stay," he reminded and stood immovable. She kissed his sparse gray head.

"Pia, take Dudie to Loki. Van!"

"I'm staying with you and Kai-ko."

Her arms fell to her sides as though she were completely exhausted.

"Go!" she commanded.

Pia released the brake and the truck lunged forward.

"I go!" he shouted back defiantly over his shoulder, "but I come back!"

They vanished and Ku-lani laid her hand on Van's shoulder. It smelled strongly of chloroform and faintly of tobacco.

"I've got to go back to Thelma, you go and keep watch and report to me every so often."

He nodded and glanced at Kai-ko, who stood with thumbs locked in his braces as though he were interposing his bulk between the angry mountain and the cool desperate girl standing in the deserted garden. In the hot crude light every leaf was distinct and the abandoned table of banana leaves and purple bougainvillea stood out against the duller green of the grass. Van saw Mene-hune waiting beside her box of puppies, her eyes fixed expectantly upon the three figures gathered into a knot under the orange trees.

"Kai-ko?"

"Yes, Sister."

"Do you want to go with Van or stay here?"

"I'll go with Van, unless you'd like me to stay."

"Absolutely not." She vanished into the house.

"Just an instant, Kai-ko," Van said. Going over and picking up the box of puppies he carried it into the office. The little bitch followed wagging her tail gratefully, then hopped in among her offspring. Van's eyes blurred. . . . Mothers. . . . He straightened up and again he heard the squealing of a pig and the resentful squawk of a surprised chicken. Then he saw with amazement a dark figure hurrying up the road.

"Kondo!"

"You think Japan man run away when other fellas no can because girl no can *hemo* her baby!" he cried in an angry, grating voice. "Ha! what for God make all same!" He stared at the titanic cloud which was thrusting steadily upward, assuming various hues and shapes, murky blue, purple, scarlet as it was more or less illuminated from below. "Thelma torr sick, if take on top truck die sure, if stopping here—"

He looked in the direction of the mountain preparing in a deliberate and awful fashion to overwhelm the district as it had done uncounted times before and since the memory of man.

LAVA

"Gar-damn!" He wiped his hands on his apron which in the pressure of events he had forgotten to remove. "Son-of-a-pitch mountain make all same. Where Ku-lani? I like talk."

Van went to the door and tapped on it and he opened it a little and he heard a hoarse, exhausted, dreadful whisper.

"Oh . . . Ku-lani. . . .!"

Van felt sick with compassion, and sweat broke out all over him.

"Ku-lani, Kondo wants you."

"Kondo!"

"I here," the man said from the steps. "Suppose you speak yes, I can help. Before Japan-stop-time I soldier mans. Japan Emperor he speak all Japan soldier must learn to help womans when they having baby. So more mans by and by. I all same doctor for this kind things."

Ku-lani thrust back her hair with shaking hands.

"Christ!" she whispered and the whisper was a prayer but her eyes were unnatural.

"Ku-lani," Thelma's voice called and Van heard her catch back a scream, "I . . . don't seem to be getting . . . anywhere!"

He caught a glimpse of her face lying on a damp pillow and saw her teeth working frantically on her lower lip trying to stifle screams of tortured woman-agony. Tears were slowly spilling down the small gray cheeks. Then seeing the three united to assist her she smiled a tiny, gallant, apologetic smile.

Ku-lani stared for the ghost of an instant at Kondo's

ugly lined face, then closed the door and returned almost instantly.

"All right, Kondo."

Van hurried out and heard the man's voice, muffled by the door.

"Gar-damn, I torr much sorry, Thelma-san."

Van took Kai-ko's arm.

"Shall we go?"

Kai-ko inclined his head.

When they gained the crest of the ridge, Kai-ko found a volcanic boulder and sat down, his strained blood-shot eyes fixed on the mountain which he could not see but which he could hear erupting its crimson fury into the night.

Van watched hills melting, ravines filling, majestic forests disappearing like tufts of feathers in flame. The fresh lava at the source many miles away was lifting slabs of old flows from their solid beds and bearing them seaward with soil and trees which after a few instants toppled over and were engulfed. The vast flood of burning matter, in a terrific state of fusion, rolled to and fro, tossed up flaming billows. Fiery whirlwinds, loaded with deadly hissing gases constantly rent the smoke column over the mountain but it rapidly re-formed and continued upward. A new stream started to make its way down the mountain but after a little disappeared underground and as the great mass forced and wrenched its way forward, rending the earth asunder, the island protested with resentful, spasmodic jerks. White hot, incandescent boulders were shot up, tremendous explosions, muffled by distance, and the roar of escaping gases tore the shuddering night. Dense misshapen clouds of smoke kept increasing and streams of burning gold poured over other streams as valve after valve opened up. At times the smoke partially obscured the night but when it lifted Van could see the mountain discharging masses of horrible bloody matter from the roaring mouths of new cones.

Van noted, uneasily, that the flow on the right was heading, roughly, toward them and wondered, dully, if they and Kilo-hana were to be wiped out, burned under millions of tons of molten lava. Then he saw, with a sort of amazed horror, a dark bent figure hurrying stealthily past. Under one arm was a struggling pig and, hanging head downward from its right hand, two chickens. He had a curious shock when he recognized Puhi, heading directly for the approaching flow.

He grasped Kai-ko's arm.

"Good God! what on earth is Puhi going to do?"

"Puhi? Where is he?" Kai-ko asked. "I thought he'd gone in one of the trucks." Then like an afterthought he added, "But he wouldn't!"

"He's going up to the flow with a pig and two chickens," Van said. "It's heading this way—now."

"Sacrifices for Pele," Kai-ko said, "to propitiate her." The old man wiped his face with the palm of his hand and his shoulders sagged more heavily.

Van sat stunned, overwhelmed at the old retainer's devotion, then looked away. It was unthinkable that any

LAVA

man, for any motive, could have the courage to approach that red tumbling stream of lava and boulders breaking through the trees of the forest.

There was a brief cessation of sound as though the night caught its breath and he heard faintly an eerie, blood-chilling chant, which was lost in a dull angry roaring from the summit.

Kai-ko sighed like a tired child.

They sat in silence and Van watched the pigmy figure making its way through the distorted silhouettes of ohia trees.

"I never dreamed lava had such velocity," he said after a minute.

"A-a, evidently," Kai-ko said, straining forward, "there are two kinds of lava, the slow-flowing kind called Paa-hoe-hoe by the Hawaiians and A-a which is sometimes as liquid as water and frequently attains a velocity of thirty or more miles an hour. Hualalai seems to specialize in the latter. Van, I'm afraid they'll have to go to Kiholo and get canoes but Pia's equal to any emergency."

Van made an assenting sound.

"By morning we'll probably be completely cut off on both sides. Suppose you go and see how things are progressing below, I'll wait here."

Van rose, laying his hand on Kai-ko's massive shoulder, appreciating the tragedy of a man keeping watch of a spectacle which he felt but could not see. He made his way back and listened to the mountain bombarding the night as unleashed forces wreaked their fury upon a protesting but helpless island, thinking about Puhi hurrying through the forest with his pitiful gifts to placate a goddess's fury. Entering the office he tapped on the door, Ku-lani appeared, shook her head and vanished leaving a trail of chloroform in the air, and Van knew as long as he lived he would never forget the expression of her face.

He went out and realized that the garden was rapidly becoming obscured with smoke which irritated his lungs at each inhalation. He threw a log onto the fire and started back to rejoin Kai-ko. Morning was coming and he shivered. When he regained the ridge he saw Puhi seated beside the old man, the Hawaiian's face was wet with sweat but he looked contented. Van glanced at the flow; a long fold in the land had turned it once more toward the sea. The two seated figures were conversing in Hawaiian and he felt strangely excluded. These people knew things he did not for they had worshiped at strange shrines and had listened all their lives to the whisper of islands set in the sapphire jewel of the sea. At sound of his footsteps they looked around.

"Things don't seem to be progressing," he said and waited.

Kai-ko did not speak for an instant, then asked:

"Van, how's the lava heading—now?"

"Toward the sea, it's getting smoky and a bit hard to see."

"I guess it's formed its channel; we might as well go back. Is it day?"

"Almost."

LAVA

"I felt it coming."

"I stop here, keep watch," Puhi said, drawing out his pipe and settling his back against a rough boulder. Kai-ko made some remark in Hawaiian and took hold of Van's arm.

Puhi called out as they started off and Kai-ko answered.

"What did he say?" Van asked, guiding Kai-ko past a tree.

The old man smiled.

"He says for us to stay with Ku-lani and tell her the lava won't come this way for he gave Pele her sacrifices."

They retraced their steps and sat down by the fire burning through the blue vapors drifting through the garden. Morning broke and a choking pall of smoke smothered the island. Through it the sun shone, red and angry, dim and diminished. Shapes of trees were distorted, shadows strange as those of an eclipse patterned the grass which looked a dirty yellow through the haze.

Once Van went to the ridge but could see absolutely nothing. Puhi had gone. The bursting noises, muffled by distance, continued and he could hear the terrific thrashing of lava at white heat, falling on cooling streams as the hidden cones continued to spout their fury from the summit.

When he returned he saw Ku-lani talking to Kai-ko and his heart slipped a beat. She smiled wanly.

"Make some coffee, Van, will you?"

"How's Thelma?"

"The baby's born." She choked with exhaustion.

"Is she all right?"

LAVA

"As well as can be expected, she wasn't physically fitted for anything like this. Kondo's with her, he sent me out for a bit. She's conscious but terribly weak."

"Does she know about—" He indicated the smoke-charged garden.

"She hasn't said anything, we hung blankets over the windows, but I think she suspects—because the women have gone. Her eyes keep following me about."

"Sit down," Van begged, but she shook her head.

"I'm going to have a look."

"I'm afraid you won't be able to see anything."

She nodded but went off.

Kai-ko found his chair and Van went to the kitchen for the necessary articles. He put the pot on to boil and set cups, milk and sugar on the box Ku-lani had used for a stand the previous afternoon when she washed her hair. He went back for crackers and when he got to the door stared at the dim shape of the hill, barely discernible through the smoke, but he felt it lowering over them. Then he saw Ku-lani's figure coming back like a white ghost through the blurred exaggerated garden. He went back to the fire and took the coffee off.

Ku-lani sat down on the grass at Kai-ko's feet without speaking and laid her arm across his knees. The old man's hand found her head and caressed it. Van filled two cups and took them over and passed the sugar and milk.

"Thanks, Van," Ku-lani said, looking up gratefully.

When she finished she rose without a word and went back to the cottage and Kondo came out.

LAVA

"Coffee got?"

Van served him, then helped himself.

"Lucky," Kondo gloated, looking over the brim of his cup at the two men. "Boy!"

Van smiled. Kondo was a true son of the Orient. The man drank his coffee noisily, wiped his mouth on the back of his hand and looked about him scowling.

"Torr much hum-buggar, all this smoke. No can see anykind. I like see which side fire go."

He disappeared in the direction of the grove and returned after a while with Puhi. They were in earnest conversation, Kondo nodding emphatically at everything the old Hawaiian said.

When night came, the world opened up again. The lava streams had swelled to gigantic proportions. The one behind the hill was filling the space between the three mountains, covering it with liquid fire, spreading out, transforming it into an ocean that illuminated the sky overhead until it glowed like a red-hot, aching oven. Van could follow the mighty eddyings and surgings, hidden by the hill, by the changing glare on the thick, copper-colored, restless smoke canopy above it.

The flow directly in front was pushing its fiery snout steadily toward the sea, which was a dull, deep rose in the light reflected from overhead, strangely stilled, as though bracing for the terrible embrace awaiting it. The ruthless, resistless mass of dull red rock, like an eternal landslide, advanced with dull, thudding explosions at the front, occasionally spilling livid red trickles out into the trees. New cones showed like fiery pimples on the summit and even from that distance Van could see continuous jets of lava issuing from them, playing like firehose against and through the rolling smoke columns.

From the horrid white throat of an aperture farther down the side of the mountain, white-hot and red-hot lava shot out alternately with deep unearthly roarings and shattering noises like discharges of artillery. It seemed as though the very ribs of the mountain were being forced apart. The titanic slopes, black save where the lava streams illuminated them, looked ready to collapse from the millions of tons of molten matter which the mountain continued to eject.

Under the dark, rolling columns of smoke, suddenly distorted by whirlwinds formed by escaping gases, he could hear the dull, colossal roaring of masses of heavy liquid matter falling back on the cones which had spouted it out, choking them. They retaliated by discharging it again more fiercely, flinging it out and over the slopes of the monster mountain and the incessant metallic rattle of a hail of cooling fragments falling back upon the flows of other ages sounded through the greater noises of the night.

He stared at the pillar of cloud above the summit and estimated it must be somewhere in the neighborhood of sixteen thousand feet. It was torn at intervals by vile lightnings, then grew ominous and dark, threatening the world and even the stars which had fled frightened to remoter regions of the heavens. Not one friendly little face

LAVA

could he see. The whole island seemed to be going upward in one, vast, steady conflagration.

He passed his hand across his eyes, then removed it to look again.

The flow circling the hill, some miles to the east, was pouring over the long slopes of the island with gathering momentum, rolling along, impelled by the irresistible power from behind. It engulfed peaceful grass lands, spilled hurriedly and wickedly over slopes, sent out tentacles to gather up forests, swallowed pastures and rises in the land. Beyond the gigantic river of living fire, redly golden, the outlines of the Kohala mountains showed huddled together as though for protection, crouching terrified under the smoke clouds unrolling solemnly over land and sea. Van watched the ruthless advance, then turned back to the smaller flow.

It moved more slowly, not having the same terrific volume behind it to give it impetus. When the fused mass became sluggish, it had the appearance of clotted blood; when it became active it resembled fresh and clotted blood thrown into violent agitation. Forests smoked at its edges sending up bluish vapors, trees, pigmy-like in the distance, writhed an instant before they were overwhelmed and a continuous grinding sound accompanied the advance of the lava which changed to rending when it broke through dense groves of trees.

The air was hot and dry and filled with a fine, cindery, parching dust that caught the throat. Van unbuttoned the neck of his shirt and thrust his tie into his pocket. In his

LAVA

absorption he had forgotten Puhi and Kai-ko were with him. The old Hawaiian stood a little distance off, chanting, and Kai-ko was sitting on the boulder, his elbows on his knees and his shoulders hunched forward. Van laid his hand on the broad, patient back.

"Kai-ko?"

"Yes."

"Are you tired, do you want to go back?"

The old man shook his head.

The night seemed to split and stagger backward, and Van jerked up, his heart pounding. The flow on the left had hit the sea. Steam jet shot up like defiant white plumes and rocks burst with mighty explosions. Water boiled for miles along the tortured coast, shattering, splitting noises, roars, muffled detonations came from the shore and still the splendid, golden Niagara continued pouring its billions of tons of hot, molten matter into the sea, convulsing it, and fish were killed for miles.

Kai-ko got up.

"I'm going to stay with Thelma and send Ku-lani up to see this."

"Let me go."

The blind man shook his head.

"Puhi can take me."

The Hawaiian took Kai-ko by the arm and they walked slowly off among the trees. After a little Van saw Ku-lani coming through the grove. She joined him and watched without speaking but her white, still face was one vehement cry for the mighty despoliation of her land. A

LAVA

tidal wave assaulted the coast and an unexpected gust of wind made a noise in the tree-tops. The girl did not move but Van took hold of her arm and she glanced up at him. Her eyes were as hard as stones and as unflinching. They went from the steam columns torturing the sea to the mountain whose appalling fires were devouring the night. In the fluctuating light the sides of Hualalai seemed to pant like the flanks of an exhausted beast bleeding to death. Occasionally the cones shot out white-hot, incandescent boulders into the smoke pillar and they described great arcs and fell back into the vermilion streams pouring incessantly and with incredible rapidity into the shuddering sea. Streams like burning arms, barring out rescue, locking them into a world of horror and tragedy that seemed in no way related to the world without.

Ku-lani's hand sought Van's and its clasp gave him an intimate, disturbing sensation of all her person and he fought down an emotion which was superfluous at such a time. There was no comfort, no consolation to offer her as she stood like a rock watching the destruction of forests she had ridden through, glades she had loved, trees and grass that she had planted and registered herds which had been her pride and her care, scattered or claimed by the lava. She was like a breath carved in flesh, infinite and impersonal, like a white statue and a burning cloud, and the tears she did not shed scalded his heart.

She moved slightly as though something hurt her inside and Van looked at her, crudely silhouetted against the terrible beauty of the night. Like the island she was enduring a baptism of fire. His fingers tightened about hers. Her eyes went upward, met his and passed on to the cruel red arch of the sky overhead and its glare was reflected in their brown depths like an afterglow burning out slowly above the sad, dark line of the sea dividing earth and water from air even as this convulsion divided her future from all that had gone before.

He thought, looking at her standing at the edge of the black shadow cast by the tall grave trees behind them that she was like a sacrifice laid uselessly on the altar of implacable gods shaking a world with their wrath, destroying it wantonly.

"I must go back," she said finally and her voice shook slightly with exhaustion or emotion or both. She started to disengage her fingers but his closed about them retaining them.

"I must, I must be alone, or I cannot bear it," she whispered, then seeing his face smiled frantically. "Don't mind?"

She pressed his hand and he released hers.

"I understand, Ku-lani."

He watched her vanish among the tall trees, then sat down on a rock, watching a cone sending out blasts of blue and white smoke streaked with red lava. The night was gradually darkening and he felt as though he, too, were being obscured. His emotions, sincere enough, were puny, dwarfed against this. The red cavern of the night and the burning streams of lava seemed to mock him.

"What have I, any man, to offer her?" he thought.

"What human being could possibly compensate for this wholesale destruction of something which is essentially part of her as she is part of it."

He got to his feet and looked at the east. Save for the dim ghostly outlines of the Kohala mountain above the livid mocking red line of the flow, the whole island seemed to be melting and pouring into the sea.

A hand was laid upon his shoulder and he turned; Kai-ko stood beside him breathing heavily.

"Magnificent, isn't it?" the old man asked, and Van looked compassionately at the solid figure remembering other eruptions, perhaps more spectacular than this.

"I've had about enough for the present," Van said, and Kai-ko nodded. They started back but Van halted for a last glimpse of the terrific invasion of the sea.

When they got back Kondo was lying face downwards by the fire, his black head buried between his arms. Puhi sat on the grass staring before him in one of those trances common to Polynesians. Kai-ko groped for his rocker and Van laid a blanket over his knees.

"Thanks, Van, it's getting chilly; it must be getting on toward morning," the old man said.

"Yes."

Van looked at the haggard features, drawn and gray, and at the heroic proportions of Kai-ko's body and thought that no one but Rodin could have reproduced the vigor and tragedy that invested his face and figure, more silent than darkness and as strong.

Van stretched himself on the lawn wondering if Ku-lani

and Thelma were sleeping, wondering how and when it would end. Mene-hune came wagging out of the office and stretched beside him, sighing a little as though she were bored at the upheaval of the only world she had ever known. Van passed his hand along her little speckled back and she smiled at him, as dogs smile. Then he heard the hoarse, angry crying of a baby and Kondo jerked erect.

"Hi-ya! Boy-san wake up," he exclaimed, and Van was compelled to smile at the man's obvious satisfaction at the sex of the child born while an island was being rent apart. The Japanese rose, stretched, and going to the fire helped himself to coffee. He confronted the tawny night which contracted and expanded as the mountain decreased and increased its activity.

"Lucky when gods make like this and boy baby come. Japan man speak when he grow up he be just like god."

"Yes?"

"I tell you true, Mr. Van. You see fifteen, twenty year more—"

Ku-lani called from the window and Kondo set his cup down and ran across the strip of lawn to the cottage. Van felt uneasy, Kondo was not given to running; when necessity demanded it he—hurried. But there had been—or had there been?—a peculiar timbre to Ku-lani's voice. He could not decide, for none of their voices had sounded natural for thirty-six hours.

He stared at the vast, shadowy garden, magnified by smoke which clung clammily about the roofs of houses and limbs of trees but the immense arch overhead was fiercely illuminated by the lava streaming out of the island's veins. Hot, angry, threatening it curved overhead, guiltless of stars.

After a while Ku-lani came out and something about her face and figure snatched at Van's heart. He sat up hastily. She glanced at Puhi and Kai-ko, saw that they were sleeping and went to Van.

"It's—*pau!*" she said, sitting down and burying her face in his lap. He felt her body shaking, and grasping her by the shoulders lifted her up that he might see her face. Not a muscle quivered but tears streamed from her eyes.

"Ku-lani!"

"She had a hemorrhage."

He released her and she hid her face again on his knees. After all her work, her fortitude, to be cheated of her victory. He found her hand and held it. She lay as still as the dead woman but an occasional long shudder ran through her limbs.

Emotion almost unmanned him.

"Ku-lani."

She made a muffled assenting sound but he could find no words adequate to express what he felt and his fingers tightened about hers. He sat for a while rubbing her head and the chill of morning increased. Kondo came out with a squirming bundle of baby and commenced pacing the cracked walk, jogging it in his arms and in the dying after-glow overhead his figure was enlarged to gigantic proportions.

Van disengaged his hand and placed Ku-lani's head gently

LAVA

on the grass and went into the house for blankets and pillows. He found them and started back toward her. Like a white flame spent, she slept on the lawn while a mountain fouled the night with the vermilion streams of an island's blood.

CHAPTER XII

Van sat for hours unable to sleep or think. His skin felt parched. It was stiflingly hot. The trunks of the trees were barely discernible, their tops lost in the thick, bluish smoke drifting heavily over the island. Overhead a sickly dun-colored glow showed the position of the sun. It was getting on toward noon.

Ku-lani was still stretched face downwards on the grass and Kondo lay sprawled on his back, legs spread apart, under a rose-bush. His face, saffron in the peculiar light, was suggestive of a gargoyle's, lined and indignant, even in sleep, and yet, the devotion behind its ugliness! Puhi sat, facing the mountain, his figure expressive of the satisfaction which is the right of one whose work is well done, and Kai-ko rocked his chair softly, one large hand guarding the baby laid across his knees.

"Kai-ko, I'm going to have a bath," Van said, rising and placing his hand on the old man's shoulder.

"All right."

He walked through the echoing rooms filled with the dim, familiar shapes of furniture swathed in sheets, but it looked strange against the dark walls veiled by slowly moving wisps of smoke drifting in through open doors and windows, then sliding out again hurriedly and guiltily.

He went to the bathroom adjoining the bedroom in which he had never slept and turned on the tap. The cool fresh rush of water surprised him. It and the porcelain tub were links with a life left behind, unreal and remote. Outside the windows the atmosphere slowly altered as the smoke curled and uncurled assuming dim, monstrous shapes. It soiled, it lightened, it groped for the blurred shapes of houses and trees, enveloped them and passed on, formless, unrelated to the world that had been.

The cold water soaked into his dry skin and he dashed it over his head again and again and the mists which had fogged his mind began clearing. Sometime in the hazy future he supposed they must go. The mere mechanical act of putting on fresh clothes, of shaving and brushing his hair worked toward restoring life more to normal. For some absurd reason he half expected to see the smoke clearing but it persisted, drifting through the garden, choking it.

He went through the kitchen and saw the box of fledglings in the corner. One of them had got out and was pecking forlornly at a match. He felt guilty. They had been completely forgotten during the past two nights and days. He found food and when their crops were filled put them back in the box and they folded their wings contentedly.

When he went out vague, brittle gray cobwebs were drifting silently down. Kai-ko was brushing himself free of them and shaking them out of the folds of the blanket wrapping the baby.

"What on earth is this stuff, Kai-ko?"

"A capillary glass known as Pele's hair," the old man said. "It's a sort of foam spun from the lava; the air currents have changed and blown it our way. In Coan's account of the 1852 flow—he was a missionary—he speaks of his children gathering it up off the streets of Hilo."

Van watched it, then seeing Kai-ko's lined face said: "Let me take the baby."

Kai-ko handed the child carefully to him and went off toward the house. Van glanced at Ku-lani. Her tired body, limp on the lawn, was like a shell housing the woman inside, strong and undefeatable. A breath of air passed over the island moving the smoke hurriedly, making it take on vast, uncouth shapes and Van heard the roaring of the distant mountain and the persistent clink of falling particles of cooled lava. An overwhelming sense of depression filled him.

The baby stirred and he paced the walk, watching the smoke. He felt as though he were walking in a dream. The child moved, jerking against him and he was amazed at its strength. It emitted an angry cry and he went below the house lest the sleepers be disturbed. He eyed the strange, tiny, resentful creature that squalled lustily, waving its bits of fists, enraged at the world which had greeted it so rudely. He saw the dim shape of the cottage and something caught inside him. Thelma was still in there. . . . The realization gave him a curious sick feeling.

He listened to the child's smothered crying and shifted it in his arms, feeling clumsy and inexperienced. Its face was scarlet and moist, and its eyes had the peculiar hard angry look common to very young babies.

After a little Puhi joined him.

LAVA

"I think maybe hungry," he said.

Van wondered why he had not thought of it.

They went to the kitchen, trying to hush the child when they passed Ku-lani's and Kondo's prostrate figures. Van placed the baby on the kitchen table while Puhi diluted some canned milk with warm water and Van envied him his experienced resourcefulness.

"Before, I feed Ku-lani when she small like this," the old Hawaiian said, smiling and sampling the mixture with a tin spoon. A drop of it trickled through the eight hairs adorning his chin which served as a beard. The child appeared to be bursting with indignation and fury. Van took it up hastily. It ceased crying but its lips quivered pathetically. Then it let out a hoarse scream that startled Van and made him vaguely angry. He was shocked at the concentrated fury in its voice; it seemed to be blaspheming the universe and everything pertaining to it.

"You feed," Puhi said, "I tink Ku-lani call," and he went out, leaving Van to the task.

He fed it a tiny spoonful and the greedy little purple lips seized the metal, clinging about it as though to suck; then its body arched backwards in a spasm of rage. Van spilt milk over its face, on the table, upon his breeches, but succeeded in getting several spoonfuls down and it grew quieter though still impatient. Its wise eyes seemed to mock his clumsiness and condemn it. He poured more milk into the small gaping mouth, then wiped the child's cheek hastily and guiltily when it got the liquid too fast and choked and overflowed.

LAVA

His feeling toward it was an impersonal compassion. It did not seem possible that it could be a human being; it was merely an atom of a creature without sex or individuality, ravenous with hunger and generally at outs with the world. One of the little pigeons with a prodigious fluttering of wings managed to get on the edge of the box and cocked an eye at the baby as though shocked at such behavior and ingratitude.

Van wiped his face and attacked his task afresh, sweating slightly. Occasionally he paused to give the child and himself a rest, watching the heavy sable atmosphere changing to dull, sickly yellows and tarnished bronzes. The doorway darkened and Ku-lani came through it.

"What on earth are you doing?" she asked in a dazed voice.

"I'm trying to feed the baby but my methods don't seem to meet with its approval."

She came over slowly as though she had not fully collected her wits, picked up the cup, tasted it and set it down.

"It should be a little warmer but won't hurt for once."

She watched him working, a mildly amused expression in her sleep-dazed eyes.

"I imagined," Van said, looking up, "I suppose because I've never seen such a new baby at close range, that they were more attractive."

"They aren't, really, but you love them anyway, perhaps because they seem so put upon at being born and so helpless to prevent it."

She picked the child up and took the spoon from Van

LAVA

and finished feeding it. He knew from the thoughtful expression of her face that her mind was occupied with thoughts which stole the last drop of blood from her cheeks. Then she straightened up and they went into the garden.

Van looked at Ku-lani's strong figure recharged with vitality from contact with the earth upon which she had slept. She was the earth's twin sister, earth upon which sun has smiled. She knelt down and placed the child on a blanket and put a fold across its face. Mene-hune came up, smelled it curiously and carefully and when her investigation of this new member of Kilo-hana was ended, retired and lay down a little distance away.

Ku-lani patted the dog and got up.

"I still feel as though I were drowning in sleep, but I've got to take a shower and wake up. There are things which have to be attended to before we go."

She glanced at the cottage, then her eyes went in the direction of the smoke-hidden hill which they could feel towering over them, as though she were looking back at a chapter of her life which had closed.

She caught her breath, then groped mechanically in her breeches pocket for cigarettes. Van stood helpless to console. She had been foully tricked, cheated, robbed by life but seemed to harbor no resentment against it, perhaps because she was still too numbed, but one look at her face sufficed to convince him of his error. She *was* life so she could hardly cherish resentment against it. Her eyes were as unreadable as ever but the quality of their wide stare made him think of a lone sea bird drifting before currents

LAVA

in the thin, high blue of the ether. Then a very human tear started down her cheek as though her strong soul melted, momentarily, leaving her at the mercy of the destructive forces about her. He heard, or thought he heard, the incessant tearing sound of lava spilling over the island and the muffled explosions from the tormented sea.

"Ku-lani, when I think—"

"I don't dare to think," she interrupted in hurried, breathless tones.

He took her hands and looked down at them.

"Gone!" she said in a husky whisper. "Practically everything I love wiped out!"

There was no appeal for sympathy in her face or her voice. Her words were a mere statement of a fact which had to be reckoned with and faced, eventually, but the tear continued to crawl down her cheek, a tear of the spirit as well as of the flesh.

It routed Van, it was beyond his, anyone's power to attempt to offer consolation or to try to make restitution for what had been taken from her. He had no thought that her loss might be his eventual gain. He could not think of himself facing that face drained of emotion. An impulse, old as life, pushed him to take her into his arms but he resisted. Only the most colossal vanity on earth could be guilty of imagining that a man's mere love . . . He discontinued his thought with disgust. . . .

He pressed her hand against his breast and her eyes came up swiftly with a sort of pleased realization. They seemed to whisper:

LAVA

"You are left, you are still here—anyway."

The expression of her face made him realize that because of his brief association with Kilo-hana he would always have an assured place in her affections but it would be brutal to attempt to take advantage at such a time or try to force himself into her mind overcrowded with stark thoughts and realizations. Then he saw her staring over his shoulder. Her body stiffened and she tore her hand free.

"David!"

Van turned and saw the slack, boyish figure coming through the smoke and Ku-lani rushing to it. Brother and sister went into each other's arms in a tragic, youthful clinch. After an instant they fell apart and seemed to have nothing to say, perhaps because of his presence. David's eyes were red from smoke or tears, his face drawn from anxieties which had eaten him.

Van walked away feeling as though a cord inside him had been suddenly and painfully severed. He realized, with a shock, the strong attachment that a person develops for another whom he has helped, but only a selfishness, of which he was not guilty, would make him attempt to take Ku-lani from those who loved her perhaps more deeply than he was capable of loving. He paced the lawn, a sort of hidden fury possessing him.

He did not attempt to think for he was forcibly struck by the imperfection of the whole situation. Ku-lani might be touched or utterly dumfounded were he to attempt to express what he felt for her. To him she was life. But the mere supposition that a man might cherish the delusion that his love might or could compensate for the loss of Kilo-hana might even move her to mirth. He winced from the thought, for like all quiet natures he was intensely sensitive.

He searched for Kai-ko and saw him sprawled asleep in a chair on the back veranda where the seismograph ticked on. His great figure looked weighted and Van went softly away.

When he thought that David and Ku-lani had been allowed sufficient time to themselves he started back and saw their figures seated side by side on the grass. As he approached he saw, or imagined he saw, a vague resentment, tinged with embarrassment, in the boy's eyes. The instinctive resentment a young brother has for an older man who he fancies is interested in, or attracted to, his sister. He saw David bend and ask Ku-lani something. She shook her head and he felt the boy's attitude change toward him. David got to his feet and advanced with an extended hand, evidently determined to make the gesture demanded by the occasion and the accepted forms of life.

"My sister told me. I want to thank you for trying to help her."

The boy choked and Van knew he too had loved Kilohana, but he got also the significance of the word, sister, slightly emphasized, and the youthful formality cloaking the speech. They put him definitely on one side of a line and the pair of them on the other. If David had said, Ku-lani, it would have made her equally theirs but the other word linked her to a common past in which he had had no share. What he had done, and Van appreciated how little it was, really, was accepted gratefully, of course, but could not weigh against the rest of their lives solidly welded together by blood, joys, sorrows and endeavors. There was a little natural jealousy in the boy's attitude because a stranger had been privileged to have a part in events which seemed hardly his right. Van smiled, inwardly, at the utter youthfulness of it.

David glanced appraisingly at him, then seemed to lower an invisible lance permitting him to approach closer.

His young face twitched and he looked about him perhaps realizing the utter futility of Van's attempt to oppose what was written and give Kilo-hana to Ku-lani. Life went its appointed way undeterred by the feeble attempts of mortals to shape it to their own ends. She had got the place only to lose it.

Ku-lani rose to her feet and laid her hand on Van's arm, making him one of them, and he realized she was a staunch comrade loyal to those who cared for her and had been devoted to her interests, making them theirs.

"Well, we've got to think of getting out of here. The baby . . ." she said, but Van read the thought in her eyes. Where could she go—now? He felt drowned in guilt.

"We can go and stop with Naps," David said.

Ku-lani directed a quick look at her brother which recalled to Van that Napier was poor.

"Well, anyway for a while," David insisted. "He'll be glad to take us all in."

Ku-lani nodded and folded her arms and Van noted a line between her eyebrows as though her whole being were focused upon some matter.

"I'll wake Kondo," she said. "He and Puhi can help you, David, to—"

Her voice caught and hung in mid-air. While she had been speaking her eyes had been fixed on the slope of the lawn vanishing into the dull, twisting smoke. An incredulous expression in them made Van turn. Dim figures, magnified monstrously, showed coming through it, the first moving angrily and briskly. . . . Pia . . . Some distance behind, a large, slow-moving fluid shape . . . Loki. . . .

The garden seemed to lighten a little.

Relief went through Van like a rush of cold water. Of course she would come, despite anything and anyone. Ku-lani grasped Van's hand mechanically and the contact sent a pang through him for it linked him to all that they had experienced together. Her face was transfigured, briefly, then he saw it getting crimson. Painful waves of color flooded it, pushing up to her hair, bringing a smarting moisture to her eyes.

Through the smoke wraiths he saw Garland's stiff figure approaching, moving as though he felt that he had no place in that garden, robbed of reality. He walked slowly, reluctantly, postponing a moment.

David thrust a bewildered hand through his hair and his eyes went to his sister's, asking a question, but she did not move or reply. She looked torn, white, distracted as though life had finally betrayed her by bringing her father to her after all that had passed between them. Shaming her—and him.

Pia grasped the girl's forearm and she smiled from a distance, and he looked put-upon, perhaps because she had deputed him to discharge duties which seemed, now, only to have been vaguely connected with her. Then he fell back beside David as though forming a bodyguard. Loki came up like a splendid mountain, wiping her heated face and wet eyes on a fold of her dress. Opening her arms with a magnificent gesture of sweeping a world torn with travail to her ample and pitying breast, she embraced them in turn, giving them exultant little pats.

"Ku-lani! Van! Oh, I scare all you fellas be dead. Where Puhi and Kai-ko? David, how you get here?"

Her face was a mixture of glee and apprehension. Perhaps she was not too certain of just how the next few minutes would go. Garland came on as though compelled by an irresistible force.

"And now," she took Van and David by the arms and signaled to Pia imperiously with her head, "better us go." There was a profound and mischievous expression in her always astonishingly young eyes. "What Ku-lani and Ha-ole Hao saying to each other only for God and them two fellas to hear."

CHAPTER XIII

Van opened his eyes; cool white plaster walls about him, cool white sheets upon him and outside the square of open window, golden green foliage, filtering light.

"Well, you waking up at last," Loki said, beaming from the door like a huge, delightful child. "I think I been up twenty times since lunch to see you."

She came over and took hold of his hand.

"Your face got funny look; Ku-lani's too, and poor old Kai-ko, and he never been seeing anything!"

Van sat up, he felt as though he had come out of a whispering darkness. His mind was hazed with memories only quenchable by death. It seemed as though life had showed him its terrible, secret formula and left, abruptly. He passed his hand over his eyes.

Loki patted his arm.

"After by and by you be forgetting all these trouble things that been knock you fellas out. You stop in bed and I bring you little some kind to eat, then you feel better. After four o'clock now and you been sleeping since yesterday when we got back."

"Don't bother to bring me anything, I'll get up."

"You be good boy and do just like I say."

She smiled, pressed his cold hand between her plump warm ones and left.

LAVA

He stared at the motionless branches outside. The afternoon was so still that he felt that if he moved he might crack it, scattering its beauty. Over green tree-tops he saw the tremendous blue peace of the sea. He tried to realize he was back in Kona, but memories, like wounds, ached in him, blurring his being, numbing the working of his mind. . . .

The eruption, its aftermath, all that had led up to it and the long trip along the coast in the little blue sampan which had brought the rescuing party. The terrible aspect of the flows from the sea. . . . They had worn for themselves deep, well-defined channels down which red torrents of lava still poured, recoiling from the somber enclosing walls of black rock, splashing over them, forming cascades, whirlpools, rolling forward like smooth majestic rivers, swirling into lurid caverns festooned with red-hot stalactites hanging from still-glowing arches which the lava had flung over itself in triumph. The downward charge of the molten mass into the sea which roared and hissed and boiled in agonizing resentment at the horrible intrusion. The steam columns rising solemnly from the coast, the dense, dark clouds hanging over the island, marking the course of the flows inland. . . . The long detour to avoid boiling water and the incredible peace of the other islands stretching their huge dim shapes upon the sea.

The speck of boat making its way placidly across the dizzying blue water. Kai-ko sleeping slumped against a thwart. Kondo jogging the baby and staring with angry eyes at the smoking slopes of the island. Ku-lani stretched

LAVA

on the forward deck with David beside her. Garland looking embarrassed and proud and Pia and Loki and Puhi conversing in Hawaiian, untroubled children of the Pacific, accepting events as they came.

He passed his hand over his eyes, trying to come back to life as it had been, unconvulsed by momentous events and titanic happenings.

He heard Loki's step. She entered the room like a cotton-clad queen, Otero at her heels carrying a loaded tray which she set on the bedside table.

Loki seated herself in the rocker, leaned forward and laid a napkin across Van's long legs, faintly outlined by the bed clothes.

"Drink coffee first; that wake you up and give you good appetite. I got nice chicken stew in coconut and fine alligator pear."

She smiled.

Van felt the warmth of the coffee permeating his being.

"I glad to have you all back, when Pia come I think sure you fellas all dead. I sorry about Thelma," she wiped her eyes furtively, "but maybe better for her that way. Sometimes God know best."

He thought of his last sight of her. Loki had woven a garland of red roses and placed it about her neck. Her head had lain like a dark flower on the pillow and her face was at rest as though her life had been fulfilled. As it had been. Because of her Ku-lani had stayed, proving her caliber, convincing her father of her worth, and the grave in the grove of eucalyptus would stand as a monument to brave hearts.

"Shame all this mess happening just when Ku-lani get Kilo-hana," Loki said, wiping her face and smiling at Van, making him feel enveloped in her affection and approval. "Half John fault because he never been making that sacrifice. I think after last time we all go over, 'Well, I wait one two more days, give him last chance,' then before I can kill pig and chickens myself all that damn lava come out. Never mind, Ha-ole Hao learn his lesson from it. He know now, like I always been telling him, that Ku-lani fine girl. She never run away and leave her friend when Hualalai blow up and inside he feel sassy and proud because he got daughter brave like that. But," she rocked and her eyes twinkled, "seem funny to see them all friends."

She rose and looked out of the window.

"I think Ku-lani lose one cook. That Kondo just like crazy about Thelma's boy. There he go carrying him again!" and she laughed indulgently.

"What is Ku-lani going to do with the child?"

"Oh, I keep," Loki said, airily. "She got enough to take care without one more kid. Hell that lava going through Kilo-hana. John lose some land too, only I not so sorry about that. Good lesson, next time he listen and do like I say and not be so smart. One stream come down on this side and spoil plenty coffee."

"What," Van hesitated and felt as though all of life was running out of him, "is Ku-lani going to do?"

"Oh, stop here, little time, then go back I guess. Got

LAVA

some land left. This kind things happening often in Hawaii so no use make a big fuss."

Van looked at her abashed.

"But I sorry about her fine cattle, sure plenty get burnt up and horses too, but more calves and colts by and by and I betting you," her eyes grew merry and wise, "that Ha-ole Hao give Ku-lani more land after little while."

"But Kilo-hana is cut off entirely on both sides from the rest of the island."

"Soon as the lava get cool supervisors make a new road. Always like this in Kau—that south part of this island. Every few year Mauno Loa kick up fuss, lava come down and cover the road. By and by make a new one and when the old mountain feel lively again—down she come! No can help and that lava not so bad," she paused effectively. "It make—Hawaii."

Van gazed at her. Her mental attitude was like a shout of victory coming out of the black gates of death.

"And now you finish up all this fine food I bringing you. I going to see if Ku-lani ready to eat. She just waking up when I come. Never mind dress, just put on bathrobe. Kai-ko in his pyjamas sitting in his old place. I have to laugh that night when he nearly get catch by the *oni-onis* and his pants off."

She gave a reminiscent chuckle and went down the stairs and Van rose and went to the window. His body seemed encased in ice. None of them who had been through that time at Kilo-hana would ever be quite as they had been for they had looked into the heart of horror and touched beauty.

LAVA

He drew a deep breath realizing that while at Kilo-hana he had ceased, absolutely, being aware of himself as a distinct entity. But now the old consciousness of self was creeping over him again.

He moved unhappily.

From below came the grumble of Kai-ko's voice and he saw Kondo strolling across a reach of lawn carrying Thelma's baby. The still, green garden breathed softly below the gaudy tangles of orange and purple flowers smothering the house. Presently he saw Ku-lani and David go down the walk. They paused to inspect Kondo's charge, then vanished around the house in the direction of the office.

His hands tightened on the sill. She belonged to this island, to this life. Who was he to try, to fancy that he could take her from it? He realized how little he knew, how poorly versed in life he was. . . . He recalled Loki's words overheard the first afternoon he had spent in Kona. "The land is stronger than you, Ha-ole Hao, no use to fight with it for the kids. They belong to Hawaii, always they hearing the heart of this island beating."

The truth of that statement applied equally to him. It was not to be thought that the beating of his own awakened heart could drown the sound of that other, stronger one to which Ku-lani had listened all her life until it had become part of her. Stripped of all she loved most, still she was richer than he was for all of the island was in her. What had he to offer her that she did not already possess?

Senseless not to face facts.

He moved restlessly. When he had come to Kona it

had been only a name, now it held for him all the secrets of life. There it was spread out before him, vital, green, stronger than the fires which had formed it. The sound of the restless sea came to him, muted to a whisper and the smell of dense, moist vegetation straining toward the sun made his heart ache dully.

"You never coming down, Van?" Loki called from the foot of the stairs.

"I'm eating—everything!" he called back.

"You—lying!" the woman said and he heard her mounting the stairs and felt routed. Did she suspect? He winced from the supposition. She entered smiling.

"Now don't you be feeling sad about anything, everything going to come out all right, just like I always telling. Look already! Ku-lani and Ha-ole Hao friends, David back again—"

She laid her hand on his arm and subjected him to an intense, candid scrutiny which disturbed him; then picked up the tray.

"Better take shower, then you be feeling fine and like eating the good supper I having by and by. Kai-ko down stairs sitting in his place and Ku-lani too. They waiting for you I guess," and she smiled archly.

Van held the door for her, then went back to the window. The sea was unbearably blue with a few small clouds floating above it. Below, the green island spilled to the shore broken by its dark, out-juttings of lava, and he felt, in the cells of his being, the push of the forests growing all about him.

LAVA

He went through the business of bathing and thought he would dress but when he got to the point felt more inclined to wear a bathrobe as Loki suggested. That marvel of a woman, kin to the island she had been born on, eternally young, undaunted, triumphant. He caught a glimpse of his face in the mirror, pale, drawn, under its tan.

He felt an intense annoyance with himself. Why keep on thinking! He had thought, reflected all his days and known absolutely nothing about life until he had come to Kona and been hurled like a star from remote and chilly spaces beyond the earth into a maelstrom of events. He felt as though he were still hurtling through space with bewildering winds blowing about him, describing an enormous arc through limitless ether.

Then he smiled his old, faint, amused smile.

Life had trapped him successfully. A person, a locality, a cause had got him off his guard. His tide had come in, he had served his hour of usefulness and it was over. Why try to cheat himself, he would go out of the lives of these people as simply and silently as he had come into them, leaving a ripple which would pass.

He tightened his bathrobe. He would go down, look on, see the end of it like a true son of his father, then go with the moon which had been born the night they went to Kilo-hana and which would die shortly to be born over again. . . . He heard Ku-lani's voice and knew her white face would burn like a star in his memory. The proof of his love must be his silence, else he loved himself more than her. No land, no person could ever mean to her what this island did. To attempt to take her from it would be like tearing a tree from the earth expecting it to live and flourish. To attempt to intrude himself into her life would be like trying to fill a cup already spilling over. . . .

At least, he thought, as he descended the stairs, he did not delude himself about the importance of his part in life.

He came upon her seated on the front steps facing the garden. She looked exhausted, still, but managed a smile.

"Recovered?" she asked.

"Sufficiently, Ku-lani."

She moved as though brushing aside cobwebs.

"I feel dazed; even this garden still seems unreal."

He stared at it, high-colored, cool, filled with aching peace.

"I keep expecting earthquakes, their feel is inside of me still," Ku-lani said. "It seems as though the island were dead underneath us."

They sat for a while in silence.

"Ku-lani."

"Yes?"

"You'll go—back?"

She nodded without looking at him, as secret as ever, as withheld. He felt defeated and baffled, horribly lonely.

Evening lurked on the edge of the sea as though reluctant to shatter its beauty. The water moved in an indiscernible way as though depths beneath the surface were still troubled. A golden haze was dying behind the sharp horizon beyond which, over the curve of the earth, the islands of the Pacific lay in their scattered constellations.

LAVA

Ku-lani sat without speaking, a strange expression upon her face. She was in a kimono gay as the garden, with her hair tied at the back of her neck and hanging over her shoulders and he remembered the last occasion he had seen her wear it that way. In her eyes was a hint of wide spaces and her face had an expression of having been blown upon by cold winds coming from beyond the stars. A dull pang passed through his body, stabbing it, and he winced slightly.

"Something hurt?" she asked, without looking at him.

"Yes, in my mind."

"Growing pains," she said, clasping her strong hands together.

Her expression was curiously peaceful, that of one who has passed beyond emotion or been emptied of it. He looked at her beautifully proportioned forehead and thought about the lava spoiled acres of Kilo-hana.

"It seems abominable, Ku-lani, that for you things always seem to be made difficult."

"Perhaps it's the way I have to be taught," she said, staring at the sea. Its vast, regular respirations lent the evening a curious, capacious quality. It seemed a blue bowl holding all of life, memories, promises, victories and defeats.

"You are feeling sad, Van," she said.

"A little," he confessed and waited for her to ask why, but she did not. He realized that she never questioned life, she accepted it, was part of it as he ought to be.

Kai-ko came out of the door.

"That you, kids?"

LAVA

Ku-lani put out a guiding hand and he sat down beside them.

"Well, we've come out of the so-called jaws of death and had more than our share of adventures but—they turned out for the best."

Ku-lani smiled oddly and Van knew she was thinking rather amusedly of her father and he suspected that Kai-ko was also. Garland, who had once declared that he wished Kona destroyed because in his estimation it was destroying his children. But it had united him to them in the end. How life mocked men!

And here he was, almost feeling resentment against these two people he loved because they were—rightly—engrossed in affairs that concerned them vitally and him not at all. Then the resentment fell away leaving emptiness, desolation and regret.

Imbued with his father's teachings, he had been and would always be to a certain extent walled within himself; because he had been in Kona he would be beating himself eternally against the walls enclosing him, trying to get out. He had forsaken safe teachings only to discover he was not equipped for a stronger creed, perhaps because of a secret reserve in his soul, a fastidiousness which prevented him from flinging himself into anything. He did not regret the experience which had awakened him but an overwhelming longing welled up, all at once, inside him to escape back to the old security of detachment.

Ku-lani moved and he rose and went down the steps and was conscious of the absolute stillness of islands and

LAVA

of people about him whom he loved but who seemed to have gone from him in some inconceivable way.

Garland called out and he retraced his steps. Once more he sat down to dinner in the room which seemed pleased with itself despite the fact that it was too small for the people who had outgrown it since first it had been built.

He studied the faces about the table; Ku-lani seated beside her father and David on her other hand. The three of them looked a little ill at ease, pleased and embarrassed, like amateur players in a first rehearsal of new rôles assigned to them. Garland's face looked like a mummy's as though he had dried up inside. The old *koa* tree had at last gone down before a stronger, younger growth and had found peace. Luke and Ben ate as though aware that they were only the chorus of this drama. Loki beamed as she superintended the filling of plates and Kai-ko sat relaxed like a man who, work finished, has won an earned rest.

In the room were echoes of days that had been gradually building toward this one, turning around on an immense invisible wheel. The splendid pattern of the years had grown slowly. The strong island had separated the threads of these lives in order that it might arrange them in better order before it gathered them together again, weaving them into a solid design which was part of itself.

Supper over Van went into the garden and seated himself upon the stone wall. He looked back at the lighted veranda and saw Ku-lani sitting on the floor against Kai-ko's knee talking to her father. He wondered, without curiosity, what had been said between the two of them that smoke-choked day at Kilo-hana. Probably very little. Ben and Luke had vanished but he saw David's graceful young silhouette seated on the rail leaning toward Loki. A thought crept to him that he crushed with a smile. From where he sat in the dark it looked as though they were ranged about Ku-lani, barring him out, guarding her for themselves and the land that they lived in. Once he heard Loki laugh and the charm of her voice filled the garden with warmth.

The night was absolutely still. Once in a while a leaf rustled or an insect buzzed past. He felt the velvet green peace of Kona enveloping him and the spell of the extravagant coast hidden from his sight by darkness.

He studied the group upon the veranda. They were all captives of the tropics, listening entranced to the symphony of stars, sea and islands. In the lighted porch Kai-ko and Loki and Garland looked bigger than life, David's slight form was a promise of days to come and Ku-lani he would always see silhouetted against the future.

He moved as though prodded from within and took a deep breath of the night. Despite its solid blackness he was conscious of the lush growth all about him. He heard the distant echo of an outlaw wave breaking on the peaceful coast and the tiny immeasurable whisper of sap pushing through the cells of juicy green-leafed things growing around. He thought of Hualalai still slowly bleeding lava and of the sun and wind and rain which would, in time, win back the land which had been taken in order that valiant forests might spring out of it again.

Loki rose, looked about her as though she missed him and

LAVA

then he heard the music of her voice calling out good night. It was the eternal voice of woman summoning man back from his errors and follies to her huge and compassionate breast. A wave of loneliness swept him. Of them all, perhaps only she was capable of understanding the motive that kept him silent.

He answered but did not go in.

He was conscious of some awful intelligence about him, older than the world, the intelligence which is in rocks and trees, in inanimate objects and in the stilled sea of evening. Faint, occasional rustlings sounded as though gods were going about their eternal work of building and destroying.

He was aware of the island beneath him, projecting itself into his consciousness as it had that first day, trying to transmit its message to him. He felt as though it were watching him with expressionless eyes, whispering, insisting. "I am here! I am here! Listen! I am torn, and tortured but I persist because I make no attempt to dissociate myself from the forces working within and about me."

He got to his feet, squared his shoulders and started back to the house. The veranda was empty. When he reached the steps he sat down. He knew he could not sleep and had no desire to be in his room. Once he glanced around as though something were creeping up on him, closer and closer. The night nestled down on the island and he felt as though he were fading out, dissolving into the universe about him, becoming part of it.

He thought of Ku-lani and her conviction that it was only when a person ceased to be aware of himself as an individual that the true vision was granted of life as a whole. A curious peace was creeping into him permeating his being. His senses tingled to the silent harmony of earth, sea and air working their eternal magic and he held his breath to hear the chorus of their old, old song.

Through the massed tree-tops he saw a solitary star burning steadily. Somewhere behind him a tired moon was rising wanly behind the smoke-hidden summit of Hualalai, washing the sky with faint light. He watched drops of moisture crawling down the glossy leaves of a banana, dropping off and being absorbed into the earth, and the beam of the star coming toward him.

"Ku-lani," he thought and his face was a mask, "Kulani."

She came like a ghost—evoked from the night by his thought—and sat down simply beside him.

"Did I call you?"

She shook her head.

"No, I didn't, actually," he said in a held voice, "but I was thinking about you and about things you've said to me which are real because you apply them to your everyday life. I was wishing—"

Her dark eyes went up to his and he felt himself being drawn into something tremendous.

"That it weren't all over?" she asked.

He picked up her hand, looked at it and held it against his heart.

"Ku-lani—"

She waited and he looked about him at the vast quiet

LAVA

night holding sea, islands and stars, making them one. His fingers tightened about hers.

"Ku-lani." He paused and filled himself with a great breath. "It's just—begun!"

THE END